THE OASIS DECEPTION

BOOK 12 THE THAW CHRONICLES

TAMAR SLOAN

HEIDI CATHERINE

SEQUEL HOUSE

FYVE

*I*n all the quiet moments, lying in his hut with hunger pangs tearing at his stomach, Fyve imagined what Terra might look like. His people pray to her. Beg her. Have faith she'll take care of them. But how many actually thought about who Terra is?

Is she some nebulous being, camouflaged amongst the clouds? Or does she have a form? Everything suggests she's female—a nurturer and carer. That would imply a kind face, maybe wide, rounded hips, eyes surrounded by wrinkles because she smiles too much.

Yet Terra is also the one who claims her people when she's unhappy. If he was pondering such a question just after his mother left on her month-long searches, or when one of his siblings died, or someone dropped to the ground during Gratitude, tears of blood on their still face, he'd imagine an old crone. One who took satisfaction in culling the unworthy or turning her back on the weak and vulnerable.

Yet, the sight before Fyve is none of those. The real Terra is nothing like he ever could have imagined.

He glances down at Halo, wanting to see if she's just as

shocked and astounded as he is. Her green eyes are wide, and if it wasn't for the gentle bobbing of The Oasis, she'd be unmoving. "It can't be…" she breathes.

Elijah is beaming like a proud father. Then he's bowing. "All hail Terra."

The young girl, probably eight or nine years old, gazes over the speechless faces staring at her in wonder. Her slight form is swathed in cream-colored robes stretching from her neck to the floor, her hands tucked inside, leaving nothing but her head visible.

"All hail Terra," shouts a girl breathlessly, the words quickly echoing over the deck of the ship.

Yet Fyve can't find his voice. Terra is a child? How is that even possible?

She angles slightly, her gaze falling on him, stilling every cell in his body. Her head is bald, making her look fragile, almost frail. Her mouth is clamped closed and unsmiling. But it's her dark eyes that grip Fyve's heart and don't let go. They're… vacant. There's no smile sparkling within them, yet no callous hardness, either.

It's like she's here in body and little else.

"Terra, give me your blessings!" someone calls from the crowd.

She blinks, her gaze slowly falling onto the young man. She blinks again, barely moves, and doesn't say a word.

"Terra does not speak in the way you or I do," says Elijah, his brows knitted in disapproval. "You are not to address her directly."

The young man instantly bows his head. "Of course. Please forgive me, Terra."

Elijah scans the rest of the crowd and one by one, they do the same. Fyve quickly follows suit, noting that Halo also does beside him. He blinks at the wooden floor of the deck, trying to get his brain to process this. But it keeps hitting a wall of disbelief. Confusion. Almost…disappointment.

How could all their fates have been resting in the hands of a child? How will he ever make sense of that?

He peeks up from beneath his brows, noting that Terra is still just as unmoving and emotionless. Maybe this is so hard to accept because there's something about her that reminds him of Sevin. Maybe it's her youth. Maybe it's the frail vulnerability. Maybe it's because he's still grieving.

What would his sister have made of all this? She wanted to be on the ship to Tomorrow Land so badly.

And yet, the bald child wrapped in more material than he's ever seen in his life took her away from him. Why?

Halo's hand slips into his and Fyve wraps his own around and holds on tightly. Even though she hasn't lost a sister, she'd be reeling just as much as he is. It reminds him more than ever that they're in this together. That as they navigate this uncharted territory, they have each other.

"Rise, my people," Elijah intones. "We have much to celebrate."

Faces lift, once more focusing on Terra even though it's Elijah who's talking. It seems he's once more her spokesman, even though she's now before them in the flesh.

Elijah lifts his arms and extends them wide. "We're on our way to find Tomorrow Land!"

Fyve glances around, noting the other teens are doing the same. Treasure Island is now gone, slipped from sight in a way that makes his gut clench painfully. He turns away, instead focusing on the wide beyond they're now carving their way through. The red ocean stretches for miles, unbroken and unapologetic. Above it, the blue sky is just as vast, interrupted by the odd, lonely wisp of cloud. Fyve's never felt so small.

Yet more determined to leave his mark.

It's the only way he can ensure Sevin, Coal, his mother, even his father and each of his siblings, didn't die for nothing. That their lives counted for something.

"Now, let us celebrate," Elijah says, looking excited. "You have cabins assigned on the lower floors, but first, Terra has prepared us a feast."

There are a few gasps, several murmurs. Fyve and Halo glance at each other and he feels his stomach grumble. He hasn't eaten today. First, he was too shredded with grief. Then there were the preparations to farewell Sevin and his mother's bodies.

And then there was the frantic run and row out to The Oasis when he realized this is where he's meant to be. Honoring his family, although it's not just that.

He's meant to be with Halo.

She blinks up at him, looking like she's just as unsure of how to feel about all of this as he is.

He grins at her. "You know, when I woke up this morning, I thought to myself it sure would be nice to take Halo to a feast today."

Her responding smile is instantaneous and blinding. "What's the chances that I thought this morning that I sure would like to go to a feast with Fyve today?"

He chuckles, even as a part of him thinks the likelihood is as high as his expectations that Terra would be a child.

Ahead, Terra turns and stops before a door. It silently slides open, eliciting gasps of wonder and surprise, then she disappears from view. A good proportion of the crowd crane their necks, not wanting to lose sight, then sag when they can no longer see her.

"Terra will lead us to the feast," Elijah announces, then quickly follows her through the door.

After a stunned moment, the crowd lurches forward to join her, taking Fyve and Halo with them. They push through, some people's shoulders hitting the doorjamb with enough force to bruise, but they don't seem to care. They don't want to lose sight of the child who they've blindly accepted as the holder of their fate.

Ahead, Fyve sees Terra walking, almost looking like she's floating beneath her long robes, to the stairs and steps down. Whispers follow her, although she doesn't seem to register them.

"She's so beautiful!"

"I knew she was real!"

"She looked straight at me. She knows how hard I've been praying to her."

Descending into the ship, Fyve is momentarily startled by the totality they're quickly surrounded by. Solid walls, a sturdy roof, absolute shade that would be night if it wasn't for the small lights illuminating their way. It feels strangely comforting and claustrophobic all at once.

Halo leans in close. "If Terra's here, who's controlling the ship?"

Fyve drags his gaze from the wonder around him. "So many questions," he says, conscious of how much of an understatement that is.

Ahead, Terra descends more stairs and Elijah and the one hundred teens dutifully follow. They reach another corridor and Fyve sees that names have been printed on some of the doors. This must be their allocated sleeping quarters. He suddenly hopes his own isn't too far away from Halo's. He's never had a space all to himself. In fact, with the too-recent loss of Sevin, any space will feel too big.

He thinks of the soft bed he and Halo saw through the window when they snuck onto the ship. It had looked so inviting, but he'd take a hard mat every night of his life if it would mean sharing it with his sister again.

After making their way through the winding corridors and never-ending stairs, Fyve realizes they've come to the same large room he and Halo discovered. She'd called it the ballroom, something about the massive expanse being dedicated to nothing but dancing.

Already bracing himself for the intimidating size of the room, Fyve is still left speechless when they enter. The teens fan out, some just as silent, others crying out in surprise.

A long table sits in the middle of the room, and on it sits the most food Fyve's ever seen in his life. Stretched over several feet are platters, stacks, and pitchers. Surely, none of it can be real.

Several teens almost fall over in their rush to get to it. But when they do, they shove handfuls into their mouth, their eyes rolling back in their heads as they chew as fast as they can. Seeing this isn't some hallucination, others rush forward. Fyve grabs Halo's hand and they join them, pushing between a guy and a girl to get to the table. He grabs the first thing he sees and passes it to her, then jams another helping into his mouth.

Salted flavor bursts over his tongue and he quickly swallows so he can repeat the heady experience. Beside him, Halo's doing the same. So is everyone. Fyve looks around in wonder, once more struggling to believe this is really happening.

Sliced meat sits on shiny platters in portions far larger than a rat. Bread is stacked periodically, but it's not the flat, hard servings he's known all his life. They're rounds of brown that fit in his hand yet are far lighter than he expects. There are foods he has no hope of recognizing. Small balls of green, strange, pointed sticks of orange, bowls of little kidney-shaped things that turn to paste in his mouth. Everything is soft and salty, and right now, it's the most delicious thing Fyve's ever tasted.

Within minutes his stomach is objecting, feeling like it's been unnaturally stretched, but Fyve doesn't stop. No one does. It's as if they have to devour this all before it disappears.

"Praise Terra," someone shouts around a mouthful of food.

Dozens echo the sentiment, looking up from the table for the first time. Fyve glances around, looking for the robed child. The door to the ballroom is closed, Elijah standing not far from it, while the teens crowd around the long table. Terra's gone. Practically disappeared.

Halo looks down at the round of bread in one hand and a slice of meat in the other, as if something just struck her. "Who prepared all this?"

Conducting another quick sweep that confirms Terra hasn't stayed around to watch the hundred teens she chose, Fyve returns his focus to Halo. All he can do is give her the same answer from earlier. "So many questions."

Someone shoves them and Fyve frowns, drawing Halo to his side but not moving.

"Make room, will you?" growls a voice.

Fyve's frown deepens when he realizes it's Ajax trying to jostle in closer to a platter of meat. The guy's own scowl dissolves when he realizes it's his sister that he just tried to bully out of the way.

"Oh, hey Halo," he says, not having the grace to look embarrassed. "I just wanted to make sure Viney got some of this stuff."

He angles his body and a red-haired girl tucks in next to him. "Thanks, Ajax," she purrs, picking up a piece of meat and slipping it into her mouth.

"Sure thing," he responds, his chest expanding.

Viney picks up another piece of meat and holds it up to him and he takes it with his teeth, his gaze holding hers.

Halo snorts then tugs Fyve's arm, tearing his gaze from the unsettling sight. Does Ajax even care that his pregnant partner is back on Treasure Island, possibly unable to feed herself or their unborn baby?

"Here," she says, passing him one of the soft orange things. "I think this is called a carrot, although I imagined them harder."

Fyve takes it and chews on it, his mind now back on Treasure Island. The food here could feed so many for so long. Guilt that he's eaten so much that his stomach is tight and he feels sick makes it a little hard to swallow.

Cee, Bloo, Rubee and Jett should be here.

He glances at Halo. "Can you see now why I could never have come without Sevin? If I were here, knowing she was missing out on this, I couldn't live with myself."

Halo blinks. Then blinks again. "Fyve..." She swallows. "Sevin would've wanted you here."

His stomach clenches painfully, multiplying the nausea. "That's not the point. What sort of brother would I be to enjoy this, while she's there, starving and fighting to survive?"

"Yes, but—"

He shakes his head, not wanting to think about things that could never have been. He slips an arm around Halo. "But I'm here." He brushes a strand of hair from her face. "With the one person I trust most."

As he says the words, Fyve realizes they're the truth. And she not only has his trust.

She has his heart.

Her lashes flicker as she nods. She opens her mouth, but before she can speak, Elijah calls out.

"Finish up," he says, indicating toward the almost-empty table. Fyve suspects pockets are just as full as stomachs. "It's time to see your sleeping quarters. Each of you will have your own room."

Fyve grabs some more bread, then a few slices of meat, and passes them to Halo. He smiles, wondering at the way she hesitates before taking it, and feeling a rush of warmth when she does. He jams some more into his own pockets, focusing on the one thing he's sure about.

So many questions, but there's one truth to cling to.

He and Halo will find the answers.

Together.

HALO

*H*alo lies on her bed and holds her stomach, unsure if she should call for help. Is it normal that eating too much can make you feel like this? Surely, not? Because if it is, then she's not certain she wants to go to another feast.

Actually, no. That's not true. The feast had been the single best moment of her life so far. Better than standing beneath her tree. Better than being chosen for The Oasis. Better than kissing Fyve under the starry sky. And *that's* saying something.

The only thing that could have made the feast better was if Sevin had been there.

"Urgh," Halo groans, shifting to her side to see if that helps and returning to her back when it only seems to make things worse.

Maybe it's the guilt that's causing her stomach to spasm like this? Because when Fyve had said he couldn't live with himself if Sevin were back on Treasure Island while he was feasting, Halo had to stop herself from crawling under the table so he couldn't see her face.

How can she possibly keep this secret from him? It was one of the reasons she'd so readily agreed to stick to the rules and sleep in separate rooms. It's easier to hide something from someone when you don't have to look at their desperately gorgeous face.

Ajax, on the other hand, doesn't seem to think the rules apply to him…

Reaching for one of her impossibly fluffy pillows, she shoves it over her face, trying to block out the evidence of just how many rules her brother is breaking through the thin wall that separates their cabins. She'd seen him slipping Viney into his room, despite their father announcing that Terra wishes for them to sleep alone.

Poor Cloud!

Halo already regrets putting Viney through to the final trial. She'd thought she looked sweet and kind, which to be fair, maybe she is. It's just that the timing is all sorts of wrong. Ajax hadn't even waited a day before moving on, proof of how much confidence he has that The Oasis will ever return for those left behind. Which brings Halo's thoughts back to Sevin, and her guilt consumes her once more.

It's too late for Fyve to jump off the ship and return, which means that maybe she should tell him what she'd seen as they'd sailed away. But it feels cruel to tell him now after what he said at the feast. The poor guy will be tortured! Maybe it's better for him to think Sevin's gone so he can go ahead and do great things with his life. Halo had already known Sevin was smart before the final Trial, but faking her own death to get her brother to board the ship had taken things to a new level. It was the most selfless act Halo's ever seen.

Deciding this bed is far too soft for anyone to possibly sleep on, Halo gets up and goes into the bathroom attached to her cabin. The whole concept of a room just to clean yourself in seems so extravagant. She takes a drink directly from the magic tap that refills itself, her mouth dry from the salty food at the feast. As she washes her face, she realizes there are no more answers inside this small room than there had been when lying in her bed. Her stomach does feel a little better for standing up though. Perhaps a walk is what she needs.

Recalling the map of the ship on the back of the stairwell door, Halo closes her eyes as she conjures it in her mind. The engine room isn't too far from here. And her father had said if she passed the final Trial, it would be hers. Which would surely mean she can visit it whenever she likes?

She goes to her cabin door and pokes out her head. The hallway is quiet. She waits a few moments in case Terra comes floating down the hallway in her voluminous robes. How strange that Terra had turned out to be a child. This is just another thing that makes no sense. Terra has been around since long before Halo was born. So, how can she be younger than her? Do her powers prevent her from aging? Is she even human?

There's only one thing Halo knows for sure. And that is she's not going to find the answers to any of these questions while she's alone in this claustrophobic cabin.

She steps out into the hallway, and walks quietly past Ajax's cabin, deciding if anyone asks that she'll tell them she's looking for her father. Which is plausible given she has no idea which one of these doors belongs to him. She passes Fyve's cabin and hesitates, resisting the urge to see if he wants to come with her. Her hand even clenches into a fist as if it's ready to knock.

But she doesn't. She walks on. Seeing Fyve means keeping secrets from him. She needs more time. She has a decision to make—keep the truth to herself and carry the weight of the guilt, or tell Fyve Sevin's still alive, passing him the burden of tortured guilt as he realizes he left his beloved sister behind.

Reaching the stairwell, Halo glances around to make sure she wasn't followed, then grips the handrail as she descends toward the engine room.

The hum of the machinery that's keeping this ship moving gets louder with each step she takes. Last time she'd come here, the ship had been stationary, and it had felt peaceful. Now it has an excitement about it, and it makes Halo's pulse pick up. Terra seems to have extraordinary access to the most miraculous things. Food enough for a feast. A gigantic ship that's slicing through the ocean. The power to take any of their lives at a moment's whim. All from a skinny, bald girl who would barely reach Halo's shoulder. She doesn't seem to speak, either, which is interesting given she's whispered Halo's father so many instructions over the years.

Halo opens the door to the engine room and steps into the brightly lit room. She looks around in fascination at how it's come to life. Pistons are pumping, generators are roaring, and lights on panels are blinking. There's the scent of fuel in the air and Halo can't help but wonder if she'd ever gotten her motor running back on Treasure Island if it would've made noises like this. It's unlikely. There's more technology in this one room than has ever washed up on Treasure Island since the currents first created her former home.

She takes a few more steps into the room and notices a cup of steaming tea has been abandoned at one of the desks. Looking around, she sees no sign of who had been drinking it.

"Hello?" she calls, walking toward the tea. "I'm looking for my father, Elijah. Is anybody in here?"

One of the boilers lets out an almighty *clank* and Halo jumps a foot in the air, making her realize just how on edge she is. She turns from the desk and walks straight into a swathe of soft fabric.

"Sorry!" Halo stumbles backward to realize it's Terra herself.

The young girl holds very still, neither smiling nor frowning.

"Who are you?" Halo asks, finding herself stepping forward again as she takes in the sight of this strange girl. "*What* are you?"

Terra blinks at her, not saying a word.

Halo lifts a hand and reaches out, her fingers hovering just inches from Terra's face. But just as she's about to make contact, Terra steps back and a sharp pain pierces Halo's temples.

"No!" Halo cries as she doubles over, certain this must be what it feels like to be claimed. Her hands fly to her face, and she feels a sticky dampness dripping from her nose. Lifting a hand away, she sees it's stained deep red.

"No," she whimpers again as she drops to her knees. "I'm sorry. I shouldn't have come here. Please, Terra. Don't claim me."

Terra tilts her head impassively as she looks down at Halo, then raises a single arm and points at the door.

Halo drags in a deep breath, trying to steady the rapid beating of her heart, as she figures out what this means. The pain has ceased, and the blood dripping from her nose has steadied.

Terra points more urgently at the door.

"Y-you w-want me to leave?" Halo drags herself into a stand. Her legs are shaking so badly she's not sure if they'll hold her, but she doesn't wait to find out.

She runs.

To the door. To the stairwell. Up to the second level of The Oasis. Down the passageway. And to her room.

She closes the door and leans against it. Sweat beads on her forehead and she propels herself to the bathroom, bends over the bowl-shaped thing and splashes water on her face, sending rivulets of red down the hole. But it's not enough to cool her down and before she knows it, the contents of her stomach rush upward and are expelled.

Turning the tap on to wash it away, she splashes more water on her face, rinses out her mouth, and looks up at herself in the mirror. Green eyes lock on green eyes and she stares at herself for long moments, hardly able to believe she's still alive.

"What were you thinking?" she asks herself, glad she'd resisted the urge to bring Fyve with her to the engine room.

Terra may not have been so merciful to him. Halo could be standing in this room right now, grieving his death, having never told him that Sevin's still alive.

There's a white fluffy cloth and she lifts it to her face, patting herself dry before going to lie down on her bed, wishing she'd never gotten up in the first place.

Despite the fact Terra hadn't uttered a single word, she'd been very clearly warning her. Terra hadn't wanted her dead but was letting her know what would happen if she wandered the corridors of this hulk of metal at night ever again. And it's a warning Halo's prepared to heed. Because whatever power it is that Terra has, it's real. She hadn't imagined the blood nose or the pain in her temples. Her life is in Terra's hands. Which means no more breaking the rules.

Halo shifts on the bed, trying to get comfortable as she sinks into the mattress. Deciding to move to the floor, she lies down on her back.

"Better," she murmurs, closing her eyes and pretending she's back at home on her sleeping mat listening to Ajax snoring on the other side of the room. She wonders if anyone has moved into their hut, taking it as their own. She hopes so. It's not like they need it now. Just as long as it's not Zake.

"*Halo,*" comes a whisper.

She sits up and looks around but sees nobody. "Who's here?"

"*Halo,*" the voice whispers again.

She gets up and goes to the door, pressing a button that fills the room with a soft glow. She looks around, searching every corner and again, finds nobody. Could Ajax be calling her from the next room?

She knocks on the wall. "Ajax, is that you?"

"I'm busy!" he shouts back, clearly annoyed at the interruption.

Viney's giggle floats through the wall.

Grimacing, Halo lies back down on the floor and closes her

eyes, deciding she must have been imagining it. After all, she had just had a terrible shock. But this time, she leaves the light on.

For a few minutes, there's nothing but silence and she concentrates on the gentle rocking of the ship in the sea.

"*Halo*," the voice comes again. "*When you saw me in the engine room just now, you asked me who I am. I'm Terra.*"

She sits up again, and blinks, looking around the room, again seeing nobody.

"*You asked me what I am*," the voice whispers. "*I am nobody. I am everybody.*"

"Where are you?" Halo asks, adding another question to her list.

"*I am everywhere. I am nowhere*," the voice says. "*Most of all, I'm inside your head. Listen to what I have to say from now on, or I'll be forced to punish you again.*"

"Whoa." Halo lies down before she falls down and stares up at the ceiling as she processes this. Terra is talking to her just like she speaks to her father.

"*Halo.*" Terra's whisper echoes inside her head. "*Be ready. Sleep well. Tomorrow is an important day.*"

"Why?" Halo lets out a slow breath. Can Terra hear her, too? "What's happening tomorrow?"

"*Tomorrow, the real Trials begin*," says Terra.

There's a hum, then a split second of static, and Halo's room is plunged into darkness.

"Terra?" she whispers, already knowing that she's gone.

Silence is followed by more silence.

Halo covers her face with her hands once more, not sure what any of this means.

They just finished the Trials. She doesn't have the strength to do it all again.

FYVE

*T*he sound that wakes Fyve is one he's never heard before. The wail is louder than anything on Treasure Island, longer, terrifyingly everywhere.

He's already on his feet before his eyes are even open. "Sevin!" he shouts. "Where are you?" The need to keep his sister safe pounds through his veins.

Three blinks and he realizes he's not in his hut. Two more and he remembers he's on The Oasis.

The next one is the sucker punch of awareness that his sister is dead.

The ear-splitting wailing still pierces the air as Fyve stands in the middle of his cabin, chest heaving, body slowly waving from side to side as everything else does. He shakes his head, unsure whether he's trying to escape the loss slicing him anew, or whether he's trying to lose the lingering effects of sleep.

It took him a long time to fall into that black oblivion last night. First, there was the ache in his stomach as he wondered if it was going to explode. Then there was the overwhelming loneliness as he'd climbed into a bed. Alone.

He's always slept beside Sevin. Sometimes his mother was

only a few feet away, Coal and his family were always in the adjacent hut. Not even the bed as soft as a cloud could make up for their absence. The need to see Halo had been overwhelming, but she'd looked so tired after the feast as she'd told him they were best off just retiring to their rooms that he hadn't wanted to disturb her. Eventually, he'd fallen asleep, lulled by the knowledge he'll be seeing her the following day. That a future that he's looking forward to still exists.

Stumbling forward as he tries to adjust to the constant, undulating movement of the ship, Fyve opens his door. He registers others standing in the hallway, looking as confused as he is. Everyone glances around, trying to understand the awful noise.

"I think it's Terra's wake up call," mutters a guy from the cabin next to Fyve's. "She sure ain't being quiet this morning."

Fyve's about to respond when he registers what others already have.

Each room has a plate sitting on a shelf beside the door. And on it is food and a cup of water. Everyone moves at once, devouring it. Another round piece of bread. Some pale slices of salty meat. A few wedges of something soft and orange and deliciously sweet. It's all gone within a few seconds, crammed into Fyve's mouth and swallowed before it can disappear.

"Terra can wake me whenever she wants," says his neighbor through a full mouth.

Fyve smiles, extending his hand. "Hi, I'm Fyve."

The guy with the mop of thick black curls grins back. "Dargo," he says, shaking a leather bracelet further down his wrist before clasping Fyve's hand. "I saw you row out in the final Trial and take on that leatherskin. Impressive."

Fyve's not sure what to say to that, but before he can formulate anything, the wailing sound stops. The ensuing silence feels almost as loud. Teens stand in the hallway, glancing between each other and the staircases on each end.

They've eaten, now what?

Fyve takes a step forward, deciding the first thing he's going to do is see Halo. They can figure out what this strange new life on The Oasis is going to look like.

Suddenly, Elijah's voice echoes loudly down the corridor. "Return to your cabins."

Dargo gasps and spins around, looking for their leader. But Fyve glances up, realizing the sound came from the ceiling. A small, round piece of mesh sits flush with the smooth white surface. Is Elijah in the ceiling?

"Terra has given you her orders," Elijah says through the mesh. "Return to your cabin and wait for further instructions."

Fyve hesitates. He wants to see Halo, to make sure she's okay. When they'd said goodbye last night, she'd not only seemed tired, but…preoccupied. He'd realized that his mad rush to The Oasis had been fueled by an assumption. The very same thought that just had him going to see her.

That she wanted to be together as much as he did.

That they'd forge this future side by side.

Dargo turns back into his room. "What Terra wants, Terra gets," he says cheerily, shutting the door behind him.

Reluctantly, Fyve does the same. Wandering around the ship right now would be blatantly defying what they were just told to do, and he doesn't want to start this voyage like that. Terra's fed them. Promised them Tomorrow Land. He needs to respect that. Which isn't easy given she claimed his sister. But if he wants to keep Halo alive, he has to survive himself. Which means obeying the rules for now.

The moment he's closed off in his cabin again, it feels like the isolation has been trapped in there with him. One person per room, lined up beside each other, close, yet disconnected, is the most alien thing Fyve's ever experienced. How can anyone be happy like this? With nothing but their own thoughts to keep them company.

"Take off your clothes."

This time, Elijah's voice comes from the round piece of mesh tucked above the door, and it's much quieter. Almost as if he's speaking to Fyve directly.

Fyve stares at it, uncomfortable with everything that's happening, and not with being undressed. Half the people on Treasure Island are barely clothed. No, it's as if the blind obedience to Terra is even more expected here on The Oasis. Somehow, he'd thought there would be more freedom.

"Terra is here to teach you," Elijah says. "She will know whether you are willing to learn."

Fyve glances around, now feeling like he's being watched. Slowly, his gaze still darting from the bed to the empty shelves lining the opposite wall, he peels his shirt off. What is going on? Next, he removes his pants, then places his clothes carefully on a small table beside the bed. They're all he owns.

"Enter the bathroom," Elijah orders. "Inside the small booth, turn the metal knobs."

Cautiously, Fyve does as he's told. There, he turns one of the strange dials, gasping when water shoots out from the flattened disc above him. It sprays him in the face and sluices down his body before he can jump back, slamming into the clear door that had closed behind him.

"Now, clean yourself." This time, Elijah's voice comes from within the bathroom, making Fyve jump again. He blinks through the water dripping down his face, trying to understand the rain that's pouring down *inside* the room.

This is how people used to wash themselves?

Fyve extends his hand, watching in fascination as the needle-thick streams of clear water hit his skin, sending dozens of tiny rivers coursing down his arm, his chest, his legs. It's cool but pleasant.

Giving himself up to the sensations, he ducks under the stream, now scrubbing everywhere. The water quickly turns brown as dirt rushes to the small hole in the middle of the cubicle. Fyve watches as his skin progressively lightens to a shade he's never seen before—a deep, warm copper, not dark and mottled like wet soil.

His whole body is tingling when the water suddenly shuts off. "Get dressed," Elijah orders.

Fyve steps out of the rain cubicle, wet in a way he's only been after a storm. He shakes his head, water droplets scattering everywhere, and slicks the rest from his arms, chest, and legs, registering that it trickles down another hole in the floor.

Back in his room, he's shocked to find his clothes are gone. He rushes to the bed, frantically throwing back the sheets, then looking all around when he doesn't find anything. Terra wants everyone naked? He flushes as the first image is of Halo.

On the next spin, Fyve registers his door is cracked open. Wired and alert, he peeks through, seeing the plate on the shelf is gone, instead, some neatly folded material sits there. He grabs it, realizing they're clean clothes. A shirt and trousers, in the same cream color as Terra's robes.

Closing the door with a frown, Fyve stares at the gift, then glances at the bathroom. For the first time, he wonders where the water went. Where it came from.

He grips the clothes. And who left these while he was in the rain cubicle, along with the food?

He assumes every other teen on this ship is receiving the same instructions and has been given fresh clothes, too. Terra has managed to be a hundred different places at once.

Quickly dressing, he also wonders how soon Halo would've been asking the same questions. Far sooner than him, he guesses. Maybe he was too stunned, maybe he was lulled by a full stomach and so many wonders, but now that the questions have formed, they're quickly added to the others.

It turns out The Oasis has more of those than answers.

Feeling strange in the new clothes with trousers that hug his legs all the way to the floor, and a strange tunic-like shirt that covers his chest and upper arms, Fyve strides back to the door. He wants to see Halo. He needs to.

"Sit down."

Elijah's words are said mildly, almost warmly, but for some reason they have a shiver running down Fyve's spine. They weren't a request. They were an order.

Once more, he looks around, wondering if Terra is watching right now. Or is Elijah? Or someone else…

"Terra has some questions for you," Elijah says through the mesh. "She wants to know her chosen teens."

Clenching his jaw, Fyve sits on the bed. Is he going to be trapped in here forever?

"How many teeth do you have?"

Fyve's eyebrows cinch, his gaze darting to the mesh circle in the ceiling. Is Terra watching as well as listening to a hundred teens in their rooms?

He runs his tongue over his teeth, mentally counting. "Twenty-eight." He briefly thinks about people like Zake, who probably can't count that high, or his own father, who lost several teeth before adulthood. How would they answer Terra?

"How many illnesses have you had in your life?"

Fyve frowns. Everyone in his family seemed to get sick but him. There were many times he felt guilty about it. "A few," he says, feeling weird talking to an empty room. "I vomited a lot once when I ate a dead rat I found stuck underneath our trap." For a day or two, he'd wondered whether he would be joining his brothers and sisters in the ocean.

"How many siblings do you have?"

Fyve shoots to his feet, pain slicing straight through his chest. "Why do you want to know?"

Silence.

He hunches his shoulders, almost feeling the weight of

Terra's dark, emotionless gaze. "Eight," he mutters darkly as he's reminded she took every one of them.

The small child who is somehow everywhere, doing everything.

"How many scratches are above your door?"

Fyve squints as he focuses, realizing there are indeed, thin scratches engraved above his door. Have they always been there? And why does Terra want to know this? "Three."

There's a pause as he waits for the next question.

"You are healthy. Terra is pleased."

Fyve freezes as the words are said. His heart stutters. His breath disintegrates.

It can't be...

Elijah didn't say them through the mesh in the ceiling. The words were said in Fyve's head. By Terra.

His knees go weak and he only stays standing by sheer force of will. Terra spoke to him, in his head, in the way she speaks to Elijah. What does that even mean?

He's never felt more terrified and blessed at the same time.

"Assemble on the deck," says Elijah, the order making Fyve startle. The softly spoken command suddenly feels like a shout in the small room.

Because a soft, pleased voice just carried through his mind.

Numbly, Fyve does as he's told, making his way out of the room. He vaguely registers Dargo exiting, barely recognizable with his clean skin and neat, pale clothes. Other teens exit, all washed, all wearing the same outfit. They don't look like their world has just been rattled. They look fresh-faced and excited. Some even jog toward the upper deck, bouncing up the stairs with anticipation.

Fyve rubs his forehead, struggling to pin an emotion down. There's a fleeting flash of elation. An echo of the others' excitement. But mostly a tidal wave of confusion.

Up on the deck, the sulfuric, briny scent of the ocean washes over him. He wipes his hand down his face, trying to get out of his head. The others congregate where they did yesterday, now almost replicas of each other with their identical outfits and wet hair. There are no more dirt-streaked faces, torn, murky-colored clothes, desperate expressions wondering when they'll see their next meals.

Fyve startles. All signs of Treasure Island are slowly ceasing to exist.

And as much as he's relishing a full stomach and a shirt that doesn't feel like it's going to disintegrate at any moment, he doesn't want to forget his home. His roots. His family.

"Fyve!"

He spins around at the sound of Halo's voice. Then stops.

Halo's always been beautiful, but he hadn't realized exactly how much was hiding beneath the layers of Treasure Island. Her long hair streams over her shoulders in damp strands, looking like spun gold. Her skin glows. The flush on her cheeks is the most fascinating thing he's ever seen.

"Fyve," she says, rushing toward him and clutching his hands. She pauses, her eyes roam over his face and hair, then she quickly shakes her head. "We need to talk."

He finds himself smiling, glad to see her as excited to see him as he was her. Maybe she was nothing more than tired last night.

"I have something to tell you," he says, his voice hushed. Will she believe him if he tells her Terra spoke to him?

"Me, too. And it's important."

Someone jostles into Fyve's shoulder, reminding him they're far from alone. Maybe he should wait. Although who knows if they'll be ordered back to their rooms. "Listen, something happened—"

"My people." Elijah's voice carries through the air, far fuller now that it's not trickling through the mesh circles. "Terra has spoken."

Fyve turns around, Halo by his side, and spots Elijah on a balcony one floor up. Terra is standing next to him, hands tucked in the folds of her robes, somber face staring at the teens. Fyve studies her lips, not only are they unmoving, they're pressed into a firm line. She spoke to Elijah. In his head. Now that Fyve's experienced it himself, he can no longer doubt the truth of Elijah's words.

"And she's excited for the next stage of our journey to begin."

Halo's hand clenches around Fyve's, almost as if she's worried. He glances down, and the furrow between her brows definitely suggests concern.

The crowd of teens shift forward, rapt faces angled up at their savior. "We are yours to command, Terra," Dargo calls out and Fyve wonders if she spoke in his head, too.

Elijah smiles as Terra doesn't react. He raises his hands in the way he always has when he's about to make a big announcement. "I have good news. The Oasis Trials continue!"

Stunned silence is the only response. They've already completed the Trials. That's how they got here.

Halo is slowly shaking her head, dread tugging down the edges of her mouth.

"Over the coming days and weeks, you will have the opportunity to demonstrate your true value to Terra. At the end of the Trials, Terra will choose fifty teens who will go on to forge the future of humankind."

The silence is no longer stunned. It's the cumulative absence of breath of a hundred people.

Fifty?

That means half of them are destined for Tomorrow Land.

And half of them aren't.

HALO

ood news. Halo is stuck on these two words that she heard her father utter. She hears them on repeat, swirling inside her mind.

Good news. Good news. Good news.

The Trials are continuing, and fifty teens will be chosen.

This. Is. Not. Good. News.

Because what's going to happen to the fifty who miss out? Halo can't imagine the ship turning around to drop them back off at Treasure Island. Which means…what exactly does it mean? She honestly has no idea. But it can't be *good news.*

Halo squeezes Fyve's hand, liking this new clean smell he has about him. The clothes suit him, too. The cream color of the fabric is making his features seem darker. His skin looks smoother. And how she'd love to run her fingers through the dampness of his hair.

She'd burst out of her cabin after that weird series of questions Terra had asked her, desperate to find out if the same thing happened to Fyve. To tell him about what happened to her last night when Terra had warned her with a claiming that she never went through with, then told her about the Trials.

But none of that seems to matter now. It's clear from the sea of cream fabric surrounding them that everyone is experiencing the same thing. The same confusion. The same terror. The same desperate disappointment. Terra must be talking to them all.

Ajax and Viney stand off to the side, clutching hands in the same way Halo is holding Fyve's. Maybe it's good that Ajax didn't mope around mourning Cloud. They're all going to need a hand to hold to get through whatever Terra is going to throw at them next.

Justice stands alone, as seems to be the theme of her life. She's leaning heavily on a set of crutches, the bulge of a bandage visible underneath her trousers. At least she's received the medical care she so desperately needed. In time, hopefully she'll make a full recovery. Sevin would like that.

Halo's father raises his arms and Terra stands steadfast by his side. Her flowing gown flutters in the breeze, making her look like she's sprouted wings and is about to take off into the clouds they all assume she came from. Her bald head catches the sunlight, giving her an ethereal glow and an innocence normally reserved for newborn babies.

"Our first Trial begins immediately," Halo's father says. "Please excuse Terra as she goes ahead to prepare."

"Prepare what?" Fyve mutters as Terra turns and disappears through the door behind her.

Halo squeezes his hand. "We can still be claimed here," she warns, her temples pulsing in memory of the pain Terra had inflicted on her in the engine room.

Fyve nods and falls silent as they wait to hear what this first Trial will involve.

Halo's father goes to a large rectangular board that's been draped in a sheet. He uncovers it with a flourish to reveal several lines of text.

"I can't read that." Fyve frowns.

"I thought your eyesight was good?" Halo looks up at the

board, clearly able to make out the words even from this distance.

"I can see it just fine." Fyve lets go of her hand to cross his arms. "I said I can't read that. There are too many words. I don't know all of them."

"Oh." Halo nods her understanding. Most people on Treasure Island have basic literacy skills, making this number of words likely to be too much for most of the teens gathered here.

She's just about to read it out loud when a voice enters her mind. The way Fyve's jaw drops open slightly as he tilts his head, she knows he's hearing it, too. The voice is young and female. The same voice Halo heard last night that must belong to Terra.

Terra reads the words from the board…

Hidden from sight, I live all around you
Never to be seen until now
Clear as light, and bright as coal
My appearance is a deception

I look like I fly, but I can't
I seem like I'm soft, but I'm strong
I feel like I'm smooth, but I'm bitter
The sound I make when we meet is all wrong

You could see right through me if only you looked
Because without you, I wouldn't be here
You need me, and now I need you
My appearance is a deception.

Who am I?

"Terra," breathes Fyve, stealing the answer from Halo's lips.

"You must solve this riddle," Halo's father says proudly. "When you have the answer, you need to find Terra and convey it to her. She will provide further instructions. You have one hour. Talking is forbidden. For this Trial, you must work alone."

Halo takes an image of the board with her mind, wanting to turn over each clue before deciding on her answer. If only she could talk to Fyve! Warn him that they need to think this one through. Terra is the obvious answer. But is it too obvious?

Halo tears herself away from Fyve and paces over to the railing of the deck. The desire to talk to him is too strong. She doesn't want them to fail this Trial before they've even started. Why are they even being put through this at all? They passed the Trials! They're supposed to be together forever. Not fighting again for a chance to survive.

And what happens if they fail?

Knowing there's no point in objecting to what's happening, she starts with the first line of the riddle, bringing it to the front of her mind as she looks out over the crimson ocean.

Hidden from sight, I live all around you. Never to be seen until now. There's no denying that clue fits Terra. Until yesterday, nobody had seen her at all.

Clear as light, and bright as coal. My appearance is a deception. This is a little more cryptic, although Terra taking the form of a young girl does seem like some kind of deception.

I look like I fly, but I can't. That has to be a reference to Terra's flowing gown. Halo had only just been thinking she'd looked like she was about to take off into the sky.

I seem like I'm soft, but I'm strong. Again, this fits the image of a small girl filled with power.

I feel like I'm smooth, but I'm bitter. This could be talking about Terra's baldness. Although, is she bitter? Perhaps killing all those people would make even a deity a little bitter.

The sound I make when we meet is all wrong. That clue has to be about Terra! Because they've all learned she's far from the silent girl who until moments ago, was standing on the balcony. She speaks in very clear terms when she has something to say. It just happens inside all their heads.

But what about the last few lines?

You could see right through me if only you looked. Halo's eyes are wide open, but she hasn't been able to see right through anything just yet. Perhaps she will in time.

Because without you, I wouldn't be here. This points to Terra as well. None of them would be here on The Oasis if Terra hadn't gathered them.

You need me, and now I need you. They are most definitely at Terra's mercy. But does Terra need them?

And then that final line repeated from before. *My appearance is a deception.*

"It sure is," she mutters, then catches herself. No talking. Her father had been very clear.

She turns back to the deck and sees teens all around grinning broadly, no doubt believing they've worked out the riddle. Fyve is watching Halo, seeming unwilling to go in search of Terra until she's ready to go with him. Once again, she's glad that Sevin isn't here. How could Fyve possibly go through all this again with the fear of losing his sister? He'd probably take his chances with Sevin on one of the lifeboats and sail off in search of Treasure Island, never to be seen again.

The riddle nags at Halo and she shakes her head at Fyve, trying to tell him to think harder. Although, how can he when he can't read the board and Terra's voice will now be a jumbled memory inside his frantic mind?

Terra is just too obvious an answer. It can't be her. But who else could it possibly be? It's not Halo's father. None of those clues fit. For a fleeting moment, she wonders if maybe it's herself. Although, none of the clues make sense for her either.

Perhaps this is the trick of the Trial. That the obvious answer is indeed correct...

Fyve walks over to Halo, but before he can reach her, she's marching across the deck, still not trusting herself to be anywhere near him. If only she'd told him the claimings are a real threat before they'd been told to be silent.

A stream of teens leaves the deck in search of Terra, and Halo crouches by the pool, watching the squishy pods swim underneath their blobs of green. It looks like they've been breeding. She's certain there's more of them today than yesterday. What a magical thought, that the future generations of these pods might feed her own great great grandchildren. And she was there when they were scooped up from the sea.

Fyve squats next to her and points up to the balcony where Terra had been standing.

Halo shakes her head as she churns over every possibility of where else the riddle might lead. There's still one line that doesn't make any sense.

Clear as light, and bright as coal.

What does that mean? And why those specific words? She'd seen a chunk of black coal once and it had been anything but bright. Although it's used to make fire, which is bright. Is that what it means?

Then it hits her, and she stands up straight.

Coal. Not the fuel source but the person. Coal!

Coal had been bright. And he was the one who'd discovered they could eat the pods she's staring at right now. Is that what the clue means?

She runs the riddle through her mind once more.

Hidden from sight, I live all around you. Never to be seen until now. The pods have always been around them, only discovered when these Trials began.

Clear as light, and bright as coal. The pods are translucent. And

Coal…he'd been smarter than any of them ever knew, just like these resilient creatures.

My appearance is a deception. That line could definitely relate to the pods. Nobody would expect these squishy looking things to be such a rich food source.

I look like I fly, but I can't. Halo studies the wings of the pods as they flap up and down, gliding through the water with no hope of ever flying to the clouds.

I seem like I'm soft, but I'm strong. The pods are most definitely strong. Barely anything else has been able to survive in the acidic depths of the ocean.

I feel like I'm smooth, but I'm bitter. The sharp taste of the pods comes back to Halo and her fingertips flutter to her lips. Bitter is exactly the right word to describe them.

The sound I make when we meet is all wrong. She looks into the pool with a frown. These creatures don't make any sound at all.

Fyve touches her on the arm and points to Ajax and Viney who are watching them, and Halo remembers the word Viney had used for the pods. Pteropods. Spelled with a 'p' yet pronounced with a 't'. That's it! The sound I make when we meet is all wrong! It has to be a pteropod.

Bouncing on her toes now, Halo runs through the final lines of the riddle.

You could see right through me if only you looked. One of the pods swims near the surface and Halo can indeed see all the way through it.

Because without you, I wouldn't be here. They caught these pods in the final Trial. That's why they're here!

You need me, and now I need you. They most definitely needed the pods to pass the Trial. And now that they're captive in the pool, these small creatures are at their mercy to keep them alive.

My appearance is a deception. Who am I?

"You're a pod," Halo whispers, before clamping a hand to her mouth. Several seconds pass and when no pain pierces her skull, she dares to draw in a breath.

Fyve crinkles his brow as he tries to figure out what's going on in her mind, and she points to the pool, hoping he'd heard her whispered words.

The answer is a pod. She looks him in the eye, begging him to understand.

He nods and tugs at her hand. The clock is ticking, and they really don't know how long it's going to take to find Terra.

They break into a run as they race to the stairwell and take the stairs two at a time in their desperation to get downstairs. There are people everywhere inside the ship. They seem panicked, opening doors and searching all the corners of the ship for Terra.

Halo stops for a moment to think. Terra is unlikely to be in one of their individual cabins. Nor is she likely to be in the engine room again. The only other place they all know is the ballroom. She has to be there!

Halo taps a few people on the arm and points toward the ballroom, but they're either too frenzied or untrusting to pay her any attention and they continue their scattered search. However, Fyve seems to understand and they continue down the corridor.

There are a few people outside the ballroom when they arrive and as Halo steps inside and glances up at the ancient chandeliers, she thinks of the fleeting dance she'd had with Fyve when they'd snuck aboard this ship. Back when life had felt confusing but was infinitely simpler than it is now.

Fyve lets go of her hand. At the very least they need to make a show of having worked on this riddle alone.

Scanning the ballroom, Halo doesn't see Terra and she thinks she's gotten it all wrong. Then she sees her sitting cross-legged in the far corner. She's wearing robes of black, with a hood that covers not only her head but her face. Only her eyes are exposed. If Halo hadn't been certain she was here, she may have left the ballroom thinking it was empty.

Terra holds up a hand as they approach.

"One at a time," she says inside their minds.

Fyve puts a steadying hand on Halo's back and urges her forward, letting her go first.

She goes to Terra and sits on folded legs in front of her.

"What is the answer to the riddle?" Terra asks inside her head, her voice little more than a whisper.

Halo keeps her voice low, using the same hushed tones. "You're a pteropod."

Terra reaches inside her robes and removes a jar. Scooping out a pod, she hands it to Halo and points to her mouth.

"Eat," her voice says. *"Then return immediately to the deck. You have passed the Trial."*

Halo slides the smooth gelatinous creature between her lips and bites down, smiling when the bitterness explodes in her mouth. She should have more than enough energy now for whatever the next Trial involves. Fyve, too, when he tells Terra the answer.

Not wanting to hold Fyve up, Halo stands and walks toward the door to wait for him.

She's only taken a few steps when she hears Fyve's voice ring out clearly across the ballroom.

"You are Terra," he says as he kneels in the corner of the room. "The answer to the riddle is Terra."

FYVE

*T*erra looks at Fyve, her impassive eyes simultaneously seeming to be bottomless and have no depth at all. Then her lashes flutter, as if she's processing his words. For a second, he almost repeats them.

The answer to the riddle is Terra.

She reaches inside her robes and removes a jar. Her face still expressionless, she hands the small, fluttering body of a pod to him and points to his mouth.

"*Eat,*" her voice says, as it floats through his mind. "*Then return immediately to the deck. You have passed the Trial.*"

Fyve can't help the blinding grin that explodes across his face. He passed! And so did Halo! He slips the pod into his mouth and bites, not even grimacing at the bitterness that floods his tongue.

"Thank you," he says to Terra, words he never expected to utter to the person who claimed his sister's life.

This win is just as much for Sevin and Coal as it is for him and Halo. Coal was the one who had the courage to put one of those gelatinous blobs in his mouth, while it was Sevin's determination to compete in the Trials that has Fyve on this ship.

Just by being here, Fyve's ensuring their deaths weren't for nothing.

Terra's lashes flutter again, the only sign she heard him, and Fyve's not sure, but he swears she retracts into her black robes as if she's seeking their shadows.

Fyve pushes to his feet, tucking away the observation to think over another time. He's too relieved right now. And he wants to talk to Halo, so they can discuss everything that's happened since they arrived.

As he walks to the door, Fyve passes Dargo, his gaze zeroed on Terra. He's clearly nervous but also steps with determination. Fyve wishes he could tell him he'll be fine. The answer wasn't hard. It was downright obvious.

He finds Halo waiting for him on the other side of the doors to the ballroom, but rather than looking excited, she looks stricken. She grabs his hand and draws him further down the corridor. "What did she say?" she hisses.

"That I've passed," he says, squeezing her hand in reassurance. "She gave me a pod and told me to return to the deck."

Halo blinks in surprise. "But you said Terra was the answer."

"Because that's what it is." Fyve frowns in confusion. "What did you say?"

"The answer was pteropod, Fyve. The riddle was a trick."

Fyve runs through what he remembers of the riddle.

I look like I fly, but I can't

I feel like I'm smooth, but I'm bitter

My appearance is a deception.

His frown deepens. The pods fit each one of those descriptions. So, how did he pass?

"Maybe there are two answers," he offers, knowing how weak that sounds.

"Then what's the point of the riddle?"

Trying to ease the tension that's creeping up both their faces, Fyve smiles a little. "Always asking the hard questions."

Halo lets out a small huff. "It's the answers that would be nice."

Dargo exits the ballroom and Fyve turns to him but before he can say anything, a girl with long, pale hair—even paler than Halo's—rushes to him.

"What did she say?"

Dargo shrugs, looking a little pale. "Not much. Just to go back to my room and wait."

The girl gasps. "What answer did you give?"

"Iva, I was so sure it was Terra," he says, his voice tight. "It was the logical answer."

"Dargo," the girl says, fear evident in her voice. "The answer was the pteropods."

Fyve's gut tightens. The conversation between the couple is almost identical to the one he and Halo just had.

Except Fyve passed. And Dargo didn't.

Iva steps in closer and wraps her arms around Dargo's waist. "I have to go to the deck. I'll come and see you as soon as I can."

He nods, visibly swallowing. "Only when Terra permits it."

"Of course," Iva says. "We owe her everything."

Iva presses a quick kiss to Dargo's lips then walks away, smiling over her shoulder at him. Dargo smiles back, but even Fyve can tell it's an effort.

He's scared.

Because Elijah's words are now hanging in the corridor as if he just spoke them.

At the end of the Trials, Terra will choose fifty teens who will go on to forge the future of humankind.

If Dargo isn't one of those fifty, what does that mean?

Without glancing their way, Dargo follows Iva down the corridor, although at the stairs he heads down rather than up. Fyve tries to tell himself it's not symbolic. He glances at Halo, noticing she's also somber. All of a sudden, the aftertaste of the pod stings Fyve's throat. Winning isn't supposed to taste like that.

Silently, they make their way up to the deck. Fyve weaves his fingers through Halo's, wishing they could talk for more than a few sentences. One moment being on The Oasis is the greatest gift he's ever received, the next it feels like being chosen is far more a burden.

Up on the deck, the few teens who have already passed are smiling and chatting, and Fyve quickly sees why. A table with food has once again been set up, although this time with plates, each piled with the same amount of meat, bread, and mushy-looking vegetables. Softly murmured comments flit around as Fyve and Halo approach it.

"Terra truly is great."

"So much food. And it just keeps appearing!"

"I knew the answer was Terra."

Fyve and Halo both stiffen at that. A barely discernible gasp to their right reveals Iva heard the last comment, too.

Just like the Trials back on Treasure Island—the ones they thought were behind them—none of this is making sense. What's more, no one seems to be acknowledging that all this comes at a cost. No one seems to be asking what's going to happen to the fifty who fail.

They reach the table and Fyve picks up a plate and passes it to Halo before taking his own. She clasps it, her turbulent green gaze holding his. He can already see the questions shifting in there.

If Terra was in the ballroom, who made all of this, then set it up on the deck?

"Will you come to my cabin after this?" Fyve asks in a low voice.

Halo glances around as if she expects Terra to suddenly pop up. "Okay. We need to talk."

Fyve smiles, brushing his fingers over her cheek. "I will

never regret the decision to come on The Oasis," he murmurs, the truth of his words echoing through his heart.

There was so little left for him back on Treasure Island.

And even with the strangeness of Terra and the mysteries, there's a future waiting for him here. One with the person he cares most about. Halo's filled the aching parts of his soul.

To his surprise, Halo's lashes flutter down, then her face does, breaking their connection. "Me too," she whispers.

But there's something about the words that's strained.

Before he can decide whether he should ask what's going on, Iva appears beside them and places her empty plate on the table. "I'm going back to my room," she murmurs, her gaze barely meeting theirs.

Fyve instantly knows she's lying.

She's going to check on Dargo.

"*Eat,*" says a calm voice in Fyve's head. "*Then you train.*"

He stills, registering that Halo and Iva heard it, too. In fact, so has every teen on the deck. Terra just spoke to them all. It's only once that shock has worn off that the actual words Terra spoke filter through.

Train? What sort of training?

Halo taps his plate. "We need to hurry and eat."

He nods, jamming some meat into his mouth. This stuff is darker than the meat they had yesterday. Just as salty but also stronger in flavor. More questions rise with each chew and swallow. What animal did it come from? And are they here on The Oasis? And what about the saltiness? And the water sitting in cups like it just comes from the metal pipes protruding from the walls in his cabin. How is that even possible?

Fyve glances around, watching as others eat. Except they're smiling, more murmurs flitting through the crowd of teens.

"I can't believe she's speaking to us."

"I feel like Elijah himself!"

"We really are blessed."

Justice is here, her plate already empty. So are Ajax and Viney. She pretends to take a piece of Ajax's bread, but he yanks his plate away, his eyebrows jamming down before he quickly smiles then presses a kiss to the end of her nose. Viney flushes as she leans into him.

Everyone's happy to comply with Terra's wishes. They eat, smile, and chat about the wonders of The Oasis.

Except maybe Iva. She stands alone, her gaze fastened on her plate as she chews slowly and deliberately, as if she's focused on that one task. When she thinks nobody's watching, Iva slips a piece of bread into her pocket, no doubt to give to Dargo later.

And then there's Halo. She's watching all this, too, the slightest furrow between her eyebrows.

Yep, they really need to talk.

"*Line up on the deck,*" Terra says. "*It is time for training.*"

Looking intrigued, the teens place their plates back on the table and do as they're told. They spread out over the open expanse beside the pool, waiting expectantly.

"Fyve," Halo whispers as she points upward.

He follows the line of her arm, registering Terra standing up on the balcony. Elijah's nowhere to be seen. Everyone else soon notices her too, and a hush falls amongst the teens.

"*Complete ten jumps.*"

Terra's lips never move. In fact, her face doesn't twitch, making the connection between the words that would've just drifted through everyone's minds and the owner one floor up difficult to make.

Ajax is the first to leap into the air, Viney quickly copying him. And then heads are bobbing around the deck as everyone unquestioningly complies with the order that was never spoken aloud.

Fyve glances at Halo as they do what they're told.

"*Complete twenty squats.*"

Once more, heads bob, this time downward, as everyone

squats, some counting underneath their breath. Iva stumbles as the boat rocks but quickly rights herself and finishes the exercises.

"Complete ten laps of the deck."

Terra remains motionless, her dark gaze seeming to watch them, yet not see them at all as she speaks in their minds. Fyve indicates with his head to Halo, and they fall into step beside each other as they circle the deck. His stomach cramps around the food it's still trying to get used to and his mouth already feels dry. He thinks wistfully of the cup of water that's now empty.

The sound of panting breaths quickly fills the air, along with the odd groan. Seems others are also struggling with adjusting to full stomachs.

Followed by rigorous exercise.

They finish the laps and Fyve comes to a stop beside Halo, deliberately brushing her hand with his. He asks her with his eyes if she's okay. She smiles faintly. "Always looking out for others," she says quietly.

"Always looking out for you," he corrects gently.

Something he promises to do as long as he lives. Because he's in love with Halo.

The thought startles him as much as Terra's first words in his mind.

Possibly because they're true. Probably because he shouldn't be surprised.

Halo's smart. Beautiful in a way that starts in her soul. Strong enough to forge her own way, despite everything and everyone expecting otherwise.

Including Terra.

Falling for her was inevitable.

"Complete ten jumps."

Fyve executes the required jumps, noting that it's the same as the first order.

"Complete twenty squats."

The muscles of his legs groaning, Fyve does that, too, matching his timing to Halo's. To his right, Viney falls over as the ship rocks again. Ajax continues his squats, throwing her a scowl. She scrambles to her feet, executing several hurried crouches to catch up.

"Complete ten laps of the deck."

Once more breaking into a run, Fyve quickly realizes they're caught in a loop. Jumps. Squats. Laps. A mass of identically clothed teens, completing regimented exercises while an emotionless child-leader watches on. She doesn't even need Elijah to speak for her anymore.

They're all obediently doing as they're told.

The ten laps have just been completed when they're told to jump again. Harsh breathing fills the air. There are so many still recovering from the toll of first Trials. Sweat stains the cream tunics. It's not long before someone vomits over the railing. Fyve grits his teeth, determined to keep every ounce of nutrition his body's had in the past day. More than it's had in years. Iva quickly follows the first person, the contents of her stomach thrown into the ocean.

Yet, they have no choice but to comply. Jumps. Squats. Laps. Halo said they could still be claimed. He's not sure how she knows, but he trusts her. She wouldn't lie to him. So he completes the monotonous exercises, just like everyone else. He wonders how long Terra will ask them to do this.

When it goes from training to torture.

And will the other teens even see it as that?

Fyve's not sure how long they're out on the deck, but the sun has almost reached its highest point when Terra tells them they're finished.

"Return to your cabins," she orders in that same emotionless tone. *"You need to rest before the next Trial."*

Relieved and breathing hard, Fyve takes Halo's hand. He's

tired, nauseous, and confused, and all he wants to do is talk to her. Try to understand what's going on.

Another Trial is coming.

They've just reached his cabin when the door from the adjacent one flies open. Iva rushes out, looking frantically up and down the corridor. "Dargo!"

There's no answer.

"No," she moans. "Please, no."

"What's wrong?" Fyve asks, dread ballooning in his gut.

"It's Dargo," Iva says, tears tracking down her cheeks. "He's gone."

HALO

"*W*hat was all that about?" Fyve throws out his arms, one hand accidentally slamming into the wall of Halo's small cabin. "Jumping, squatting, running. So much fuss for absolutely no purpose. It wasn't even a Trial."

"Terra wants to make sure we're strong." Halo sits down on her bed, still surprised by how soft it feels. "She's feeding us and making us exercise. She's building us up."

"What for?" Fyve runs a hand through his shiny, clean hair.

She shrugs, although she suspects she knows exactly what it's for.

"It's for Tomorrow Land, isn't it?" He sits beside her and the bed dips.

"I think so." She slides into the divot, not resisting the pull to be closer to him. It's a comfort to have her thigh pressed up against his. "If the chosen fifty are going to survive on Tomorrow Land, then Terra wants to make sure we're strong."

He lets out a long sigh. "Did you get asked that list of questions yesterday? About how many teeth you have, how many times you've been sick, how many siblings you have?"

"I think she wants good breeding stock," she says. "Did you get asked how many lines were carved above your door?"

Fyve glances up at her door as he nods. "You only have two scratches. I have three."

"It was an eye test. She's checking to make sure we don't have any deficiencies." She winces, already knowing he'll relate this back to his sister.

"Sevin wasn't deficient," he says right on cue.

"No, she wasn't." Halo slides her hand onto his thigh. "Quite the opposite, actually. But Terra doesn't seem to see it like that."

"In that case, I think the Trials are rigged," he says. "It didn't matter what answer we came up with for that stupid riddle, Terra eliminated whoever she wanted. I wonder how many teeth Dargo had?"

"We don't know any of that for sure," she says, cautiously. "Although, it would explain a lot. We'll have to see what happens in the next Trial."

"There were five missing after the Trial." He wraps an arm around her. "I counted. It wasn't supposed to be like this."

"Where do you think they've gone?" She snuggles in a little closer, ignoring the guilt that's clawing at her thanks to the secret she's keeping from him.

"I don't know, but we need to find out." Fyve tightens his grip on her, and she understands what it must've been like for Sevin to grow up with the unwavering protection of this guy beside her.

"Maybe the people who didn't pass the original Trials were actually the lucky ones?" she suggests, deciding if she can convince him of this, then maybe it will hurt less when she tells him the truth about Sevin.

"Well, we're on the ship now." Fyve turns to her, his voice taking on a husky tone. "And no matter what, we're staying together. You're all I've got."

"And you're all I want," she replies, stretching up to press her lips to his.

He spears his fingers into her hair, almost like he'd been waiting for her to do exactly that. Deepening the kiss, his desire for her is clear. And it's intoxicating. The minty taste of him is only matched by his fresh almost earthy smell, and a fire lights deep inside her belly.

She runs her fingertips across the firmness of his chest, and they fall backward until they're lying on her bed, lips and tongues exploring while desperate hands fumble in their quest to discover more. To *feel* more. Anything except the fear that's been wrapped around their chests like tight bands ever since the new Trials were announced.

Losing herself in all things Fyve, Halo lets out a small moan. It's a sound of exquisite pleasure, but it has him pulling back.

"Are you okay?" he pants. "I mean, is this okay?"

She nods, trying to close the gap between them once more. "I want this."

That's all he needs to hear. He runs his hands down her torso, his eyes burning with heat as he toys with the hem of her shirt. He kisses her again and just as she's pressing herself closer to him, he jumps back like he's been electrocuted.

Fyve gets to his feet and paces the room with his hands on his temples.

"What's wrong?" she asks, sitting up.

"I heard..." He looks at her, his handsome face filled with anguish. "I heard a voice. Except, it wasn't Terra. It was a man's voice."

"What did it say?" Halo's eyes widen and she leaps to her feet. "What did he tell you?"

"He told me to stop," he says. "Did you hear it, too?"

She shakes her head. "Nobody spoke to me."

"What's going on?" He looks up at the ceiling. "Is Terra watching us? And why does she suddenly sound like a man?"

Halo sits back down on the edge of the bed and lets out a long sigh, wishing she had answers to any of those questions. Fyve goes to sit beside her but changes his mind and heads for the door.

"Where are you going?" she asks, quick to follow him.

"If she's watching us, then I think it's about time we started watching her," he says with one hand on the door. "I'm going to find Terra. She has to be somewhere on this ship."

"That's too dangerous." She puts a hand on his arm to stop him.

"Is it any more dangerous than a one in two chance of...we don't know what?" His eyes flare with anger. "I can't just sit by and let this happen again."

"Then I'm coming with you," she says, realizing she can't stop him. "She was watching me, too."

Fyve looks to the ceiling. "Did you hear that, Terra? We're coming to find you!"

He yanks open the door and they march down the hallway.

"Let's start with the upper decks," Halo suggests. She has the map of the ship in her mind, realizing she's been mentally crossing off sections one by one as she's discovered them. So far, she's probably only seen a quarter of this ship. And so much for her father telling her the engine room would be hers. It seems perhaps he doesn't have as much say around here as she thought he did.

They reach the stairwell and glance around before entering and climbing upward.

"This one," says Halo, when they reach the seventh floor.

"Why?" Fyve pauses, staring at the number on the back of the door.

"It's my lucky number." She winks, wondering if she'll think of Fyve's bright sister every time she sees that number. If only those thoughts weren't laced with so many layers of guilt. She really had grown to love Sevin very much. "Besides, look at the footprints."

Fyve looks down and sees what she'd noticed. There's a pattern of scattered footsteps on the landing, not present on the other floors. Someone's been using this door on a regular basis. And recently by the look of it.

They enter the corridor to the seventh floor and glance around. It's dark, with only dim lights to mark the path.

"What do you think's up here?" Halo asks in a whisper.

Fyve shrugs. "More cabins?"

He opens the nearest door. It's an empty room apart from the same set of built-in furniture in all the other cabins. The musty smell tells them nobody's been inside for many years. Perhaps decades.

They continue down the corridor, their steps brought to an abrupt halt when they hear a terrified scream.

Halo spins to look at Fyve. "Who was that?"

The scream comes again, and she puts a hand on Fyve's back. Maybe coming up here was a bad idea.

"Someone needs help!" Fyve takes off down the corridor in the direction of the terrified sound.

Halo's pulse rate picks up as she flings open cabin doors, looking for the source of the scream, which is now a pained groaning sound.

"Here!" cries Fyve from an open door on the opposite side of the corridor. "Oh my—"

"Help me," a female sobs.

Halo is by Fyve's side in a matter of seconds, her eyes widening when she takes in what's inside. Or rather, who.

"Cloud!" Halo rushes to the bed where Ajax's former partner lays sprawled on her back with pink liquid radiating across the sheets beneath her. "What are you doing here?"

"Halo," Cloud sobs, ignoring her question. "I need help. It

hurts." Her stomach is bulging even more than the last time Halo saw her, except it's much lower now. It seems her baby's decided it wants to join them in Tomorrow Land.

Halo looks from Cloud and back to Fyve, frozen in her own panic and confusion. She's heard the cries of women in labor on Treasure Island, but she's never...

"I don't know what to do," Halo gasps, her heart rate tripping into overdrive.

"It's okay," says Fyve, his voice calm and firm. "I've seen my mother and aunt do this lots of times. You're going to be fine, Cloud. You can do this."

"But it hurts so much," she moans.

Fyve moves to Cloud's head and perches beside the bed as he holds out his palm. "Squeeze my hand as hard as you like."

She snatches it like an offering and does exactly as she's told. Fyve winces in response to the tightness of her grip and Halo has to suppress a smile.

"Halo." Fyve tilts his head toward the end of the bed. "You need to...go down that end."

Her eyes flare as she realizes what he means. "But. I...You see—"

"Just do it," he says. "You need to feel for a head."

Swallowing down her fear and reminding herself that Cloud is in far more discomfort than she is, Halo lifts Cloud's skirt and lets out a little gasp.

"I can see the top of the baby's head," she cries.

Cloud lets out a yelp. "I'm not ready!"

"Breathe, Cloud," Fyve commands. "You *are* ready. Guide the baby out smoothly. Give us one nice, big, even push. Come on. I'll breathe with you."

Halo positions her hands ready to catch her niece or nephew should they come shooting out.

"It's coming," she reports, her excitement catching in her

throat at what she's witnessing. She thinks of her own mother, eternally grateful for what she must have suffered to bring her into the world. "Come on, Cloud. You're nearly there."

Cloud lets out an almighty scream that's surely heard throughout the entire ship and a perfectly formed baby slides into Halo's shaking hands. Covered in fluid and far tinier than any other baby Halo's ever seen, it's a little girl.

For one precious moment, the rest of the world disappears and it's just Halo and her niece. The first female relative she's seen since her mother died, and the bond she feels catches her by surprise. She knows she'd do anything for this girl. Die for her if she has to. And for the first time, the way Fyve feels about Sevin makes complete and total sense. This child is her own flesh and blood.

The baby lets out an angry cry and Halo quickly places her on her mother's chest, mourning the break in contact the moment she lets go.

"She's a perfect baby girl," Halo announces.

"You did it, Cloud," says Fyve, massaging his hand. "You're amazing. She's a little miracle."

"That's exactly what I'm going to call her." Cloud drops a kiss on her daughter's crinkled forehead. "Her name is Miracle. A beautiful gift from Terra."

Halo blanches at this last bit. While she likes the name, she's no longer convinced Terra had anything to do with the birth of this beautiful child.

"I should get Ajax." Halo takes a step toward the door. "He needs to meet his daughter."

"Not yet," says Fyve. "The sac the baby grew in needs to come out."

"Oh." Halo rubs her hands on her pants, then realizes her mistake as she leaves pink streaks on the cream fabric.

"Something's not right." Cloud grimaces, handing Miracle to

Fyve, and clutching at her stomach. Fyve expertly holds Miracle against his chest and covers her in one of the blankets he pulls from the bed.

"Let me see," says Halo, returning to her position near the foot of the bed, even though she has no way of knowing if what she's about to see is normal.

"It hurts," says Cloud. "Is it supposed to hurt like this?"

Halo takes a look and lets out another gasp. "Cloud! There's another head. You're having twins."

It's no wonder Cloud's belly had grown so rapidly, and these babies were born so soon. There are two of them!

Cloud groans in a way that's impossible to tell if she's pleased or terrified. Perhaps she's both. Or it could just be the pure agony of being torn in two like this.

"Remember what you did last time," Fyve instructs. "Push the baby out smoothly."

Cloud moans, quieter this time than when Miracle had been birthed, and another tiny baby slides into Halo's waiting hands.

"It's a boy!" she squeals, delighting in the fact she now has a nephew.

But this time the baby isn't crying or angry. He's completely silent.

Halo clutches him to her chest, afraid she's going to break him. That is, if he's not broken already. "Fyve…"

"What's wrong?" Cloud asks, immediately sensing the shift in Halo's mood.

Fyve places her daughter back in Cloud's arms. "You look after Miracle. Give us a moment."

"Give me my son!" Cloud demands, the force in her voice a direct contrast to the gentle way she cradles Miracle to her chest.

Ignoring her, Fyve takes the baby boy from Halo and places him on the foot of the bed. Halo rushes for a blanket to wrap him in. The air temperature is warm, but he must be feeling so cold out here in this cruel new world that's greeting him.

"Come on, little guy," Fyve says, rubbing the baby vigorously on the chest. "Breathe for us. You can do it."

Halo finds herself holding her own breath as she waits, internally begging Terra if she has any power over this to please let her nephew live.

Cloud dissolves into a howling sob that pierces its way directly to Halo's breaking heart. She already can't bear the loss of this sweet baby who until a few moments ago, she hadn't even known existed.

"Breathe," she begs, hovering beside Fyve. "Please."

Leaning forward, Fyve covers the baby's mouth with his own and provides several puffs of air, continuing to rub his tiny chest as he does so.

He pulls back and the cabin fills with the glorious sound of the baby's cries as a rosy color rushes to his cheeks. Baby Miracle cries in response and Halo smiles, imagining she's scolding her twin for scaring them all so much.

Fyve rushes the baby boy over to join his sister. Cloud snuggles both her children to her chest and they quieten instantly, as if simply being together is the only elixir they needed.

"He's a fighter," Fyve says, his voice breaking with relief.

Halo wraps her arm around him, pulling him closer. "I'm so proud of you. You were amazing. You *are* amazing."

"His name is Marvel," Cloud announces. "I've been blessed with two gifts from Terra."

Halo had briefly thought Cloud might name the child after Fyve but, somehow, Miracle and Marvel are a whole lot more fitting for children of Terra's most faithful servant. She's not entirely sure what Ajax will think of the names, though.

"Does Ajax know you're here?" she asks gently.

Cloud shakes her head, not looking up from the bundle of love she's holding in her arms.

"Then how did you get here?" Halo asks. "Did Terra allow it?"

There's a small cough behind them and Halo spins around to find her father standing in the doorway.

"I snuck her on board," Halo's father says, his eyes shining with pride at the sight of his two baby grandchildren. "It had nothing to do with Terra. It was me."

FYVE

*F*yve watches, feeling as astounded as Halo looks, when Elijah closes the door and rushes to Cloud.

"Two babies!" he gasps.

She beams up at him. "A boy and a girl. Miracle and Marvel." Her face twists with pain. "Oh no, not more."

"It's the afterbirth," says Fyve, moving closer as he reassures her. "And it's a lot smaller than a baby."

Halo quickly moves to the end of the bed again, her face turning stoic as Cloud pushes again.

Fyve almost grins. "Blood and mess are inevitable."

She throws him an unimpressed look. "I can see that."

"She'll be quiet though?" Elijah asks as he hovers by the door.

Fyve doesn't say anything, but the reminder of Cloud's screams, quickly followed by Elijah's confession that he secretly brought her here, have his shoulders constricting. Are these babies in danger?

There's no time to dwell on the troubling question, because the two sacs that nurtured Miracle and Marvel are expelled. Halo looks a little pale as she quickly bundles them in bloody sheets and Fyve wishes he could kiss a little color back into her

53

cheeks. She was amazing. This birth was a total surprise, yet she was calm. Comforting and encouraging.

Then seeing her with baby Miracle, instantly suffused with love, had practically taken his breath away.

Miracle lets out a little mewl and Fyve's about to tell Cloud the babies are hungry, but she instinctively brings one baby to her breast, then the other, only to frown. Unashamed about her state of undress, she looks up at Fyve in consternation. "Two at once?"

Although Fyve's never had any experience with twins, he knows Cloud needs someone to be confident right now. So he takes a pillow from the other side of the bed and props it under Miracle. "There, now we just need to get Marvel sorted."

Cloud smiles at him like she just realized he's as smart as Halo or Sevin, then quickly tucks Marvel in. He latches on as if he's been doing it for weeks, making Cloud gasp. She melts a moment later, relaxing into the soft bed as she looks as if she's falling even deeper in love with her babies.

Elijah sits on the edge, his face soft with wonder. "We've truly been blessed." He smiles a smile Fyve's never seen before. One that makes him look far more like a proud grandfather than the leader who announced the second set of Trials. "Terra is great."

"Terra is going to be pissed," Fyve points out. "You've deliberately disobeyed her."

Elijah flashes a glare his way. "She didn't understand." He looks back at his newborn grandchildren, pride suffusing his features. "But she will."

Halo moves closer to Fyve, frowning. "But Terra doesn't know Cloud is on The Oasis?" she checks.

Elijah's mouth clamps closed. "No, she doesn't."

There's a soft popping sound as Miracle finishes her first feed and she instantly starts fussing. Cloud's brow wrinkles as she tries to see if the baby's still hungry, but little Miracle isn't interested in feeding again. She scrunches up her little red face, then her whole body. Her arms shoot out of the loose blanket Fyve wrapped around her, two tiny fists waving in the air. A thin wail climbs into the air.

Elijah rushes to the door as if he's expecting someone to come storming in. "We need to keep the babies quiet!"

Cloud bounces Miracle, anxiousness twisting her face. "She's not hungry. I don't know what to do!"

Fyve quickly walks over. "May I?"

Cloud nods, her eyes taking on a panicked edge. "Yes. Please. She needs to be quiet."

Fyve takes the squirming bundle of baby and quickly lays her at the foot of the bed. With deft movements, he rewraps Miracle tightly, swaddling her. She instantly calms and Fyve picks her up, holding her upright as he tucks her head into the crook of his neck. "Little Ate loved to be bundled up too." He gently rubs Miracle's back. "And you'll need to do this every time they've fed."

Cloud nods, looking a little dazed now that there's no threat of noise. She settles further into the bed, gazing down at Marvel. "I'll do whatever I need to," she vows. "No matter what."

Halo approaches Fyve, smiling softly. "You're so good with them."

He grins. "Bloo in particular was a fussy baby. I'd take some of the early morning shifts so Cee could get some sleep."

A soft gurgle bubbles up from Miracle and her body relaxes even more. Halo moves around to gaze at her face. "She's asleep," she whispers.

"Babies don't usually mind noise," Fyve tells her. He holds Miracle out to her. "Here, you hold her."

A sweet, tender, rather breathtaking smile blooms across Halo's face. "Yes, please," she says, still whispering, but this time it's with awe.

Crooning nonsensical words, Halo takes baby Miracle,

instinctively rocking her as she tucks her into her arms. Elijah gravitates toward them, the same tenderness mirrored in his soft, smiling eyes as he strokes Miracle's downy hair.

Marvel finishes feeding, too, and Cloud looks at Fyve. He takes the baby without needing to be asked, swaddling Marvel and burping him. Warmth fills his chest as the newborn instantly settles and Fyve breathes in the familiar scent. Memories of not only Bloo, but Ate and Nyne, filter through his mind, tugging at his heart. Protectiveness wells up next, solidifying the same promise he made to every other baby he's held. The same words that echo Cloud's.

He'll do whatever he needs to ensure they stay safe.

"They're so loved," Cloud says, clasping the sheets to her chest. "I'm so happy."

Halo tears her gaze from Miracle to look at her father. "We should tell Ajax."

Elijah pulls back sharply, shaking his head vigorously. "We can't tell your brother. It's not safe."

Fyve can't help but agree. Ajax doesn't know the meaning of loyalty.

"Ajax should know, Elijah," says Cloud, tucking Marvel in a little closer. "They're his children, too."

"Ajax has already moved on," Elijah says bluntly. "He's with Viney now."

Cloud rears back as if she's been slapped, her eyes filling with tears a second later. Halo sits beside her and wraps an arm around her shoulder. "He thought he had to leave you behind," she quickly assures her.

Cloud wraps herself around her babies even more. "I don't want him to know."

Elijah relaxes. "Yes, you're right. We need to keep this a secret for now."

"I'm so tired," Cloud murmurs, sinking deeper into the bed. "And hungry."

"You rest," Halo says, patting her on the arm. "And we'll find you something to eat."

Cloud nods, turning to lie on her side as she tucks Miracle and Marvel into her chest. She's asleep almost instantly, weariness tugging at the lines of her face.

Halo pulls the blankets up around them, then turns to Fyve and her father. "She can't stay here. Someone may have heard her."

Fyve's about to agree that they need to move Cloud, except Elijah is shaking his head. "Terra will be pleased. I know it."

"You snuck Cloud onto the ship," Fyve says, keeping his voice low. "I doubt she'll be happy with that."

"She blessed us with twins," Elijah points out. "Of course, she's happy."

"So, she does know about the twins, then?"

Elijah's eyes widen and Fyve swears he sees a flash of fear. "No, there's no way she can know. I made sure to hide Cloud."

Fyve doesn't respond, wondering if Elijah is aware that he's not making any sense. Either Terra knows the babies are here, or she doesn't. And he has no way of knowing what her response is going to be to either of those situations.

Or how Terra will respond to discovering her faithful servant has been keeping a secret.

Fyve steps to the door. "I'll find Cloud some food. She's going to need her energy." Both for the move and to sustain the two lives now dependent on her.

"I think I saw an area on the map that might be used for food preparation on the sixth floor," Halo offers. "Toward the stern."

Fyve nods, glad she understands this is what they need to do, and even more glad for that amazing memory of hers. He can't afford to be wandering around the ship in the middle of the night. He slips out into the dark corridor, registering Elijah's words to Halo. "I've been Terra's loyal servant all my life. She'll understand why I did this. I know she will."

Wishing there was time to hear Halo's response, Fyve walks away. If there's one thing he's learned throughout his life on Treasure Island and even more on The Oasis, it's that nothing can be assumed.

Making his way to the stairs as silently as possible, he heads to the next floor down. The small lights that dot each corridor and stairs illuminate his way as he keeps every sense alert. He doubts anyone is awake, let alone roaming the ship. But the memory of the voice that stabbed through his mind in Halo's room is far too fresh.

"Stop!"

And it was a male voice. Loud and insistent.

There's far more going on with Terra and The Oasis than they realize. Either that, or he's going crazy… Hearing Terra is plausible. Elijah always has. Now everyone is.

But a male voice. One who seems to know what Fyve and Halo were doing, and wanted them to stop. Realization had been a punch to the gut.

Someone's watching him. And it may not be Terra.

Fyve walks past the rooms lining the corridor he's now in, seeing a large set of double doors at the end. Reaching them, he glances down, noting what Halo had when they went to the seventh floor—footprints.

Others have been here, and he doubts it's the teens. No one's had an opportunity. And no one seems to want to ask too many questions.

Pushing one of the doors, Fyve enters, discovering a large room lined with metal. Metal walls. Metal benches. Metal shelves.

And stacked against the back wall are dozens of wooden crates.

Pausing, Fyve listens hard, but the room is silent. Curious, he makes his way to the crates, finding one open. He peers over the side that almost reaches his waist, eyes widening when he sees row upon row of silver-colored cans. Picking one up, he notices it's heavy. It's not empty like the ones on Treasure Island that they'd use as cups or to collect water.

There's something inside.

Taking a step back, Fyve tries to process what he's stumbled on. There are dozens of crates, stacked ten high. And they must all be full of cans.

This is the food that Terra has been providing them. And there's more of it than Fyve could have ever imagined. His stomach leaps with joy and contracts at the same time, overwhelmed at the thought. This could easily feed a hundred teens or more.

Surely, there's no need for the Trials to continue.

Pressing his fingers to a temple, Fyve shakes his head. How many more revelations is he going to have to jam in there? It feels even fuller than his stomach did after the feast.

Focusing back on the can, and the issue at hand, he wonders how to get to the food inside. Cloud is the priority right now. The accumulating mysteries are going to have to wait.

Looking around, Fyve notices a small gadget sitting on the edge of the crate. What's more, an open can is on the floor not far away. Grabbing it, he runs back to the doors and out into the corridor. This will give Cloud her sustenance after giving birth. Next, they have to find somewhere safe for her.

Away from Terra's prying eyes.

Fyve's just at the stairs that will take him back to the seventh floor when a sound has him freezing.

Soft, muffled sobbing.

It carries down the stairwell. Or is it up? It's hard to tell where it's coming from. Fyve shakes his head. If Halo was here, would she even hear it? This could be like the male voice he heard earlier—only for him.

Or nothing but his imagination.

Especially when the sound reminds him of Sevin. The

stifled, girlish cries she tried to hide in the middle of the night in the weeks after their mom left. The same sounds that would eventually stop as he held her, promising he'd never leave.

Rushing up the steps, Fyve now runs as fast as he can back to the room Cloud gave birth in. The need to move her is suddenly overwhelming, as is the feeling that Miracle and Marvel are in danger.

The Oasis is carrying more than just the promise of Tomorrow Land. Something disturbing.

Or he's losing his mind.

Either way, he needs to act before one of those is proven true.

HALO

*H*alo paces Cloud's cabin with Miracle held to her chest. She should have insisted on going with Fyve to look for food. He's taking too long.

Cloud has fallen asleep, pure exhaustion winning over her need to keep her babies close. Halo's father is cradling Marvel, looking down at him like he can't dare to believe he's real. She wonders if he looked at her like that when she was small.

"Dad," she says, noticing the dark circles underneath his eyes. He seems thinner, too. "Are you okay?"

He drags his gaze from his grandchild to look at her, and swallows.

"Dad?" she prompts. "What's going on? We haven't even spoken since we got on this ship. What's happening with you?"

His blue eyes brim with tears and he shrugs. "I don't know."

Halo kicks herself for not checking in on her father sooner. She's never seen him like this. He's always been so capable. So sure of himself and his purpose. Right now, he just looks like an ordinary old man, not the all-seeing Elijah who'd stalk around Treasure Island, knowing everybody's name.

"I think I made a mistake," he whispers, glancing at Cloud

who's snoring softly. "I shouldn't have snuck her on the ship. Nor should I have encouraged you or Ajax to enter the Trials."

Halo studies him. "What's changed? Have you lost faith in Terra?"

"Terra's no longer speaking to me." He keeps his voice low. "I think she might know about Cloud. She's punishing me. I'm scared she might also punish my family."

Halo holds Miracle a little tighter. She understands now why her father hadn't made much sense when Fyve had questioned him. He's scared out of his mind. All the power he'd had on Treasure Island has been stripped away. A punishment for disobeying the almighty Terra. And he'd done it all for his family, unable to leave his grandbabies behind, in the same way Fyve had refused to leave Sevin until he'd believed her to be dead.

Halo tucks Miracle in beside Cloud and goes to her father. She wraps her arms around him gently, careful not to disturb Marvel who's sleeping contentedly, unaware of the turmoil bubbling around him.

"I love you, Dad," she whispers, uncertain of the last time she'd told him this.

"I love you, too," he replies without hesitation. "But I fear I've also failed you."

The door swings open and Fyve steps into the cabin clutching a can of food. He has a look of panic on his face. Halo steps back from the first man she ever loved and toward the last man she ever wants to love.

"What's the matter?" she asks.

"We need to move Cloud and the babies." His dark eyes dart around the cabin. "It's not safe here."

Halo holds up a hand. "Cloud's asleep. She needs her rest."

"What happened?" her father asks him. "What did you see?"

"I saw nothing," says Fyve. "But I did hear something. Someone was crying. I didn't realize how much sound travels in this ship. Cloud made a whole lot more noise earlier. We need to move her. Anyone who heard her will know exactly where to find her."

Halo looks to her father, who's nodding his agreement.

"We're on a ship," Halo reminds them. "Where exactly are we going to move them?"

"I know somewhere," her father whispers. "Somewhere nobody would ever think to look. I'd have taken her there in the first place, only I just found it yesterday."

Fyve rushes over to Cloud and gently rouses her. "Wake up and eat this," he says, holding out the tin of food. "It's time to go."

Cloud sits up with a start, frantically looking around until she sees Miracle tucked beside her and Marvel safely in his grandfather's arms. "What happened?"

"We need to move you. It's not safe here. But first you should eat. You need your strength." He hands her the tin. "It's called pineapple."

Cloud holds the tin to her lips and drinks the liquid then scoops out some yellow fruit that's been cut into perfect rings.

"Why isn't it safe?" she asks between mouthfuls. "Terra will take care of us."

"Terra is great," Halo's father replies, his words missing the usual sincerity he injects into them. "But it's different out here. Fyve's right. We need to move you somewhere nobody will think to look. And I know just the place."

Cloud nods, so conditioned to taking orders from Halo's father that she drops any further questions. She finishes the pineapple, gently picks up Miracle and swings her legs out of bed.

"Urgh," she groans, clearly still sore from her ordeal.

If Fyve hadn't looked so spooked when he'd returned, there's no way Halo would agree to moving her. But Cloud made a lot of noise when the twins were born. Which means it's better to be safe. The longer they can be kept hidden, the safer they'll be.

"Let me take Miracle," Halo says. "I'll be careful with her."

Cloud holds out her daughter and Halo snuggles her into the crook of her neck, positioning the blanket around her and supporting her head in the way Fyve had shown her. She never realized he knew so much about babies. And as much as she never wants to experience what she witnessed Cloud going through again, she has to admit it's made him even more appealing. Who would have thought that a guy holding a baby could be so hot!

Fyve helps Cloud to stand, offering to carry her, but she refuses.

"If we move slowly, I can do it," she says, leaning heavily on him.

Pressing a finger to his lips, Halo's father leads them out of the cabin and into the dimly lit hallway.

They reach the stairwell and head down a few floors, then enter another corridor. Halo tries to bring the map to her mind but is too distracted with fear and worry. This precious baby she's holding needs to be kept safe. As does her nephew, who's tucked against the chest of his grandfather.

A flickering shadow down the far end of the corridor has Halo halting. She grabs the back of her father's shirt and draws him to a stop, pointing.

Fyve quietly opens the door behind them and he and Cloud step into a cabin. Halo and her father follow, just as the shadow rounds the corner and morphs from gray to a solid black.

Fyve closes the door without making a sound and they stand in the pitch-dark cabin, holding their breath. Halo's certain the shape she'd glimpsed had been a person. Someone too tall and broad to be a teenager. It most definitely hadn't been Terra. So, who could it have been? As far as she's aware, her father is the only adult aboard this ship and he's standing right beside her. Her only hope is that whoever it was, hadn't seen them, too.

Miracle grizzles in Halo's arms and she jiggles her into a different position, cradling her tighter as she moves to her father so the twins can be nearer to each other.

Please don't wake up and cry now!

Miracle settles and footsteps replace her soft baby sounds. Someone is walking down the corridor, confirming all of Halo's fears.

Fyve and Cloud stand like statues, while Halo and her father gently rock the two babies, willing them to stay silent. Seconds feel like excruciating minutes, and the footsteps grow louder and louder, then begin to fade away.

"Who was that?" Cloud eventually whispers when all is silent once more.

"We don't know," Fyve says, opening the door a crack and peering out. "And right now, we don't want to know."

"We need to keep moving," Halo says. "Quickly and quietly."

Fyve opens the door fully and steps back, letting Halo's father lead the way. Halo follows closely behind, aware that Cloud is a little slower. They enter another stairwell and head down two more floors and through another shorter hallway, making a series of turns. Unless Halo is completely disoriented, they must be in the stern of the ship now.

She keeps her eyes peeled for more shadows and her ears tuned for the crying Fyve had mentioned but hears and sees nothing.

Just like they suspected, it seems they're not alone on this ship. Someone has to be helping Terra to produce the feasts that keep appearing, let alone steering the ship. But why aren't they showing their faces? Is this all part of some grand illusion? Perhaps Terra is nothing more than an ordinary little girl and these faceless people are the ones in charge? How then does Terra manage to speak inside their minds?

She lets out a long sigh as she walks. Terra is not an ordinary little girl. She's more than proven that. She does things. Impossible things. Maybe none of this will ever make any sense.

"Nearly there," her father whispers, leading the slow procession, with Cloud and Fyve trailing only a short distance behind.

They reach a thick door and her father hauls it open with his free hand to reveal a small room with thickly padded walls, a bed and a bucket.

"What is this place?" Halo asks, a shiver running down her spine.

"It's called the brig," her father says. "It's the ship's prison. It's also completely soundproof. Nobody will hear the babies cry."

"You're putting Cloud in prison?" Halo is horrified. She can practically feel the misery seeping from these walls. A prison is no place for a woman to raise her two babies.

"It's the safest place," he says. "Nobody will think to look here. Plus, it's the one place I know for sure isn't bugged."

"I haven't seen any bugs on the ship." Halo steps inside and looks down, expecting to see a line of cockroaches scurrying across the floor.

"Not bugs," her father corrects. "Bugged. It means wired up so that Terra can listen to us."

"I didn't think she needed wires to do that," Halo says, remembering how people had been claimed on Treasure Island for nothing more than their thoughts.

Fyve helps Cloud through the door and to the bed. She sits down immediately and sighs.

"It's fine, Halo," she says weakly. "I trust Elijah. I'll be safe here."

"And we won't lock the door," her father says. "Which means, it's not really a prison. Just a safe place to rest."

Miracle begins to fuss, and Halo passes her to Cloud, who lifts her shirt to feed her daughter.

"And you're sure this place is safe?" Fyve asks, scoping out the tiny room. "We'll need to bring some supplies. Food, water, more blankets, some sheets that can be used as diapers."

"I'll do that," says Elijah. "After all, I've been looking after her just fine this whole time. You two need to get back to your cabins before you're missed."

"I'm pretty sure Terra already realizes we're not in our cabins," says Halo.

"Well, get back before you're punished then," her father says firmly. "I can take care of Cloud."

"We'll be fine," Cloud says again. "Terra won't let me come to any harm."

Halo frowns, hoping there won't come a day where Cloud's unwavering faith in Terra gets put to the test.

Her father places a hand on her arm. "There's a Trial tomorrow."

"What will we have to do?" she asks.

The sad expression from earlier returns to his face. "I told you. Terra is no longer talking to me. I don't know."

"That's no different to normal for us," says Fyve from the doorway. "We never know."

"But it's different for me," her father says, letting his hand fall. "Which means you need to have your wits about you. If I'm in danger, then so is my daughter."

"Dad." This time it's Halo who puts her hands on him. "We've been in danger this whole time. The only thing that's changed, is that now you know it, too."

Tears fill her father's eyes. "Leave now, and be careful," he says, just as Marvel wakes up and lets out a loud cry.

Fyve and Halo step outside and slide the door closed. Marvel's cries are instantly swallowed up as the room is sealed off. Halo can't help but feel like she's just closed them into a tomb.

"I don't like this," she says.

"It's only for a little while," Fyve reassures as he drops a kiss on her forehead. "Everything will be okay."

She nods, aware he's just saying this to make her feel better. He can't possibly believe that, can he? Because so far, nothing has turned out to be okay. The further this ship sails, the more troubled are the waters it floats across.

And there's no turning back now.

Just like Cloud inside the brig, their fates are already sealed.

FYVE

*F*yve wakes with a dull headache pulsing at his temples. He's not surprised, to be honest. He slept terribly after everything that happened yesterday. He stares at the pale ceiling above him, realizing he barely notices the movement of the ship anymore. He's not sure how he feels about adapting to this new life.

Especially when he's not sure what this new life *is*.

Apart from confusing.

Unsettling.

And full of secrets.

Fyve sits up and pulls on his tunic shirt, the walls feeling like they're closing in on him again. Of all the things that kept him up last night, it was the memory of the soft cries he heard while getting Cloud some food. Probably because they'd reminded him so much of Sevin. There had been a familiarity to the sound. A bittersweet tug at his heart as he was reminded of the sister he lost.

Or maybe it's because it was so out of place. A child was crying, and the only person on the ship who's a child is Terra, and she doesn't speak.

Rubbing his hand down his face, Fyve wonders what time it is. He's never lived in a place where he was so disconnected from the time of day, the weather, his very surroundings. Pushing to his feet, he walks to his door and opens it. Just like yesterday, a plate of food sits on the shelf beside his door. Yet, he's now experiencing something he's never felt before.

He's not hungry.

Especially when he registers there's no plate of food beside the neighboring door. Dargo's cabin. Glancing around, Fyve sees he's alone, possibly the first to wake up. He wonders if it's even morning. The thought of staying in his own cabin has restless, anxious energy firing through him, so he quietly slips out. There are too many questions, and not enough answers.

Padding softly, he tries Dargo's door and finds it unlocked. He peeks inside, not sure what he's going to find, if anything. The first thing he registers is it's dark. Dargo's room doesn't have the soft lighting that's always on, no matter what time it is. Fyve suppresses a shudder. It almost feels prophetic.

He's about to slide the door closed when a soft sob reaches him. Stilling, Fyve peers a little harder, registering a body curled up on the bed, pale blonde hair spilling over her face. Iva. And she's mourning the loss of her partner.

Fyve quietly shuts the door, not wanting to disturb her. Sevin had sometimes crawled over to their mother's mat in the days after she'd gone, craving her scent and wanting to be close to all she had left of her. He frowns. Maybe that's what he heard when he was sneaking around the ship—someone's grief. Others have left loved ones behind on Treasure Island. A handful have now lost loved ones to these new Trials.

Has his own grief meant he's attributing something to the crying he heard? Maybe it was just another teen shedding tears for what they've also lost...

Shaking his head, Fyve turns away from Dargo's cabin, and also his own. He can't go back into the tiny space with only his thoughts for company. He's slowly going mad. Plus, he wants to check on Cloud. Grabbing his plate of food, he makes his way down the corridor and to the stairs. He knows how vulnerable babies are.

He's held them as they took their last breath.

Hurrying to the brig, Fyve keeps his eyes and ears open. Whoever had been investigating the seventh-floor last night certainly hadn't been a teen. Their outline was too large, their footsteps too heavy.

Cloud isn't the only surprise hiding on The Oasis.

Thankfully, Fyve doesn't see or hear anyone on the way. He opens the door to the brig carefully, just in case Cloud's still asleep. He's pretty sure it's close to dawn, but there's no way of knowing for sure in the depths of this ship.

Cloud is sitting up in bed, one baby on her lap, the other in her arms. She beams when she sees Fyve. "Good morning."

Surprised but pleased at her broad smile, he enters fully and closes the door. Extending the plate, he smiles too. "I brought you some breakfast."

Cloud giggles, indicating toward an empty plate and cup beside her on the bed. "Elijah was just here. He already brought me some food."

Fyve shrugs as he grins, placing the food on her other side. "More for later, then." He studies the babies, even more pleased to see them sleeping peacefully. "You're in a good mood this morning," he observes. It's a direct contrast to the tenuous place she's in right now.

Cloud's eyes shine. "Terra spoke to me last night. After everyone had gone." She clasps the baby she's holding tighter. "Isn't it wonderful?"

That has Fyve stilling. "She did?"

"Yes," says Cloud, nodding enthusiastically. "She welcomed me to The Oasis. And my babies. I feel so blessed!"

"That's, ah, great."

"It really is," she gushes. "Elijah also said she spoke to him. That she understands why he hid me."

Fyve blinks. "That's also great." He knows he's repeating himself, but his mind is struggling to keep up with this development.

Terra knows. And she's happy.

Yet Elijah was borderline terrified. He snuck Cloud down here so she couldn't be found.

Cloud's nodding again. "Elijah said he'd been worried for nothing. Of course, Terra would welcome me, and the twins."

"Wow." Fyve glances around. "That means you don't have to stay here."

"Exactly. Terra said I'd have my own room. She also said—" Cloud clamps her mouth shut even though Fyve hasn't spoken.

"She also said what?" he asks, suspicion instantly raised.

Cloud smiles secretively, tucking her face down to press a kiss to her baby's head. "I'm not allowed to tell you. It's a surprise."

"Surprises haven't always been pleasant on The Oasis," Fyve warns. "What else did she tell you?"

But now Cloud is shaking her head with just as much enthusiasm. "You'll find out," she says. "I will tell you I'm excited. I'm going to be part of the chosen who will find Tomorrow Land."

Fyve's about to press for more information when she shoos him with her free hand. "You'd better get going." She even winks. "Halo's probably looking for you."

Realizing there's no way Cloud is going to talk—she'd never defy Terra—he walks back to the door. "So you've got everything you need?"

Cloud tucks the cloth wrapped around the baby on her knees a little more snugly. "I will," she murmurs happily. "Even Ajax is going to be happy to see me. I just know it."

Fyve closes the door on Cloud's fervent, "Terra is great."

As he makes his way back to his cabin, he knows he should

be happy for her, and even Elijah. Her presence here has been welcomed. Her babies will be looked after.

But uneasiness has been Fyve's new companion since the continuation of the Trials were announced. The Trials that were defined by death and loss, all in the name of Terra and finding Tomorrow Land.

He's just reached the floor of his cabin when a gasp echoes in the narrow space. "Fyve! I was so worried!"

Halo runs toward him and launches into his arms. He catches her, holding her to him, confused. "What's happened? Who's been hurt?"

She clings to him, burying her head in his chest. "I came looking for you. When you weren't in your cabin, I thought you'd…"

Disappeared.

Died.

Fyve wraps his arms tightly around her. "I'm so sorry. I went to check on Cloud."

"Oh." Halo looks up, her hands twisting in his shirt. "That makes sense," she says sheepishly. "How is she?"

"She's fine. And so are the babies." He cups her face as his chest tightens. "I should've told you I was going."

There's too much going on. Their world is no longer defined by certainty. He doesn't need to glance at Dargo's door to be reminded of that.

She smiles weakly. "I just freaked out, that's all." She pushes up on her toes. "I can't imagine being here without you, Fyve."

His breath whooshes out as he leans down. "You'll never have to," he promises.

Their lips brush, gently, tenderly. Their bodies relax into the comfort the other provides. The only sure thing they have right now.

This sweet, exquisite, once-in-a-lifetime emotion that's grown between them.

They pull back, resting their foreheads against each other's. There's so much to say. So much feeling filling up inside of him. "Halo—"

"Report to the deck," says a voice in Fyve's mind. Terra's voice.

He pulls back. "Did you hear that?"

Halo nods, her body tensing. "The next Trial is about to start."

Not liking how ominous that sounds, Fyve takes Halo's hand and leads her up the stairs. The other teens join as they leave their cabins, forming a crowd that pours up the stairs. Everyone's quiet as they glance at each other.

It seems the glow of the first arrival onto The Oasis is wearing off. Everyone's nervous.

Up on the deck, Elijah's already standing beside a table not far from the railing. He beams as he sees the crowd of teens fan out, proudly wearing the same expression Fyve's seen at the beginning of every other Trial. It seems their leader is feeling confident again.

Terra appears on the upper deck and although the crowd was quiet, total silence now settles on the ship. The only sound is the soft lapping of the waves far below and the hum of the engine. After a cursory glance over the teens, Terra focuses her gaze on the table. A length of cloth is spread across it, raised in the center like a tent. There's no way to know what's beneath it.

"Welcome," Elijah calls, pride inflating his chest. "Terra has informed me that she will communicate the instructions of this Trial directly through me."

Halo shifts beside Fyve, looking troubled. The uncertain, scared Elijah of last night is gone. The old Elijah who personified faith in Terra and these Trials is back.

"Remove the cloth."

Fyve startles as the words filter through his mind. Halo also jolts and their gazes fly to the other. Fyve nods. So does Halo.

She heard it, too.

74

The other teens are also looking around, clearly wondering what to do with the instruction. One that was surely meant for Elijah.

He steps forward and grips the edge of the material, obviously having heard the words, too. "Now, I am honored to reveal the object central to today's Trial."

He yanks back the cloth with a sharp motion, his gaze on the crowd as he gauges their reaction.

Halo gasps.

Fyve almost does a double take.

Someone cries out.

Elijah's eyes shoot to the table and he stumbles back. "No," he moans.

Miracle and Marvel are nestled beside each other, a stick protruding between them to hold the cloth away. Hiding the two sleeping infants.

Elijah spins to face Terra. "No! These are my grandchildren!"

There's a loud gasp from Viney, and Ajax's eyes bulge to realize these are his children.

Terra's gaze lifts from the table, past the teens, and locks onto the horizon. There's no acknowledgement of Elijah's pain.

"*Elijah decided that three more lives should board our ship. His grandchildren and their mother.*" Her voice slips through Fyve's mind, and from the way Elijah stiffens, he also hears it. "*Balance must be maintained. Order will be restored. For Cloud and her babies to remain on The Oasis, three people must volunteer to lose their place.*"

Gasps ricochet through the crowd. Halo staggers and Fyve quickly clasps her to his side. "No," she moans. "This is wrong."

Anger and disgust coil through Fyve. No Trial has been right.

"You said she was welcome!" Elijah cries. "You can't ask this of us!"

Fyve notices that Elijah suddenly aligns himself with the group of teens. He's realized he's just as powerless as they are.

Terra doesn't tear her gaze from the horizon. "*Those who volunteer so Cloud and her babies may stay must move to the left side of the pool,*" she says calmly as she points to their left. "*Those who do not volunteer and do not wish these stowaways to remain on The Oasis, move to the right side of the pool.*"

Every teen shifts uncomfortably, several no longer able to meet the gaze of anyone else. Fyve searches the crowd, wondering what one person thinks of all this.

Ajax is frozen, staring at the two bundles on the table. His children. Fyve's not sure what that means. If it were him, he would've run toward the babies the moment he learned they existed.

A movement beside the table reveals Elijah's decided to do just that. He leaps for the twins, desperation etched on his face. He's just extended his hand toward his grandchildren when a cry is wrenched from him. Elijah drops to the ground, holding his head as he howls in pain.

Fyve grips Halo as she tries to go to him. There's no point in both of them being punished, even if it means having to watch her father being claimed.

But Elijah's cries stop and he falls still. He lies on the deck, breathing raggedly as blood trickles from his nose.

"It was a warning," Fyve says in a low voice. "He'll survive."

Halo sags. "The babies, Fyve. Miracle and Marvel are innocent in all this."

"I know," he says, trying to be reassuring as he wonders how they're supposed to respond to the awful decision they have to make.

Someone on his left moves away. "I worked hard to get here," they mutter, then stalk to the right side of the pool.

"I almost died getting here, then they just go ahead and sneak on," a girl adds as she follows him. "That's not okay."

"Babies die all the time." This time it's Viney who speaks, and she's looking at Ajax as she does. "There's no point giving up my place for that."

Ajax watches her walk away, still rooted to the spot. All that moves is his head as his gaze bounces from his children to Viney. Surely, he wouldn't…

Halo tugs on Fyve's hand. He looks at her, seeing the decision she's made in her resolute expression. He nods, having come to the same conclusion himself.

They step forward simultaneously. "I volunteer," Halo says clearly.

"So do I," adds Fyve.

Together, they walk to the left side of the pool. They turn to face the surprised crowd of teens, holding their heads high.

No place on The Oasis is worth having at the expense of the lives of innocent children.

One or two teens frown at them, then join the others on the right side. Iva breaks away, eyes still puffy from her crying this morning, and joins Fyve and Halo.

She smiles weakly at them. "Dargo would've chosen this, too."

They're soon joined by a tall guy, then another girl Fyve recognizes from Treasure Island. Sica's wild tangle of black hair was always noticeable. Even Justice hobbles her way over to join them, and they all know much she wanted to be on this ship. Within the space of a minute, almost twenty teens join them on the left side of the deck. Each and every one willing to lose the place they fought so hard for so Miracle, Marvel, and Cloud can be safe.

The remainder walk to the right.

"Ajax," Halo gasps.

He's not only in the larger group of those who aren't willing to volunteer, but he's also tucked behind Viney, clearly trying to hide.

"Coward," Fyve growls.

Now that everyone has chosen, all eyes turn to Terra. She shifts slowly, her vacant gaze settling on the small group of volunteers.

"Thank you to those who volunteered," she says collectively in their minds. *"You are now safe."*

HALO

"Safe?" Halo repeats Terra's last word. "How can we be safe? We were the ones who volunteered to give Cloud and the twins our place."

"It was a trick," says Fyve. "Some kind of twisted reward for doing the right thing."

"So, what happens next?" Halo shifts her gaze to the seventy teens standing on the other side of the pod pool. They're not in the slightest bit happy about what just happened. Is it possible that in addition to wanting a group of teens who are strong and smart, that Terra is also looking for them to be kind? But what's kind about inviting one hundred people on a ship to then tell them that only half of them can stay?

Ajax has stepped out from behind Viney and is cursing loudly. These are his own babies! How can he be upset about the possibility of them taking his place?

"Round two." Terra's voice enters their minds. *"Those of you who are safe may remain where you are. The rest of you must choose again."*

A frenzied murmur ripples over the group of teens as they

speculate whether this second round will also be a trick, or if this time they can take Terra at her word.

"Move toward the bow of the ship if you wish to volunteer your place," says Terra, pointing to show which direction she means. *"Move toward the stern if you do not."*

"Do the right thing, Ajax," Fyve growls. Halo can't blame him. He's only saying what everyone is thinking. His words carry over the rippling water of the pool and Ajax snaps up his head.

"I misunderstood the instructions last time." He scowls at Fyve with venom in his gaze. "Of course, I volunteer."

Ajax moves to the end of the pool at the bow of the ship, runs a hand through his blond curls, then firmly crosses his arms as if daring anyone else to criticize him. Viney follows to stand beside him, determined to align her fate with the guy she seems to think so highly of. But he's not fooling Halo with this show of selflessness. Terra's instructions in the first round had been more than clear. He hadn't misunderstood anything. He's merely banking on Terra continuing to play by the same rules and declaring him safe.

About half the teens go to Ajax's end of the pool and the other half try their luck at the stern. None of the teens in either group want to offer up their place, they already made that abundantly clear.

Halo's father wrings his hands beside Terra with his shoulders slumped and dried blood staining his cheeks. He'd been so proud to announce that the instructions for the Trial were going to be delivered through him. It was like he had his old self back and was filled with purpose once more. But then the babies had been revealed and he'd questioned Terra in front of them all, the anger unmistakable in his voice. And suddenly the instructions were being issued by Terra directly into their minds, showing everyone just how superfluous their leader really is.

The babies remain asleep in their basket, curled into each other. Miracle has her little arm across Marvel's body, her ruby lips pursed as if she's waiting for her next feed. It takes all of Halo's strength not to run to them. She has to hold on to the hope that they're safe. Terra said they can stay in the place of three of the teens. It's not exactly a fair deal, but it does seem to be one that guarantees their safety for now.

The last of the teens still in the Trial shuffle reluctantly into place. Once everyone has made their decision, Terra's voice enters their minds as she turns to the group at the stern. *"Those of you who have once again decided not to volunteer their place are excused from the Trial,"* she says. *"You may join those who were declared safe in the first round."*

Uncomfortable satisfaction blooms in Halo's belly. Even though it feels disloyal, she's unable to help being glad that Ajax's plan had backfired. He's now one of about thirty teens who will move on to the next round. His face is scrunched into a displeased frown, confirming to all that he hadn't been genuine in his offer to give his children his place.

Maybe this Trial isn't such a bad one, Halo decides. Although, it's still unclear as to what's happening to those who are eliminated from the Trials. They're disappearing from their cabins, but where are they being taken? Is that who was crying on the upper levels of the ship? Or are they being tossed overboard as food for the leatherskins? It would be nice to believe they're being sent back on a raft to Treasure Island, but with the distance they've covered by now, that's seeming less and less plausible. She just hopes that salty meat they're being fed doesn't turn out to be anything more sinister...

Terra turns to Ajax and the terrified teens beside him. Their odds of being selected to volunteer their place just got a whole lot greater.

"Thank you for being so kind as to volunteer your place," says Terra. *"Round three will now begin."*

"How do I even know they're my babies?" Ajax protests, clearly getting desperate. "They could be anyone's. I don't see Cloud here, do you?" He makes a show of looking around, then shrugs.

Terra raises her palm, then sweeps her hand in the direction of the door to the stairwell. As always, her expression remains neutral, her thoughts inscrutable.

The door slides open and Cloud strides out onto the deck, smiling broadly. She walks directly to Ajax and kisses him on the cheek.

"I knew you'd protect your children," she says, her eyes shining with pride. "Just as I knew Terra wouldn't let harm come to innocent children."

"Sevin was a child," Fyve mutters beside Halo.

The satisfaction that had been blooming in Halo's belly extinguishes immediately. Even if Fyve's mistaken about what happened to Sevin, what he's saying is correct. Terra hasn't exactly got a great track record when it comes to protecting the children of Treasure Island. Cloud made a catastrophic mistake allowing her children to be used as part of this Trial.

Cloud loops her hand into the crook of Ajax's arm, leaving Viney biting her lip on his other side as she seems to be wondering how much she'll have to fight to keep him. Straightening her back, she takes possession of Ajax's other arm, gripping onto it so tightly that her knuckles turn white.

"*Round three begins.*" Terra's words have everyone on the deck stilling as they wait for her next instructions. "*Step forward if you volunteer to allow Cloud and her children to take your place.*"

"This isn't fair," calls out a girl standing behind Viney, who Halo recognizes as one of her sisters. "The rules keep changing. How are we meant to know what to choose?"

"She's trying to divide us," says Viney's other sister. "She'll keep doing it until there are only three left."

"Then we stick together," says Viney's sister. "All of us. We all make the same choice."

Justice lets out a low chuckle behind Halo. "That's actually really smart."

Halo turns to her, not feeling the same sense of enjoyment. "Terra won't allow herself to be outsmarted."

Justice nods, a more serious expression crossing her face. "Good point."

"*Step forward if you volunteer your place,*" Terra repeats, ignoring the rebellion brewing on the deck.

Nobody steps forward. In fact, the teens who remain in the Trial cross their arms and raise their chins, daring Terra to eliminate them all. Halo holds her breath. She wouldn't put it past Terra to do exactly that.

"*Is that your final decision?*" Terra's voice reverberates inside their minds. "*Is nobody willing to offer their place for Cloud and her two innocent babies?*"

"You should all step forward!" Cloud suggests, her confidence seeming to slip just a little. "It's the same thing and it shows Terra that you're willing to participate in the Trial."

The teens look at each other. Some whisper in each other's ears. But, still, nobody steps forward. Perhaps they're afraid that nobody else will follow suit.

"*Very well,*" says Terra, turning to Halo's father and looking him directly in the eye.

Halo's blood turns to ice, fearing Terra is about to follow through on the warning she gave him earlier when she threatened to claim him.

She watches on as Terra delivers her father a message that's only for him. His face cracks with lines and his entire body sags when he hears her words. Whatever Terra is saying to him, it's crushing the pieces of his spirit he has left.

"I won't do that," he says, sinking to his knees. "I won't."

A sharp pain shoots to Halo's temples, and she cries out as

her legs give way. Fyve catches her before she hits the hard surface of the deck and scoops her into his arms. She thinks he might call out something, but she can no longer hear. Her world is a thick fog of agony as a familiar sticky wetness pours from her nose. This is more intense than the last time Terra had warned her in the engine room.

This claiming must be for real.

"I love you, Fyve," she sobs, wanting her last words to come from the dwindling light that remains in her soul.

The pain lessens just enough to allow some of her other senses to return and a howling fills her ears.

It's Ajax, making the same keening noise that had escaped his lungs when their mother died. Halo uses every ounce of energy she has and turns her head. She sees her brother collapse on the deck with Cloud and Viney hovering over him as he convulses and clutches at his skull.

Terra is claiming both of Elijah's children as punishment. He was right to be fearful for his family.

But just as quickly as the pain had gripped her, it subsides.

"Halo!" Fyve sobs, still cradling her in his arms. "Halo, fight this. Breathe. You have to hold on. I can't lose you, too."

She focuses on his voice, doing as he tells her, dragging in oxygen and urging her heart to return to a normal rhythm.

"I'm okay," she manages to say as she rests her head against his chest.

He kisses her on the forehead, his relief palpable. Then using the sleeve of his tunic, he wipes the blood clear from her face.

She does her best to give him a reassuring smile. "Is Ajax—"

"He's okay, too," Fyve replies, his voice developing a harder edge. He sets Halo back onto her feet, making sure she can stand, then keeping a steady arm around her shoulders.

Her father is still on his knees, his eyes sweeping between Halo and Ajax, then landing on the babies. It seems that what-ever Terra is asking him to do, has something to do with his grandchildren. And she's using his children's lives as the incentive for him to comply.

Terra stands over him again, saying words only he can seem to hear.

This time, he stands, his legs shaking and tears pouring down his face as he goes to Miracle and Marvel and lifts their basket by the handle. He carries them to the railing of the deck and lifts the basket higher, looking back at Terra, his eyes pleading with her to make it stop.

"No," breathes Halo. "He's not..."

The basket is lifted until it's resting on the timber railing.

Fyve tightens his hold on Halo, his own body vibrating with rage, as Terra's voice enters their minds. *"I call on those who remain in the Trial once more. Who is willing to volunteer to give these babies their place on the ship?"*

"No!" Halo screams, trying to wrench herself free. "I volunteer! Choose me. Don't do this, Terra. Dad, you can't let go!"

Cloud lets out a whimper, seeming to fully realize what the rest of them had known all along. Miracle and Marvel are in mortal danger.

"The babies and their mother are safe," says Terra. *"As long as I have three volunteers from those who remain in the Trial."*

"Ajax!" Cloud's scream pierces their frayed nerves as she pushes him forward. "Ajax volunteers."

Ajax is still weak from his near-claiming and stumbles, blinking at Terra in confusion as Viney tries to pull him back.

Cloud grabs his arm again, holding him in place. "And I volunteer with him. That's two for two. Please don't hurt our babies."

"You don't have a place to volunteer," Terra replies, a hint of impatience in her normally impassive tone. *"Ajax, go to your children and choose which one of them will be saved."*

There's a collective whisper across the crowd. Ajax may not have shown much compassion for the twins so far, but asking any parent to choose between their children isn't something that should ever happen.

"She volunteers as well." Cloud points a finger directly at Viney. "It's the least she can do."

Viney shakes her head firmly, a look of horror spreading across her pale features. Halo almost feels sorry for her for getting herself involved in this mess. "I refuse."

These words wipe any sympathy from Halo's mind. How can anybody choose themselves over the life of an innocent child? Cloud seems to feel the same way as she releases her grip on Ajax and lets out a growl. She lunges at Viney and shoves her hard, sending her flying into the pod pool.

There's a gasp as onlookers are splashed when Viney plunges underneath the green blobs of plant life the pods feed from. She fights her way back to the surface, screaming her protest as she hurls out a bunch of words Halo's never heard before. Picking green slime from her red hair, she reaches out a hand in Ajax's direction.

"Help me out," she cries. "The acid stings."

Ajax looks the other way, as do the rest of the teens.

Fyve lets out a frustrated sigh and lets go of Halo to walk to the pool, reaching down and hauling Viney out. She stands on the edge and shakes off the water, her pale skin now a deep pink.

"It hurts," she sobs, directing a scowl at Cloud.

"How do you think it would feel on a newborn baby's skin?" Fyve asks, leaving her to return to Halo's side.

"*It's time for Ajax to make his choice,*" Terra's voice booms inside their minds.

Ajax makes no move, so Halo launches forward, running toward the basket, aware that Fyve is right behind her. She hadn't even had time to think this move through. It's like her body's propelled itself without her brain's permission, so strong is the need to protect her niece and nephew.

"No!" she cries to Terra as she takes hold of the handle of the basket. With Fyve's help, she forces it away from her father and the dangers of the railing. Miracle opens her eyes, her arm still firmly across her twin's chest.

Cloud runs forward and throws herself at the basket, covering her babies' cheeks with kisses as tears pour down her face. "My children," she sobs. "My precious babies."

Terra stands firm, her expression not giving away any of her thoughts, even though she must be furious with these acts of defiance. Not even the threat of death had been enough to keep them in line.

"*I've seen enough,*" Terra says firmly, her words reverberating through Halo's mind as fear slices down her spine. This must be where it all comes to an end. Surely, Terra will claim her for real this time.

Halo looks up at Fyve and he nods, letting her know Terra is talking to all of them.

"*As a group, you have proven that you are unable to make the decision required of you,*" Terra continues. "*Which means you all fail the second Trial and it will be left to me to decide what happens next. Return to your cabins immediately.*"

Grateful to have been spared from being claimed for now, Halo goes to her father and wraps her arms around him. He seems smaller somehow, not at all like the powerful force she's always known him to be. He melts into her arms and holds her tight.

"I'm so sorry," he sobs. "This is all my fault."

She hugs her father back, knowing they need to talk. Properly this time.

Fyve puts a gentle hand on her back, reminding her she doesn't have time for that right now.

They need to return to their cabins and await their fate.

FYVE

*F*yve watches a sobbing Cloud clutch her babies as she runs and disappears back through the door. He suspects she'll go straight to the brig and shut herself in, as if that will protect her.

When it's clear there's nowhere that's safe on The Oasis.

Halo turns to him, her eyes heavy with the same knowledge. She just watched her father almost be claimed. She experienced the same pain herself. The dried blood smeared across her cheek is proof.

Fury whips through Fyve with such intensity, it almost takes his breath away. Hot and scalding, it fires his veins and inflames his determination.

He'll find out what's going on.

And they will survive whatever it is they're now part of.

Ajax storms past them, glaring at his father as if Elijah's done something wrong, then barely acknowledging Halo. No doubt because she fought for his children's lives when he didn't. Fyve narrows his eyes as he watches Ajax stalk away, Viney trotting after him, disgust churning through the fury. How could he choose himself over two vulnerable babies? *His* vulnerable babies?

Halo grips his arm. "Come on, we need to get back to our cabins."

Because Terra has ordered it.

Fyve takes her hand. "Yeah, let's go."

The majority of the teens have already scurried below deck, most no doubt carrying their shame with them. How many are genuinely remorseful for the choices they made? And how many are like Ajax, selfish and self-serving and worried about no one but themselves?

Halo passes through the door, looking drained, and Fyve's heart clenches. This strong, beautiful girl has been through so much today. Yesterday. And from the moment these Trials began.

The one who said she loves him as she thought she was dying.

This time, his heart constricts. It wraps around those words, knowing it will cherish them as long as he lives. Ready to set free the same ones it's been holding.

One last glance over Fyve's shoulder before he heads down the stairs reveals Terra is still up on the balcony. Unmoving. Emotionless.

The one who was going to let two babies die, when she's nothing more than a child herself. The same one who let his sister die.

Below her, someone moves so they're cloaked by the shadows of the overhang. Elijah's gaze is wide as it latches onto Fyve.

"Please," he mouths, pale tracks streaking through the blood on his face.

Tears. Of regret? Of despair? Or ones carrying the knowledge he's living in a nightmare of his own making?

Possibly all of the above.

And what exactly is he begging Fyve to do?

Elijah's lips form one more word. "Halo."

Fyve straightens. Elijah's asking him to protect Halo. Probably because he just learned he can't.

One nod is all it takes to seal the promise Fyve's already made. Halo will survive this. So will he.

And they'll uncover each and every secret hidden behind Terra's blank mask.

Downstairs, Fyve walks Halo to her cabin, noting the way her shoulders sag and her feet scrape. The corridors are empty, the remaining teens disappearing into their cabins as they try to appease the one who holds their lives in her small hands. But Fyve has no intention of doing that. The time for following orders is over.

But first, Halo needs to rest and recover. He leans down, her words still echoing through his mind as he breathes her in.

I love you, Fyve.

Halo pulls back. "Just give me a sec," she says, cheeks flushed. She ducks into her cabin before he can answer.

Fyve waits, tensions slowly tightening his gut. Does Halo regret what she said? Maybe she didn't really mean it. It was nothing more than an emotional reaction to being claimed.

She reappears a moment later, her face freshly washed. "Blood streaks aren't exactly attractive," she says, crinkling her nose.

Relief has a big smile climbing up his face. "Halo, you could be covered in that weird green stuff floating on the pod pool and I'd still want to kiss you."

She blinks. "Oh."

Fyve steps in closer, his heart thudding harder. She wasn't pulling away from him. He cups her beautiful face, the blush climbing up her cheeks, burning his palms. "By the way, I love you, too."

Her eyes widen. The blush deepens.

And then a blazing smile blooms across her face like a breathtaking dawn. "I wanted you to know, in case…"

She was claimed.

His heart had almost stopped as she'd crumpled. It can't take any more loss. It's barely holding together as it is.

And it's Halo's presence that's doing that.

"Well, I want you to know. Period." He leans down and brushes his lips across hers. "I love you, Halo."

Her breath puffs out, warm and moist. "I love you, Fyve. With everything I have."

They kiss, sinking into the aching truth that's now set free. Their mouths open, soft gasps filling the air as tongues tangle and bodies mold. Halo's hands band around his waist as she presses closer. Fyve almost instantly combusts. Desire clamps around his gut, and his hands tighten. They want to move. To delve deeper. To see exactly how hot this can get.

But he pulls away. The echoes of the male voice demanding he stop last time they kissed like this are still fresh in his mind.

And he needs to explore The Oasis while everyone is tucked away in their cabins.

Before Terra decides the outcome of the last Trial.

Fyve clears his throat. "You need to rest."

Halo flicks her tongue over her wet lips. "I know." She hesitates, smiling a little. "I wish you could come in."

Fyve almost groans. "Have a lie down while you can. Today's Trial was intense on a whole lot of levels."

Her eyebrows flutter as if they're considering a frown, then quickly smooth out. "It really was."

Fyve presses a quick kiss to her cheek. It's a good thing she needs rest right now—it's harder to leave than he expected. Especially with the invitation still lingering in her eyes.

But he can't stay. Not when he needs to find answers. It's the only way he can protect her, just like Elijah asked.

Stepping back, he turns away and heads for the stairs,

straight past his own cabin. He's going to the seventh floor. The open can he found there last night was far more of a clue than he realized.

Who opened it? Who ate the contents?

Who's been distributing food to the teens?

"Ahem."

Fyve spins around, his heart lurching. He lowers the foot that was about to reach the first step. He'd been so preoccupied he hadn't noticed Halo's door never closed.

She's standing a few feet away, her arms crossed. "That's not the way to your cabin," she points out.

He rubs the back of his head sheepishly. "I never said I was going to my room."

Halo arches a brow as she takes a step closer. "I can see that." Her arms unwind so she can prop her hands on her hips. "I'm coming with you."

"You need—"

"Answers," she interjects. "Just like you do."

Fyve opens his mouth, but this time, he doesn't even get a word out.

"I know you protect those you care about, Fyve. But I'm not Sevin or any of your siblings. I fully intend on looking out for you as much as you look out for me."

Now it's his turn to blink. Then blink again. What does he say to that? And what the hell does he do with the strange combination of frustration and warmth warring in his heart?

Turns out, Halo makes the decision for him. She walks straight past him and up the stairs. "Come on. We don't know how much time we have before Terra calls us all back."

Watching her sassy hips sway as she heads to the next floor, Fyve finds his lips twitching. He never stood a chance. Falling in love with Halo was as inevitable as his next breath.

He breaks into a jog to catch up.

"I thought I'd check out the food stash I found," he says as they fall into step. "If there's anyone else on this ship, they would've had to have gone there."

"Good thinking," says Halo, twining her fingers through his. "Let's start there."

They make their way to the large food preparation room Fyve found. Reaching the double doors they pause, listening hard. But there's no sound outside of the gentle rocking of the ship.

Fyve glances down and frowns. "There were footprints here last night."

Halo squats. "Are you sure?" She looks up. "It's all clear now."

His frown deepens. It was dark, but... "Very sure," he says emphatically. It was just like at the door to the seventh floor when we found Cloud."

Pushing up, Halo's frown echoes his. "Interesting."

She carefully slides open the door before he can ask her what she means by that, and he becomes instantly vigilant again. The soft gleaming metal covering most surfaces glints as they enter, looking exactly as he'd found it last night.

Except for one glaring difference.

"They're gone," Fyve gasps.

Halo looks around. "What?"

He strides to the rear end of the large room, trying to understand what he's seeing. Or rather, not seeing. "The crates. They're all gone."

The ones stacked several high, supposedly full of canned food.

Halo joins him, eyes scanning the floor that's just as clean and spotless as it was near the door. "That's a lot of crates to move in a short space of time," she muses.

Fyve stiffens. "I know it sounds crazy." Just like hearing voices does. "But—"

Soft crying filters through the doors, making them both stop.

"Can you hear that?" Fyve asks, just to make sure.

Halo nods. "Yes." She takes a couple of steps in the direction it's coming from. "Who is it?"

Fyve's heart thuds in his too-tight chest. Memories of Sevin curled up and crying broken heartedly on their mother's sleeping mat are crowding in. Drawn to the sound, he overtakes Halo and leaves the metallic room, pausing in the hallway with his head angled. "This way."

They head down a level, and then another. The crying grows louder the deeper they sink into the bowels of The Oasis.

"We're getting close to the engine room," Halo says, gripping the back of his shirt.

Fyve looks over his shoulder. "Oh yes, we are." There's a steady thrumming vibrating up through his feet. He'd been so focused on the crying he hadn't noticed. "Another floor or two, I'd say."

"One more," she says tensely. "We need to be careful."

"What's up," he asks, looking around. Is Halo also hearing voices no one else is?

Except the crying suddenly stops.

They both straighten and still, listening hard. But all that carries through the air is the steady hum of the engines beneath them.

"No," Fyve whispers.

He's not sure why it's so important he knows the origins of the crying, but it is. He strides down the corridor, following where he last heard the sound. Two large doors are at the end, these ones far fancier than the ones to the metal room.

The crying was definitely coming from the other side.

"Be careful," Halo murmurs, eyeing the door cautiously. "We have no idea what's waiting for us."

"Well, we're about to find out," Fyve mutters with determination, his hand reaching out to push it open.

"No! Stay away!"

Fyve freezes. "Did you hear that?" He spins around. "It's the man again!"

Halo also turns, looking around frantically. "Hear what? What man?"

Ice snakes through Fyve's veins. It was the voice that told him to stop when they were in his cabin. The one Halo didn't hear then, either.

The voice that only speaks to him.

"*Stay away from the door. Leave. Now!*"

Fyve's heart is pumping like a piston. He wants to jam his hands over his ears, but he knows it won't make a difference. The voice is inside him.

"Fyve?" Halo asks, sounding worried. "What's going on?"

He's going crazy, that's what's going on.

His gaze returns to the doors. "There's something behind there we're not supposed to see," he says, voicing the only truth he's certain of right now.

Halo's hand presses onto his arm. "Is everything okay? You're pale."

And sweating. And breathing like he just ran up and down every set of stairs on this monstrous ship.

But none of those things are going to stop him from finding out who's crying and why. Not even the voice that's somehow shouting orders yet sounding desperate all at the same time.

Fyve reaches out, placing his palm on the door and pushes. Two things hit him simultaneously.

The realization the door's locked.

And blinding pain at the side of his head.

There's no time to process either before everything goes black.

HALO

*H*alo gasps as Fyve crashes to the floor. Her first thought is that he's been claimed. Then she sees the figure behind him, holding a tin can in the air.

"Zake!" Halo shouts as she crouches beside Fyve. "What are you doing here?"

She doesn't wait for his answer as she checks Fyve is alive and breathing. He groans and his hand comes to his head where a sizable lump is blossoming. She breathes out a sigh before her lungs immediately fill with anger.

"You hit him with a can," she growls, looking up at the guy she thought she was never going to have to see again. His brown hair seems darker in the shadows, his lanky frame taller as he looms over her with a sneer.

"He was snooping." Zake lets his hand fall to his side but keeps hold of the can. "And so were you. You can count yourself lucky."

Fyve sits up, his expression thunderous. "You didn't have to hit me."

The Oasis tilts as if it, too, is expressing its disgust with this most awful of human beings.

"It's called payback," says Zake, as the ship rights itself. "For that time you got jealous and hit me over the head on the beach."

Halo hides a grimace, not wanting him to know how the memory of what he tried to do to her still fills her with fear.

"I'm not jealous of you." Fyve gets to his feet, not pointing out it was Sevin who hit Zake, even though she's safe from any repercussions now.

"You didn't like the way your girlfriend was panting all over me," Zake says, his lecherous gaze raking Halo. "If ya ask me, she was enjoying it."

Halo is on her feet in no time, anticipating the way Fyve lunges at him. She manages to get between them, flinching as she makes contact with Zake.

"He's not worth it," she says to Fyve, pushing him back. "That's exactly the reaction he wanted."

Fyve backs off and Halo steps away with him.

Zake seems to find this funny. "I'd never let a girl overpower me."

"You do realize it was Fyve's baby sister who hit you over the head that time, don't you?" Halo says before she can stop herself. The satisfaction of letting him know he'd been bested by a girl was too tempting.

"Except it won't be a girl who finishes you," snarls Fyve, stepping forward. "You'd better watch yourself."

"Terra wants you to stop snooping," says Zake, ignoring his threat. "I'm her messenger now. And she says you were instructed to return to your cabins. So, if anyone had better watch themselves, it's you two."

"We don't take orders from you." Fyve pulls back his shoulders. "You're not even supposed to be here."

"They're not from me," he sneers. "They're from Terra. I told you both. I'm her messenger now."

"What are you even doing here?" Halo asks. "I saw you carry Justice on board, but you weren't supposed to stay."

Zake laughs at this. "Seems I'm not very good at following orders."

"Some messenger you'll make then," Halo retorts.

All amusement slips from Zake's face as he raises the tin can in the air once more. "Go back to your cabins. Now!"

"Open the door behind you first," says Fyve. "We heard someone crying. Who have you got in there?" He steps forward, but just as he's about to push his nemesis out of the way, something stops him. He puts his hands to his temples and groans.

"Fyve!" Halo pulls him back. She'd been unable to protect him from Zake's unexpected blow, but she has to get him out of danger now. He's not thinking clearly after that knock to the head.

Zake waves the can threateningly, standing firmly in front of the door.

"Don't worry, we're going," she says, practically dragging Fyve down the corridor, back toward the stairwell.

He's still clutching his head, his eyes darting from left to right.

"We can come back later," she whispers. "Zake's not worth being claimed for."

"I wasn't being claimed," he says, letting his hands fall. "I heard the man's voice again."

Halo pushes open the door to the stairwell and holds it open for Fyve. He walks through and stops on the landing when she closes it behind him.

"What did he say?" she asks.

"He didn't say it this time." Fyve rubs at his sore head. "He shouted it. He told me to stay away from the door. And he was pretty clear about it."

"The voice doesn't sound like my father, does it?" she asks, unsure if she wants the answer.

Fyve shakes his head. "It's definitely not Elijah. And it's not Zake, either. This isn't a voice I've heard before."

Halo slides her hands around Fyve's waist. "You scared me back there. I'm so glad you're okay."

"But am I?" Fyve moans. "Are any of us okay?"

Halo steps back so she can look at him. This isn't like Fyve. "What's wrong?"

"It's that voice." His eyes fill with anguish. "Why am I the only one hearing it?"

She sighs. "Another mystery to add to our list, I suppose."

"And…" He turns away, seeming to change his mind about whatever he'd been about to say.

"And what?" She grabs the back of his shirt. "What?"

He puts a hand to his forehead. "My head hurts."

"Of course, it does!" She smiles reassuringly. "You just got thumped over the head with a tin can."

"It's been hurting all day," he says as they walk slowly back down the stairs. "I didn't want to say anything, but I've had this dull ache I've never felt before."

These words have Halo pausing. "Me too. I thought it was from when Terra warned me with the claiming. But now that I think of it, I've had a mild headache since I woke up."

"Maybe it's stress," says Fyve. "Seeing Zake's ugly face will do that to anyone."

She doesn't point out that they hadn't seen his face until just now. "I can't believe he snuck on the ship. Actually, I can believe that. What I can't believe is that Terra's allowing it."

"I can," he says with a bitter tone. "After that last Trial, I'll believe anything."

"At least with Zake here, Sevin won't have to deal with him back home." As soon as the words are out of Halo's mouth, she realizes her mistake.

Fyve stops on the landing and stares at her. "What did you say?"

"I'm sorry!" she says, trying her best to act cool. "I forgot for a moment. It's just so hard to believe she's gone."

He nods as he lets out a long sigh. "I know you loved her, too. She was a special kid."

"Fyve..." She has to tell him. It's not right to keep this secret. Here he is, believing what she's saying when she's hiding something huge from him. He's so trusting, so loyal, so kind. And she's nothing more than a liar.

"What?" he asks, tilting his head as he waits for her to find the words she's struggling to form.

"It's about Se—"

The door to the lower level bursts open and Justice hobbles through.

"Oh," she says when she looks up and sees them. "We're supposed to be in our cabins."

"Exactly," says Halo, unsure if she's annoyed or relieved at the interruption.

"Where are you going?" Fyve asks.

"Nowhere," says Justice. "Just needed to exercise my bad leg. I thought the stairs would help to strengthen it."

"And where are you really going?" Halo asks as they walk down the steps to meet her on the landing.

Justice flinches. "I told you. Just getting some exercise. And besides, I could ask the same of you two."

"We were trying to find some answers," says Fyve.

"There are no answers on this ship." Justice's shoulders sag. "Only questions."

"We saw Zake." Halo studies Justice's face to see if this is a surprise.

She looks down at her feet, then back up again and nods.

"You knew he was here." Fyve doesn't seem impressed. "And you didn't tell us."

"He's my brother!" Justice throws out her hands, then losing her balance on her injured leg, she clutches one of the handrails.

"A brother we thought you were glad to leave behind," says Fyve.

"Brothers are complicated." Justice points at Halo. "She should understand that."

"There's not much that's complicated about Zake," Fyve mutters, rubbing at the lump on his head. "He's a clear-cut douchebag."

"Wait, Fyve," Halo says gently. "Justice is right. Not everyone got as lucky in the brother department as Sevin. It's very possible to both love and hate your brother all at the same time. They can be exceptionally complicated."

Justice nods, seeming glad to have Halo's support. "I didn't know he'd stayed on the ship until he snuck into my room not long after we left Treasure Island."

"So, you've been hiding him?" Fyve asks.

"I didn't know what else to do." Justice's eyes fill with tears and Halo puts a hand on her shoulder, knowing she wouldn't have turned in Ajax either. "I shared my food with him on the first day. It was still more food than we've ever eaten at once. I thought maybe I could get away with it all the way until Tomorrow Land. But then he disappeared."

"What do you mean?" asks Halo.

"I haven't seen him for days," says Justice. "I thought Terra found out and, you know, vanished him like the others."

"Sadly, he hasn't vanished," says Halo, deciding that's a good term for what's been happening to those who haven't passed the Trials. It really has felt like they've disappeared into thin air. "He's up on the next floor."

"I wouldn't recommend sneaking up on him." Fyve points to the lump on his head. "He's not in a good mood."

"He told us he's Terra's messenger," Halo adds.

"But she doesn't need a messenger," says Justice, rubbing at her temples and wincing. "She talks directly in our heads."

"Do you happen to have a headache?" Halo asks.

"All day," she sighs, leaning more heavily on the handrail. "It's just been sitting there in the background thumping away. I don't normally get headaches."

Halo glances over at Fyve whose brows shoot up.

"What?" Justice seems confused by this exchange.

"We have headaches, too," Halo explains. "They all started today."

"Oh." Justice shrugs. "I did tell you this was a ship filled with questions. We really shouldn't expect to find a cause."

"Why were you looking for your brother if you don't want answers?" asks Fyve.

Justice sighs. "I actually was just trying to strengthen my leg. Those exercises Terra made us do on the deck have me worried. She wants strong people on Tomorrow Land. I'm a liability like this."

Fyve doesn't look like he believes her, but Halo does. Justice proved on Treasure Island how tough she is. She hadn't shied away from the leatherskin on the final Trial, and she's not giving up on this new set of Trials now. She wants a better life for herself and she's prepared to put in whatever hard work it takes to achieve it.

"You should be resting your leg, not exercising it," says Fyve, holding out his elbow. "Use me as a crutch. It's not safe out here. We need to get back to our cabins."

Justice nods and they make their way down the corridor. Halo follows behind as Justice leans heavily on Fyve in much the same way Cloud had after giving birth.

The sound of babies crying fills the cavernous space and Halo's head snaps up.

"The twins," she says. "Where are they?"

"Cloud and the babies have moved in with Ajax," Justice explains. "You missed quite the commotion when you were off looking for your answers."

"I'm guessing Viney wasn't happy?" Halo imagines the tussle

that would have taken place. She's glad Cloud won out in the end.

"You could say that." Justice glances back at Halo. "You could also say that Ajax wasn't all that pleased, either."

Anger boils in Halo's gut. "I'll talk to him in the morning. I really don't know what's wrong with him."

"Brothers," mutters Justice.

They reach their rooms and Halo gives Fyve a quick kiss on the cheek.

"I'll see you tomorrow," she says.

"You don't want me to come to your cabin?" he asks. "It seemed like you wanted to tell me something earlier?"

She shakes her head, not able to cope with the idea of picking that conversation up again just now. Her headache is worsening. And now she has Ajax to worry about on top of everything else. She'll have better luck finding the right words after a good night's sleep.

"It was nothing," she says. "I'm tired, and you need your rest. It's been a very long day."

"Okay." Fyve nods in his forever understanding way. She really does need to talk to him. She's not the sort of person to keep secrets from people. The problem is that she may have already left it too late. He'll never forgive her for keeping it from him for so long.

She flops down on her bed, her headache worsening. So much has happened and yet still she has more questions than answers. Something very sinister is going on in this ship. They need to find out what's behind that door Zake was guarding.

But will it answer any of their questions, or will it only raise a thousand more?

FYVE

"*W*ake up, Fyve."

Fyve's eyes fly open. He goes from asleep to alarmed before the whispered voice is finished. His gaze darts around the cabin as his heart thuds heavily, even though he knows he's the only one here.

The voice is in his head. His still-aching head.

"*I mean you no harm.*"

Yet Fyve's erratic pulse doesn't slow. He has no idea who's speaking to him or how. Or why. There's nothing on this ship that he trusts, apart from Halo.

"Get out of my head," he growls, hating that he's now answering the voice.

"*I'm here to help. The next Trial starts soon.*"

He sits up, getting his breathing under control. The next Trial? They haven't even heard the result of yesterday's.

"*I'll prove to you I only want to help. I know things.*"

Fyve frowns, uneasiness slithering up his spine. He doesn't speak, but one question slips past his defenses.

What things?

"*There will be no breakfast this morning,*" the voice answers as if it heard his unspoken question.

Frowning, Fyve stalks to the door. He opens it, unsure how he feels when he looks at the shelf to the right.

And finds it empty.

Just like every shelf beside every door.

Shutting himself back in, he stands in the middle of his cabin. The voice can't be his own mind. The relief that he's not going crazy is short-lived, though.

Someone else apart from Terra has taken residence in there.

"*Shower, dress, and be on the deck in thirty minutes.*"

This time it's actually Terra who speaks, no doubt to every teen on the ship. Fyve rubs his eyes hard enough to see bright spots. It's starting to feel crowded in there.

"*The showers will be short this morning. You must wash quickly,*" says the male voice.

Now curious as well as unsettled, Fyve enters the little room with the indoor rain. Undressing, he steps into the cubicle and turns the metal knob. Water gushes out and he quickly scrubs himself down. The water's still running once that's done, so he turns his face into the stream. The steady coolness is a balm to the ache throbbing at his temples. He almost shakes his head at his naivety. He can't believe how quickly he'd been willing to listen. It's clear the showers aren't going to be cut—

The water abruptly stops.

Fyve blinks the droplets from his eyelashes. The voice was telling the truth.

He steps out, absentmindedly slicking the water from his body.

"*There are towels, cloth to dry yourself, in the cupboard on your right.*"

Fyve glances around, deeply unsure about how to feel about any of this. It's clear the voice can see him. Cautiously, he reaches out to the small handle on the cupboard, no longer surprised to find two neatly folded towels on the shelf within. He dries himself off, marveling at the luxury of a length of material used to do such a thing as simply absorb water.

Back in his room, he dresses quickly and quietly. The headache is only increasing, but considering what's happening inside his head, that's not surprising either. He straightens, realizing he's waiting. As unwelcome as the new voice is, it's proven in a short period of time that it knows things about The Oasis and the Trials.

A voice that claims it wants to help him.

A voice that holds a strange note of sincerity.

Fyve shakes his head. He's right back to feeling like he's losing it.

"Follow my advice, and you will pass these Trials, Fyve."

He freezes. "What's your name?" he growls softly.

There's a pause long enough that Fyve assumes he doesn't get to do things like ask his own questions.

"My name is Jiro."

"And who are you?"

This time, there's no pause. *"I will take care of you, my child."*

"I don't understand. Why me?"

Silence stretches out for long seconds as Fyve holds his breath. But no answer comes. Seems he's exhausted his quota of questions.

Rapid footsteps beyond his cabin have Fyve spinning around.

"Holly!" a panicked voice calls out. "Misty!"

Exiting, Fyve sees other teens standing in their doorways, looking confused. And nervous.

Viney streaks past. "Please! Has anyone seen them?"

Fyve grabs her arm as she frantically runs back. "What's wrong? Who are you looking for?"

"My sisters," she wails. "They're missing!"

His stomach sinks, and it has nothing to do with the dipping and swaying of the ship. "They're not in their cabins?"

Viney shakes her head as tears track down her cheeks. "I've checked everywhere. Not on the deck, and the ballroom's locked, but I'm sure they're not in there."

Someone appears beside Fyve. "They've been taken," says Iva. "Just like Dargo. Because they didn't pass the last Trial."

"No!" Viney shrieks, her fingers spearing in her red hair. "They can't be!"

Another person jostles past Fyve. "Sh, Viney," Ajax croons. "I've got you."

She collapses in his arms, sobbing. "Oh, Ajax. They can't be... gone."

Iva drags her unsympathetic gaze from Viney to Fyve. "My neighbor's missing, too." She shrugs. "I don't remember his name."

Either because Iva's been spending more time in Dargo's room, grieving his loss, or because she's decided she's not going to the effort of learning people's names if they're just going to disappear without a trace. Or a bit of both.

"Not Holly and Misty," Viney moans. "They're all I have."

Ajax's arms tighten around her. "You've got me, Viney."

She looks up, blinking tear-soaked lashes. "I do?"

"You do?"

Fyve spins around to find Cloud a few feet away, her face pale as she clutches Miracle and Marvel. "What about me? And our babies?"

Ajax huffs in frustration. "I can't do this right now, Cloud," he snaps. "Can't you see I'm helping Viney? She just lost her sisters, for Terra's sake."

Cloud frowns, blinks, then frowns a little deeper. She lifts one of the babies and presses her lips to their forehead. It's impossible to tell whether she feels chastised or frustrated. Halo appears behind her and wraps her arms around the young mother's shoulders, clearly opting for the second emotion. She glares at her brother. "Ajax—"

"Spare me the lecture," he grumbles. "I'm doing my best here, okay?" Taking Viney by the shoulders, he leads her away. "Come on, let's go to your cabin."

So he can comfort her, Fyve thinks in disgust.

With a small whimper, Cloud spins around and hurries back to her cabin. The remaining teens retreat to their own spaces, leaving Halo and Fyve standing in the corridor.

He gravitates toward her. His anchor is this sea of unknowns. His foundation in a world that won't stop moving in more ways than one.

Fyve finds he's smiling, despite the headache. The tightness in his chest. The confusion in his mind.

"Hey," he murmurs.

Halo leans into him the moment they're close enough. "Hey."

A caress of his lips on hers cements the greeting. Conveys how glad he is that she's here.

She looks up at him. "Three more people have disappeared," she says worriedly.

"I know." He sighs. "And there's another Trial about to start."

She pulls back in surprise. "There is?"

Fyve blinks, realizing the voice, Jiro, told him that. Not willing to have any secrets from Halo, he nods. "I—"

"*Don't trust her.*"

Halo's eyebrows angle down as she waits. "Fyve?"

"*She's hiding something.*"

He shakes his head, trying to ignore the voice he suddenly doesn't want. "Sorry. There's just so much going on and my brain feels like it's going to explode."

Halo smiles, her face softening. "My headache is worse today, too."

Fyve's hands tighten on her upper arms. "I can trust you, can't I, Halo?" He hates that he asks, but Jiro's words have hit a nerve. They tug at the one thread that could unravel everything.

Halo, and what's blossomed between them, is the only good thing he can cling to right now.

He loves her with a totality that is the one absolute he has.

And she said she loves him, too.

She smiles. She leans in again. Yet her words are a heartbeat slower than they should be. "Of course, you can trust me, Fyve."

"She has a secret!"

Jiro's words trigger a memory. Fyve watches Halo closely, not liking that he's doing this, but needing the reassurance. "You wanted to tell me something last night?"

The tension that shoots through Halo's body is subtle yet undeniable. She goes from pliant and open, to still enough that she's barely breathing.

Terra filters through their mind. *"Report to the deck. The next Trial begins."*

Halo's eyes widen. "How did you know?"

"I, ah, assumed when she told us to report there in half an hour." The lie whooshes out before Fyve can stop it. It leaves a bitter film on his tongue and a tightness in his gut.

But he doesn't take it back.

Doors down the corridor open as teens exit their cabins and Fyve steps back. "Come on. We don't want to leave Terra waiting."

Halo frowns but doesn't have time to object. The corridor quickly fills with teens, all carrying various shades of their own frowns. There hasn't been enough time to process the disappearance of three more peers from the last Trial and they're already about to start another.

Up on the deck, Fyve discovers the teens haven't moved very far. The crowd is still standing near the door, and he quickly sees why.

A large table stretches across the deck, chairs lined up on

either side. Plates of food sit before each chair, meat, the bread rounds, and some sort of deep red vegetable sitting in equal portions on each one.

"Welcome to the next Trial," booms a voice from the balcony.

A voice that has Halo gasping. "Where's my father?" she whispers frantically.

Because it's Zake who's standing beside Terra, his arms extended in the same way Elijah would have.

But his grin is gloating. Almost sinister. Not Elijah's serene smile born of faith.

Faith that was clearly misplaced.

Because Elijah's nowhere to be seen.

Zake puffs out his chest as a murmur ripples through the crowd. "Surprise," he crows. "I'm your new messenger."

More unease shifts through the teens. Zake didn't earn his place on The Oasis like they all did, risking their lives to be here. And yet, he's standing beside the still and silent Terra, boasting.

"Get down from there," someone shouts. "You're no leader."

Zake's gaze hardens as it falls on the young man. "Did you not learn yesterday that everything's gotta be balanced on The Oasis?" His grin grows. "If I'm here, with Terra's blessings, as ya can see, one of you has to go."

A collective gasp rises from the teens. Even across the several feet between them, Fyve can see that the young man who spoke has gone deathly white. Before the sound of shocked horror has been carried away by the breeze, the young man cries out and falls to his knees. His hands clamp onto his ears in a way Fyve wishes he hasn't seen before.

The cry morphs to a scream drenched in pain.

"Stop it!" Halo cries.

Fyve launches into action, having no idea what he can do to stop this, but knowing he has to try.

"Don't move!" Jiro shouts in his head. *"This is Terra's wish!"*

Although Fyve ignores the order, the young man staggers to his feet before he can reach him. Blood seeps from between the fingers clasping his head, and as he glances over his shoulder at the crowd, more tracks down from his eyes in jagged lines.

"I will not be claimed," he screams hoarsely. With stumbling steps, he lurches to the side of the ship, hitting the railing hard but barely noticing it. Without releasing his head, he throws himself over, his feet the last thing to disappear from view.

Fyve blinks as his stomach churns. Someone behind him retches. The young man chose the acidic depths of the ocean rather than his mind imploding. Both deaths are tortured ones, but he did it on his own terms.

"And now we are balanced," Zake says as if he just announced another feast.

Beside him, Terra is still a statue. From what Fyve can tell, she didn't even watch the young man take his life before she could.

Halo clutches Fyve's hand, looking as if she wants to be sick, too. Up until now, people have disappeared, but they just watched the first confirmed death on The Oasis. They haven't escaped the horror of the Trials on Treasure Island.

They're still in them. Not only that, they're trapped.

"I will make sure you're safe, Fyve. I promise you that."

Jiro's voice is fervent. A heartfelt vow.

"But you will have to do everything I say."

HALO

*S*omething's going on with Fyve. Halo just can't figure out what it is. One minute he's kissing her like she's the last person on this dying planet, and the next he's asking if he can trust her. Where had that question come from? He's trusted her since these cruel Trials began, way back on Treasure Island. What changed in the moments between that kiss and that question?

Guilt tugs at her insides. She's keeping a secret from him…

Yet, all she wants is to spare him the pain of knowing he did the one thing he'd sworn he'd never do—leave his sister behind. Sevin wouldn't want him to hurt like that, and Halo doesn't either. Except now it's becoming clear the pain he's feeling is worse than the one she's sparing him. It's a lose-lose situation, in the same way these Trials have been all along.

"Where were we before we got distracted by that traitor?" Zake's voice booms across the terrified teens. They all jump, not wanting to be the next to be claimed. "That's right. I was telling you I'm Terra's messenger."

Halo winces, trying to push down her headache as she searches the deck for any sign of her father. That should be him standing up there on the balcony beside Terra, not that knuck-lehead. Her only hope right now is that her dad hasn't vanished. As soon as she can get away, she has to find him. And she knows exactly where to look.

"The door," she whispers to Fyve. "With Zake and Terra here, nobody's guarding it. If we hurry after the Trial, we can get there first."

Fyve's face lights up and he begins to nod. Then a look of confusion crosses his features and his nod morphs into a shake. "I'm not sure that's a good idea."

"Zake will gloat after the Trial for at least a few minutes," she says.

Fyve keeps his gaze forward. "It's not safe."

"Hey," Justice hisses from behind them. "Keep quiet. Are you mad?"

Zake raises his hands in the same way Halo's father did when he wanted his people's attention. But Zake is taller than her father, with only a few scraggly hairs clinging to his chin as a beard, and somehow the gesture looks all wrong. "Look in fronta ya, and you'll see a table with your breakfast. One plate for each of ya."

Halo's stomach groans, and she realizes how quickly she's adjusted to being fed on a regular basis. Food wouldn't have even crossed her mind at this time of day if she were back on Treasure Island.

"When I say so, Terra wants ya all to choose a plate," Zake instructs.

Halo wonders how eating breakfast could possibly be a Trial. Will Terra be watching to see who eats the fastest? Or who savors every mouthful? So far, it's all a bit unusual, which is completely *usual* for a Trial.

"I reckon you should choose wisely," Zake adds, his dark eyes glowing with amusement. "Yesterday, you proved you're not very good at deciding who stays and who goes. So, this time, Terra is leaving it up to chance."

Halo shifts her gaze to the long line of plates, squinting to see if she can notice anything different about any of them. They all look exactly the same, with a portion of meat, rounds of bread, and a strange red vegetable off to the side. She decides to give the meat a miss after that horrifying thought she'd had yesterday about the people who've vanished.

"You hafta eat everything on ya plate," says Zake as if reading Halo's mind. "If ya don't, Terra will be upset. So upset she won't ever feed ya again."

Halo's shoulders slump. She really hopes she's wrong about the meat. Because not being fed would mean a slow death on board this ship. Being claimed would almost be preferable. It looks like she has no choice but to choose a plate and lick it clean.

"Oh, and one udder thing." Zake smiles broadly. "Some plates have been poisoned."

A gasp zings its way through the crowd as jaws fall open. Halo's heart rate picks up and she feels sweat bead on her forehead. Surely, this can't be happening!

"How many plates have been poisoned?" someone dares to ask. It's a fair question. The least Zake can do is tell them their odds of making it through breakfast.

"If I told ya that, it would ruin the surprise." Zake laughs, enjoying himself in a way that Halo's father never would have. He's making a mockery of the dignity her dad brought to his position as leader. "As a treat, Terra is gonna pour ya a glass of wine. You hafta wait to eat until everyone has their glass so we can toast Terra. Then you can enjoy it all."

Halo bites her tongue to stop herself from reacting. This has to be a joke. Some of the teens here are as young as thirteen. Surely, serving them wine isn't a great idea. Although, the wine really is the least of their problems. The randomly poisoned plates pose a far greater threat.

Iva takes a step toward the table, wringing her hands, seeming anxious to select her plate.

"Wait for the signal," Halo warns, holding her gently by the arm.

"Why are you so keen?" Justice asks in a low voice. "This is the worst Trial ever."

Iva shakes her head. "At least it's an honest one."

Halo tilts her head in surprise.

Iva leans in closer to them. "I'd rather be told I might die while eating my breakfast than be stolen from my bed like Dargo and taken who-knows-where."

Nodding, Halo can't deny the truth in these words. This is the first time Terra has been up-front with her plans. Of all the teens who died in the other Trials, not one of them saw it coming. This time, they know what they're dealing with. If only they knew how many of them were about to eat their last meal. Are they looking at one poisoned plate or twenty?

"I think I know where Dargo might be," whispers Halo, deciding if Fyve isn't interested in going with her to find out what's behind that door then maybe Iva is. "Follow me as soon as this Trial is over."

Iva's blue eyes widen and her lips pop open. She nods without hesitation. She'd do anything to find out what happened to the guy she loves. Halo gets it. There's nothing that would stop her from finding Fyve if he was torn from her side. Just as she knows if Sevin or Halo were behind that door, he would've broken it down long before now.

Zake raises his hands again and scans the restless crowd. People are already eyeing plates and sharing theories on which ones might be the unlucky ones. Halo's not sure what strategy to try.

"Take one on the end of the table," says Justice. "The middle ones are sure to be poisoned."

"Not the very end ones though," says Iva. "We want plates that aren't unusual."

Halo looks at Fyve, who still seems distracted. "What do you think?"

He shrugs, not seeming to want to commit to any theory. She slips her hand into his and he squeezes tightly, then lets go. She tries not to read too much into this. They're about to begin a deadly Trial. It's no wonder he's freaking out. She's freaking out!

Zake claps his hands. "Go on then. You may choose ya plate now. Bone appetite!"

"It's bon appétit, you moron," Fyve mumbles.

Halo smiles. That's the Fyve she knows and loves. She knew she was just imagining his strange behavior.

The teens surge toward the table. Some go directly to a plate and stand firmly behind it, letting all others know it's taken. Others cruise around the table, studying each plate before moving on to the next one.

Fyve heads for the middle of the table.

Halo pulls him back. "Justice said—"

"It doesn't matter what she said," Fyve snaps, then seems to remember himself. "Sorry, Halo. I've just got a lot going on right now."

"It's okay." She rubs at her head, unable to deny that it's aching a little more now that a decision needs to be made.

"These ones," says Fyve pointing to two unclaimed plates that are sitting side-by-side.

"Are you sure?" she asks, feeling uneasy about having her own opinion taken out of this potentially life altering—or life ending—decision. But Fyve had asked if he can trust her, and he can. So, it's important she shows that she can trust him, too.

Fyve stands behind one of the plates he'd pointed at, a confident posture that makes it obvious his decision's been made. Halo stands beside him and stares down at her plate. The piece of meat looks soft and the bread a little soggy, but it's the vegetable that holds her gaze. It's a deep red color, bordering on purple. Shaped like a ball, it would fit neatly in the palm of her hand. Juice seeps from it and swirls around her plate, reminding her of a bleeding heart and she can't help but suspect Terra's done this on purpose. As if they weren't all already on edge enough.

Cloud is on the other side of the table, standing a few places down. Ajax and Viney are down at the far end, not far from Justice and Iva.

Halo catches Cloud's eye and smiles. "We'll be okay."

Cloud nods, but it's clear just how terrified she is. She has two babies to think of in all this. "Will you look after the twins if…" Cloud glances over to the basket beside the table where Miracle and Marvel are sleeping.

"That's not going to happen," Halo says, even though she can make no such promise. "But I'll always look after my niece and nephew. No matter what."

Cloud's eyes fill with tears, and she nods her gratitude. "I know you will."

Fyve puts a hand on Halo's back, seeming to be touched by what she said. He knows what it's like to be prepared to lay down your life for someone you love.

"One minute!" Zake calls out. "Make ya final decision. Hurry, hurry!"

As much as Halo hates hearing orders from this knuckle-head, it's a nice change from having Terra's voice rattling about inside her aching head. Her headache is far worse today than it was yesterday. It's like a tiny army has set up camp in her temples and is hammering away on the inside of her skull. Hopefully having a full stomach will take away some of the pain. Unless it kills her, of course. She looks back at her plate and her stomach growls, betraying her hunger despite how much she really doesn't want to eat this food.

The final person settles behind a plate and Zake raises his arms to signal their time is up. But before he can bring them fully above his head, Fyve dives behind Halo and shoves her to the side, so she's now standing behind his plate, and he has hers.

"No more changes!" Zake declares. "Your decision is now final."

Halo rubs at her arm as she gapes at Fyve, trying to take in what he just did. If it were anybody else, she'd think they'd had a bad feeling about their plate in the last second. But this is Fyve. Which means he must've had a bad feeling about Halo's plate. There's no doubt in her pounding head that he was protecting her, which makes her want to both kiss him and shake him at the same time.

"Did I hurt you?" Fyve whispers. "That plate has more food. You should have it."

"I'm fine," she replies, desperately hoping he hasn't just sacrificed himself for her. There's no way she could survive on this ship without him.

Terra and Zake make their way from the balcony to the main deck. Terra takes a bottle of wine from a nearby table and begins filling their glasses. Her long sleeves fall across the table, yet somehow, she manages not to stain her flowing robe with purple juice from the bleeding hearts. This makes her seem even more robotic. Halo's certain she'd be purple right up to her elbows by now if this task were up to her.

Looking up and down the table while she waits, Halo notices there are three empty places. One would be for that poor guy who jumped overboard, but who are the other two for?

"Who's missing?" she asks Fyve.

"I'm not sure." He shrugs.

They study the faces at the table, although with this many teens still in the Trial, it's impossible to tell.

"They're not for Zake and Terra, are they?" She feels silly the moment the question leaves her mouth. Of course, they're not. There's no way either of them would put themselves at risk like that.

"Doubt it," says Fyve. "Maybe your dad will be joining us?"

Her heart sparks with hope and she quickly extinguishes it. If there were only one empty place that might make some kind of sense, but there are two she can't account for? Who else could be joining them? Iva has noticed the same thing and is jiggling from foot to foot. Somehow, Halo doubts one of the places is for Dargo. They would both do well to keep their expectations in check. Because she also knows Terra doesn't make mistakes. These places have been set on purpose. But, for what? Or who?

Terra steps between Halo and Fyve to fill their glasses and Halo finds her gaze drawn to Terra's bald head. It's not as smooth as it looks from a distance. There's a fine sheen of stubble visible just underneath the skin, which means she has hair. For some reason, she's choosing to shave it. Halo's not sure if this clear sign of humanity makes her feel better or worse.

Halo's glass is filled and she bites her tongue when she automatically goes to say thank you. She doesn't want to thank this human-but-not-human for anything. Not unless she announces she's turning this ship back and taking them all home to Treasure Island. A pang of homesickness stabs her in the gut to join her throbbing head. They should never have gotten on this ship. Right now, she highly doubts Tomorrow Land even exists.

Terra steps back and moves on to the next glass and Halo eyes off her wine, deciding maybe it's the perfect accompaniment for the meal. It might take the edge off her nerves. Either that or it will fray them altogether.

Once all their glasses have been filled, Zake and Terra head back to the safety of their balcony.

Zake is clutching a bottle of wine and he raises it in front of him. "Here's to Terra. Thanks for ya goodness, and all that stuff."

Halo winces, wondering if everyone else is missing her father as much as she is. He'd have found far more appropriate words than Zake, who can barely string a sentence together. It seems that while Terra might be providing him with messages, she's most definitely not giving him the words.

The teens lift their glasses. "To Terra," they mumble before taking a sip. It's sour and not at all like what Halo imagined wine would taste like.

Zake guzzles his wine directly from the bottle, red liquid pouring from the edges of his revolting mouth, and Halo focuses on her plate. Her stomach churns at the thought of having to eat what's on it.

"Fill ya bellies!" Zake announces. "Remember you must eat every last crumb."

"Are you ready?" Fyve asks as he plunges his fork into his piece of meat.

Halo locks eyes with him and nods slowly.

She's not ready.

She'll never be ready.

But still, she takes her first bite.

FYVE

"*Y*ou *disobeyed me,*" Jiro says in Fyve's mind, the words sounding like a frown.

Fyve clenches his jaw for the hundredth time. Jiro doesn't seem to hear him unless he speaks aloud, which Fyve has no intention of doing in front of Halo and dozens of other teens.

"*I told you. I can only help you if you do exactly as I say.*"

Yet Fyve doesn't regret his decision. The moment Jiro told him the plate he stood in front of was safe, he knew it would be Halo's.

She may be hiding something from him, but he doubts it's that bad. They need to stick together. Now, more than ever.

Someone on Fyve's right jams a forkful of the awful-looking red vegetable in their mouth, chews, then gags. Sica doubles over, clearly struggling to keep the food in her mouth. Everyone stills, waiting to see if she's one of the unlucky ones... But she straightens and doggedly spears another forkful of food. This time she manages to swallow it with only a short retch.

This has to be the ultimate test of their faith in Terra.

Keeping food that may be poisoned in your mouth, knowing it could kill you, is asking far too much.

And yet teen after teen is doing it.

Or maybe it's not about faith anymore. Maybe it's because they have no choice. It's play Russian roulette or die of starvation.

Fyve's never felt more trapped. He's not even in his small cabin and it feels like the looming sides of The Oasis are closing in around him. Like Terra is pulling the strings of every body around him, angling a knife straight for their heart and deciding which one will have their thread savagely tugged.

Halo's fork trembles on its way to her mouth. She seems to struggle with unlocking her jaw so she can open it.

"You'll be fine," Fyve assures her, lifting his own morsel of meat. "I know you will be."

Looking like she wants to be sick, she shakes her head. "It's sweet that you're trying to reassure me, but there's no way you can know that."

Without waiting for a response, she jams her own small piece of meat in her mouth and chews. Fyve wishes he could tell her she'll be fine. Jiro said that plate was safe. He looks down at his own.

The one that may not be.

Not wanting to dwell on exactly what this poison is going to do to the unlucky teens, Fyve swiftly eats his morsel. He even manages to smile at Halo, wanting to let her know it'll be okay.

Even as he's not sure whether that's true.

The meat sticks at the back of his throat, but Fyve forcefully swallows it. He waits for a bitter taste. A burn in his gut.

But nothing happens.

Halo blinks. "I'm fine so far."

"I'm not the kind of guy to say I told you so..." he says with a soft nudge.

She throws him a wry glance. "I'm pretty sure you just did."

The good news is, he's okay so far, too. A quick glance around reveals no one has felt any ill-effects yet. Everyone's terrified but alive.

The girl across from Fyve is cutting her food up into tiny pieces, as if that will allow the poison to leach out. A guy at the other side of the table is sobbing as he chews. Justice is wolfing her food down, obviously deciding to learn her fate sooner rather than later.

"Your plate is safe."

Even though Fyve isn't sure whether he can trust Jiro, whoever he is, relief still has the fist around his throat loosening. Jiro hasn't lied to him yet.

And Jiro claims to be the real Terra.

Fyve glances at the bald child standing at the end of the table. Her hands are tucked back in her sleeves, her vacant gaze glued to the horizon. If Jiro is behind all this, who is she?

And does that make Jiro the heartless soul who's orchestrating these brutal Trials?

Reconciling that with the voice in Fyve's mind, the one who seems to care and is so intent on helping, is almost as hard to swallow as the piece of meat was.

"I'm taking Justice's lead," Halo says, picking the round of bread that's now stained with red juice and taking a large bite.

"Good idea," Fyve says, jabbing his fork into the blood-colored vegetable.

He's surprised to find it's sweet and quite delicious. If it didn't have the potential to kill him, he'd be enjoying it. Halo quickly finishes her plate, even though she grows paler and paler with each mouthful. Once she's finished, she gulps down the wine, then places the cup back on the table. She holds it for long seconds, staring at it as she waits.

Waits to see if she's going to die.

And if Jiro is telling the truth, she won't.

The moments are counted out by hiccupping cries and soft

gagging. Fyve also finishes his plate and the wine, which is also a taste he wishes he could appreciate.

Nothing happens.

Not to Halo. Or him. Or anyone else either picking at their food or shoving it in and swallowing it, as if not tasting it means avoiding any potential poison.

"Maybe it was all a trick," Halo says hopefully. "To see if we'd do it."

Her sentence isn't even finished when a girl at the other end stumbles away from the table, clutching her throat. Her eyes widen, terror expanding them until they seem to dominate her white face. She gurgles, and red foam froths from her mouth and down her chin.

Blood? Wine? Or the crimson vegetable?

Acid churns in Fyve's stomach as he realizes it's probably all three.

The girl drops to her knees, her hands still wrapped around her throat, her mouth now working as she fights the inevitable. Each time it opens, more foam spurts out, becoming thicker and darker each time.

Her eyes roll back in their sockets and she falls to the side, convulses once, and goes still.

This wasn't a trick. Some of these plates have been poisoned.

The teens around the table glance between each other and the mostly empty plates. Some look as if they're not breathing at all. A few are breathing so fast it's audible. Everyone is as pale as their new clothes.

A guy at the other end of the table, one who looks like he's barely older than Sevin, gasps. "No." He takes a shaky step backward, his hands flying to his stomach. Then his throat, just like the girl. And finally, to his mouth.

But the tightly clamped fingers don't stop the blood-colored froth from spurting out. He coughs and it spatters across the table, making a few teens leap back. He dies far quicker than the girl, dropping to the ground as bloody fluid pours from his mouth and nose. There's no convulsion, just a thud on the deck and stillness.

Fyve pulls Halo close to him. No one should have to watch this, helpless, wondering if they're next.

"You're safe," he murmurs in her hair, giving her what little comfort he can.

She glances up at him, eyes large in her pale face. "You keep saying that. How do you know?"

He clamps his mouth shut. How is it that this girl's amazing mind always knows how to get to the heart of something?

"You cannot tell her I exist, Fyve. She will not be allowed to live."

He freezes as those words slice straight through his heart.

Without warning, the girl on Halo's other side drops. The guy across the table from her does the same. The next cry that rings out has Halo spinning around. "No!"

Ajax is clutching his stomach. "Sweet Terra," he moans. "No, not me."

Halo tears away from Fyve's side and rushes to her brother. He reaches out and clamps a hand on her shoulder, eyes wide and panicked. "Halo, my stomach hurts."

Viney rushes over, too, wailing. "No, Ajax. You can't leave me!"

Cloud, on the other hand, stands back. She's finished her plate and is now holding her twins. Tears track down her cheeks, yet she doesn't move. Ajax may be the father of her children, but he turned his back on them.

Halo frowns. "There's no foam, Ajax."

The other deaths had been quick, probably Terra's version of mercy. But Ajax is still standing, his face clear of red froth.

He blinks, then straightens. "Thank, Terra," he breathes. "I got a pain and thought…"

Viney throws herself at his chest. "I'm so relieved!"

Halo steps back then returns to Fyve's side, still frowning.

He drags his gaze away from Ajax, disgust filling the space created when he lost all respect for the guy. He just scared those who care about him because of a cramp.

Then Fyve is looking back, realizing something. Long seconds have passed and no one else has dropped. Poisoned to death.

The teens glance between each other, cautious hope waiting to loosen their tight shoulders and pinched faces. A foul scent of sweet and sour bile hangs in the air alongside the bated breaths.

Five teens have died. Everyone else is alive, a meal nourishing their body.

It's quiet enough for Fyve to realize the headache that had been shoved aside has the opportunity to come galloping back. He rubs his temple, noting that Halo's doing the same. Surely, that can't be a coincidence—

"You think you're finished, don't ya?"

Zake's voice yanks Fyve out of his thoughts, and he's not sure if it's the words, or the way they're said. He slowly draws his gaze back to the balcony, finding the dirtwad up there, the smile in his voice a sneering grin on his face.

Zake indicates toward the far end of the table where three plates sit, still stacked with food. "One of 'em was for that coward who dared to question me, but surelies you are wondering who the other two are for."

A few teens shuffle uneasily. Many more are frozen as they wait.

And Zake is loving the undivided attention. His grin is an insult to the five dead bodies lying in a pool of bloody fluid and froth. Let alone that young man who jumped overboard to avoid being claimed.

Zake's gaze falls on Cloud. "Someone snuck on this ship with extra lives. And Terra is all about being fair."

Those words have the now-familiar anger flashing hot through Fyve. Terra has been anything but fair. The fact Zake is standing up there, when others have died, is evidence of that.

"So, she gotta eat two more plates, one for each of her babies," says Zake with glee.

"No," Halo moans under her breath.

Cloud survived this game of chance, and now she has to play it again, because she's been blessed with two children.

That's far from fair.

To Cloud's credit, she straightens her shoulders and walks to two of the empty plates. She quietly and efficiently eats the contents of one, then the other. A single tear escapes, but she wipes it away. When more follow, she ignores them, picking up the first cup of wine and emptying it. She puts it down and pauses, draws in a shuddering breath, then gulps the second.

The moment she's done, Cloud scoops up Miracle and Marvel. "I love you." Although she whispers the words, Fyve hears them, no doubt as do many others.

It's possible every teen heard the heartbreaking words of a mother who knows she may never be able to say them again.

Tension is vibrating through Halo as she watches Cloud do this with as much grace as she can. She grips Fyve's hand so tightly it takes away the focus from the pain in his head. "Please, please, please," she whispers over and over.

Cloud holds her babies tightly, drawing in their scent with deep breaths. She presses her cheek to one, then the other, her eyes closed as more tears leak past her lashes.

But she doesn't seize up with pain. No froth blooms from her mouth as poison erodes her insides.

She remains alive and well.

Halo sags against Fyve and he gives her a squeeze. "It's over," he murmurs with relief.

"This Trial is done," Zake announces. "I don't know about you, but I can't wait for da next one!"

Fyve's muscles coil with the need to punch the sick bastard.

How could Terra choose him as her messenger? Which means Jiro has, too, if he's telling Fyve the truth.

"Now go to ya cabins until ya get called back," Zake says dismissively. "I got some cleanin' up to do."

The teens gratefully scamper to the door, moving as if they can't disappear quick enough. They scoot around the dead bodies that Zake seems to be looking forward to throwing in the ocean, eyes averted.

Iva, though, quickly approaches them. "This is an opportunity we can't pass up," she says in a low, urgent voice.

Halo nods. "We need to get to the door before Zake does."

She glances at Fyve, hesitating, and he realizes she hasn't assumed he's coming with her, when he obviously will. The headaches and voices in his head are starting to take their toll.

He can't afford for anything to come between him and Halo.

He juts his chin toward the door. "Let's go."

Answers. They're the only thing that's going to stop any of this.

Halo's smile is one of gladness but also relief. One that wraps right around Fyve's heart and buoys and anchors it all at once. Their love is the only good thing to come out of these merciless Trials.

"No! You cannot go to the door! Under no circumstances will you go there!"

Fyve winces as Jiro's shouted words feel like a hot knife in his brain.

"Fyve?" Halo asks. "Is everything okay?"

"You cannot tell her about me. Nor can you go to the door."

Jiro's words are stated flatly. They're an order. But Fyve shakes his head. Just like the plate, it's an order he can't follow.

"I'm fine," he says to Halo as he tries to smile. "You're right, we don't have much time."

Although her brows flutter with the shadow of a frown,

Halo turns and slips through the door, following Iva. He takes one step, only to stop.

"If you do not listen to me, I will leave, Fyve. You'll be on your own."

He freezes, trapped by indecision as completely as he's trapped in the middle of the ocean.

He can't tell Halo Jiro exists, or she'll be killed.

And yet, Fyve needs him.

If he loses Jiro, he loses the ability to protect Halo.

HALO

*H*alo runs through the corridors of The Oasis with Iva close behind. The map of the ship is clear in her mind as she leads her new friend through these once unfamiliar twists and turns of the labyrinthine floor plan. They enter the stairwell and begin to climb.

Fyve hesitated too long, seeming physically unable to decide if he'd come with them, so she'd had no choice but to leave him behind. Every minute counts. They have to get to the door before Zake returns to guard it. There's no way Halo's dad would have missed the Trial if he'd had a choice in the matter. It hadn't felt right without him there. And it certainly hadn't felt right to have Zake standing in his place.

She exits the stairwell and decides nothing about that Trial had felt right. It had been cruel. What kind of sick mind even thinks up a Trial like that? If Dargo and the others who were eliminated in earlier Trials are still alive, then they have to get to them before it's too late. Although, after the deaths she just witnessed, she's starting to doubt it. It really doesn't seem like Terra is too interested in having to continue to feed those she's deemed to be unworthy of Tomorrow Land.

If such a place even exists.

"This way," she says to Iva as they run toward the door. The light is dim, but she can't see any shadows looming at the end of the corridor. There's no way Zake could have beaten them here. He'll still be on the deck, gloating over his new position as Terra's messenger as he throws the bodies of those who failed into the hungry ocean.

Iva's panting, but no matter how out of breath she is, her steps haven't slowed. Moping in Dargo's cabin hasn't solved anything. This is her chance to find him. Or at the very least, find out what happened to him.

Halo reaches the door and comes to a sudden stop, her entire body contracting in confusion.

"The door," she puffs, scanning the space in front of her. "It's…the door's gone."

"What do you mean, it's gone?" Iva bends over as she drags stale air into her lungs. "Maybe we're in the wrong place."

Halo shakes her head as she sweeps her palms down the smooth wall in front of them. "We're not in the wrong place. I'm certain of it. The door should be right here."

Iva stands up straight and runs a hand through her shoulder-length blonde hair, eyeing Halo suspiciously. "Okay, so assuming there was actually a door here, why are you so convinced Dargo was behind it?"

"We heard crying," she explains, her hands still searching for a handle or a catch. "And Zake was guarding the door. He wouldn't have been doing that if it didn't mean anything."

"What kind of crying?" Iva asks. "A guy crying?"

"More like a child," says Halo, her head aching worse than ever with the stress of the situation. "I'm not sure. It was muffled."

"There are no children on this ship," says Iva, coolly. "Apart from your niece and nephew. And Terra herself, who doesn't actually speak. You must be mistaken."

"I'm sorry, Iva." Halo reaches out for her, but she takes a step back. "I swear this is the right spot. I thought—"

"You thought you'd risk my life on some kind of hunch," Iva spits out. "I knew I shouldn't have gotten my hopes up. Dargo's not here. And nor is your father."

"Listen," says Halo, pressing her ear against the wall. "We might hear something."

Iva crosses her arms and waits, but all that greets Halo on the other side of the wall is silence. How does she prove she's not going mad? This is definitely the right place. And she knows what she heard. If only Fyve were here to back her up.

"I'm going to my cabin before we get caught," says Iva.

Halo nods, although isn't ready to give up just yet. Her father has to be on this ship somewhere. She's certain Terra wouldn't have killed him. Not after everything he's done for her over the years. She must still have a purpose for him. Surely?

Iva walks off with her shoulders slumped, and the echo of hurried footsteps fills the corridor.

"Iva!" Halo darts after her, hoping to haul her into one of the empty cabins, but it's too late.

Iva turns in a panic to face Halo just as a figure rushes around the corner a few feet away.

Halo stretches out her arms and envelops Iva as the figure slams into them, knocking them both to the floor. She curses. Zake has them now and there's absolutely nothing she can do about it!

"It's okay," a familiar voice pants. "Halo, it's me!"

She looks up to see Fyve hovering above them with his hands outstretched.

Breath whooshes from her lungs and she reaches up, allowing him to haul her to her feet. Iva waves his hands away, feeling along the carpet for something she must've dropped.

"You scared me," Halo admonishes. "I thought you were Zake."

"I'm sorry." He drops a kiss on her forehead. "I was anxious to find you. I shouldn't have let you go without me."

She nods, not prepared to disagree with that. "Look. The door's gone."

"Are you sure this is the spot?" He squints at the solid wall.

"Not you as well," she groans. "This is definitely it."

He nods. "But that doesn't make se—"

Iva yelps from the floor and they both squat down to see what's wrong.

She's holding something to her chest in a tightly clasped fist.

"What is it?" Halo asks, reaching for Iva's hand. But her grip is like iron. Whatever she has, she's not going to let it go.

Halo withdraws and waits for Iva to tell them in her own time.

"It's Dargo's," she eventually says, holding out her clenched fist. There's a strap of brown leather poking out from between her fingers. "It's a bracelet. I made it for him back home. He never takes it off."

"And you found it just here?" Fyve asks.

Iva nods. "If you hadn't knocked me over, I'd have walked right past it."

"He was here." Hope lights Halo's heart. "He must've been."

"I think he dropped it, so I'd find it," says Iva. "I'm so sorry I doubted you, Halo."

Halo shakes her head, not wanting this broken-hearted girl to feel any worse than she already does. "Don't apologize. It's hard to know what to believe right now. I get it."

"We need to get out of here," says Fyve, standing up. "Like, right now."

Halo is just about to ask how he knows that but decides to stop second guessing him. His gut instinct is part of the reason they both survived the last Trial.

"Come on," she says to Iva as she stands. "Take the bracelet and let's go."

Iva nods and scrambles to her feet. They follow Fyve down around the bend in the corridor, heading toward the stairwell. Just before they reach it, Fyve slides one of the cabin doors open and ushers them inside, holding a finger to his lips.

Halo and Iva scurry inside and Fyve closes the door silently.

"What?" Halo mouths, raising her palms.

"Someone's coming," Fyve whispers.

She remains quiet, reminding herself that she'd only just decided to trust his instincts.

Sure enough, heavy footsteps rattle their way past the door and down the hallway. It has to be Zake. But why is he checking on a bare wall where there used to be a door? There has to be something behind it.

Breaking down a wall is going to take planning. Halo's determined to do it, though. Especially after Iva found Dargo's bracelet. They must be close to finding out what's really going on in this ship.

The footsteps fade away and Fyve opens the door without hesitation.

"It's safe," he tells them.

"How do you know?" Halo can't help asking.

He steps out into the corridor. "There's nobody here."

She follows him, glancing around even though she's certain he'd never put her in danger. The corridor is empty, just as he said it would be.

Iva keeps close to Halo as they make their way to the stairwell.

"Do you think Zake boarded up the door?" she asks, not seeming to have any trouble believing the story now.

Fyve grunts. "I'm not sure he's capable of such a good job. But someone has."

"We need to break it down," says Halo, as they head down the stairs. "There's something behind it."

"There has to be another way to access it," Fyve says.

"Then we need to follow Zake." Iva is still clutching Dargo's bracelet with white knuckles. "He'll lead us to it."

Halo nods, impressed with her thinking. "Maybe we should head back up and see where he's gone."

"No," Fyve practically shouts. "I mean, that's not a good idea. You know where your dad is, Halo. Just think."

"I don't know." She grabs his arm and hauls him to a stop. "Where is he?"

"The one place they know for sure he can't escape," he says.

She rolls her eyes. "That would be this entire ship."

"Come on," he says. "You know this. Where might you keep someone captive?"

She thinks for a moment, then her mind sparks with understanding. "The brig."

Fyve raises his eyebrows. "She said it. I mean...that's right. I knew I didn't have to tell you where he was. Which is why I didn't tell you."

Halo frowns at the strange way he's talking. It's almost like he's not directing his words at her.

"What's the brig?" Iva asks, not noticing anything amiss. Then again, she doesn't know Fyve as well as Halo does. "Is Dargo there, too?"

"It's the ship's prison," Halo explains. "Cloud hid there after having the twins. Although, I'm not sure it's big enough for more than one person."

Iva's shoulders slump. The poor girl looks exhausted. It's doubtful she's slept much since Dargo went missing. And then the stress of the last Trial coupled with the constant swaying and moving of this ship as they head further away from home, and closer to none-of-them-know-what.

"My dad might know something," Halo says gently. "Why don't you head back to your cabin? I promise if I find out anything useful, I'll let you know straight away."

"Okay." Iva nods. "I'll be in Dargo's cabin." She pushes her way through the door and out of the stairwell.

Halo takes a few steps to go immediately to the brig but stops when she realizes Fyve isn't following.

"I'm not coming," he says in a voice laced with pain. "You have to go on your own."

She spins around and goes to him, slamming the tip of her index finger into his chest. "What's the matter with you? The Fyve I know would never let me go on my own." The fact he'd followed her just now proves that. Something had clearly been stopping him, but whatever it was, it hadn't been enough to overrule his protective instincts.

"Nothing's the matter." He looks to his feet. "It's just better if you go by yourself."

"Fyve!" She uses his name like it's a curse. "Something's up with you. Is Terra talking to you?"

He shakes his head, keeping his eyes cast down. "She's not."

Halo isn't sure she believes this. How else does he know all these things he shouldn't? And that whole conversation about the brig was just downright weird. It was like he knew where her dad was and had been forbidden to tell her, so he'd hinted instead.

She flattens her palm against the firmness of his chest, then runs her hand around to his back. He doesn't retract but makes no move to hold her.

"I know something's going on," she says. "And I know there must be a good reason you can't tell me, so I'm not going to push you on it."

He nods, daring to raise his gaze to look at her. Her heart aches at the grief pooling in his dark eyes. He's trying to talk to her without using any words, and it's breaking her.

She presses up to her tiptoes and kisses him on the cheek. "I love you, Fyve."

He softens at her touch but keeps himself distant, so she

breaks away and darts up the stairs, leaving him standing in the gloomy light to deal with whatever it is that he has going on.

Keeping her footsteps light and her ears tuned to even the smallest of sounds, she weaves her way through The Oasis to the brig. The door's closed and her heart sinks to realize that if it's locked, she's not going to be able to see if Fyve's hunch is right.

She looks around to make sure nobody followed her, then tries the door handle, surprised to find that it slides open an inch. She pulls hard and the door slides open the rest of the way.

"Dad," she hisses into the darkness. "Are you in there?"

Opening the door fully, the soft glow of the hallway spills into the dark cell. The lights have been turned off and Halo blinks, scanning for any movement.

A soft groan lures her in and she squints at the bed. Her eyes adjust to the dim light and she sees a rounded shape underneath a blanket with a mass of gray hair poking out from the top.

"Dad?" She reaches out and touches the blanket.

Her father rolls over and she gasps to see his face is blackened with bruises.

"Dad! What did they do to you?" Her hands fly to her own mouth as she struggles to comprehend what she's seeing. Her father is normally so well put together, his long beard and hair meticulously combed into place. If she didn't know the man before her so well, she wouldn't recognize him.

"Go away," her father hisses through several missing teeth. "Please, Halo. Go!"

"I'm not going anywhere," she says, crouching beside the bed. "Not until you give me some answers."

"Don't ask questions." Her father tries to sit up, but he's clearly in too much pain and he collapses back to the mattress. It's no wonder the door was unlocked. He can't get out of this bed, let alone run away. "Don't resist Terra."

"Did Zake do this to you?" she asks, ignoring his advice.

He nods and a line of blood trails from the corner of his mouth. "Do whatever Terra says. Don't be like me. Don't resist."

"I can't do what she says," she sobs. "People died in today's Trial, Dad. And they were doing what Terra said. If we don't stand up to her, the rest of us will soon be dead, too."

He shakes his head. "You can get through this. It's too late for me. You can make it to Tomorrow Land."

She lets out a moan. "Does Tomorrow Land exist, Dad? Is it even a real place?"

He reaches for her hand and squeezes with surprising strength. "It's real. And it's beautiful. Almost as beautiful as you. You have to make it there."

Halo blinks back both her tears and her surprise. "Will Terra really take fifty of us?"

"Yes," her father whispers, seeming to be losing strength. "It's all real, Halo. Tomorrow Land. Terra. A future so bright it will blind you. It's just that..." His eyes drift shut as his mouth droops open.

"It's just that what, Dad?" she prompts, trying to rouse him from the stupor that's quickly claiming him. "What is it?"

"It's not what you think," he says. "Terra isn't who you think..."

He lapses into sleep, his depleted body unable to keep him conscious a moment longer.

She stays beside him, holding his hand, and turning his words over in her mind. Her father believes Tomorrow Land is real. And a future there with Fyve is within her grasp.

But Terra isn't who she thinks she is.

She can't say this is much of a surprise. Ever since she laid eyes on that skinny young girl, she's questioned exactly that.

And just as always, as soon as she's answered one question, more pop up.

If Terra isn't the girl, who is Terra?

But even more intriguing is if the girl isn't Terra, then who is the girl?

FYVE

*F*yve stands in the half-light, staring at the end of the corridor where Halo just disappeared. The pain in his head is growing.

But the ache in his heart is what has him rubbing at his sternum.

He wants to follow Halo with every shred of his soul. Tell her he loves her, too. Be there with her when she finds her father.

"No more warnings, Fyve. You follow her and I'm gone."

Jiro's voice is hard and clipped. An expertly aimed warning.

The mysterious being no one else seems to hear was the one who told Fyve which plate was safe to eat. From the moment he woke Fyve up, Jiro knew what was coming. And he protected Fyve.

Who then protected Halo.

Which means Fyve doesn't move. His feet have turned to lead. In fact, his whole body has. He can't afford to alienate the strange ally in his mind.

"I'm sorry," he mutters. "I needed to make sure she's safe."

Zake's enjoyment of today's tortuous Trial proved his love of violence and power is soul deep. Fyve had to make sure Halo was okay if she was going back to the door.

He glances in the direction it would be. The door that no longer exists…

"*I understand why you followed her.*"

Fyve straightens a little, surprised by the words that were just spoken in his mind. Jiro sounded as if he…respects the decision.

Is this why Jiro told him that Elijah's in the brig? Because he likes that Fyve is trying to help Halo?

"*But it stops. Now.*" Jiro's voice is steely once more, instantly dashing the thought. "*I cannot continue to risk helping you if you don't listen.*"

Fyve returns to frozen. "Risk helping me?"

"*In fact, you need to prove yourself.*"

The confusion that had joined the ache in Fyve's head swirls to a stop. As ominous as Jiro's words are, as much as they mean driving a wedge even further between himself and Halo, Fyve doesn't move as he mutters one word. "How?"

"*You need to collect some items for tomorrow's Trial.*"

Fyve's stomach tightens even as acid churns within it. Another Trial. And so soon.

"*They will help you stay alive.*"

Even as the acid tries to climb up his throat, Fyve's already nodding. If these items can help him, they can help Halo. "What do you need me to do?"

"*Thank you, Fyve.*"

Although the whole conversation is nothing but surprising, Fyve's eyebrows hike up at Jiro's statement. Who is this voice ordering him one minute, then thanking him the next? One who promises protection as if he cares but makes it dependent on blind obedience.

"*Now, return to your cabin.*" Jiro is all business once more. "*I have something there for you.*"

With a last glance at where Halo exited, and a silent hope she finds Elijah still alive, Fyve turns on his heel and walks the other way.

As he makes his way through the cramped, artificially lit corridors, he realizes he misses Treasure Island. He misses sunlight. And space.

Even the faint stench of the place.

At least it was consistent. Familiar.

He knew what the threats were.

Fyve enters his cabin, noting that lunch plates are sitting outside several of the others, untouched. The blind faith in Terra is crumbling. Seems several people aren't hungry enough to face more food after this morning's Trial.

He takes his own plate and puts it inside. His head is thudding too hard for him to be hungry. Plus, his stomach is too busy trying to digest the awfulness of what was asked of them.

The moment Fyve closes the door, Jiro speaks.

"Under your mattress is a small oval chip."

Fyve hesitates. "Mattress?"

"The soft thing you sleep on." Fyve can't tell if Jiro is amused or annoyed. *"Under that."*

Fyve does as he's told, peering as he scans the shadows beneath. Wide slats reach from one side of the bed to the other, and on one of them sits a small oval chip, just like Jiro said. He picks it up cautiously, registering the smooth, metallic surface. "What is it?"

"Put it in your pocket. No one can see it."

Unsure how he's supposed to feel about this, Fyve once more does as he's told.

"Now, follow my directions. You need to be quick."

The urgency creeping into Jiro's voice is undeniable. Unable to ask any questions, even if he knew what to ask, Fyve slips out of his cabin and keeps his mouth tightly closed. He knows enough that he can't be caught snooping around The Oasis with this strange chip in his pocket.

Jiro leads him through the ship and at first, Fyve can keep up with where he is. Although, as the endless turns and long corridors continue, the floors quickly seem to be nothing but a duplicate of the one he was just on. It all starts to blur as his headache intensifies, and he realizes having Halo with him would be invaluable right now. She would've memorized every turn and set of stairs.

His breath rasping in and out of his throat, not because he's puffed but because the physical exertion progressively exerts pressure on his skull, Fyve finds himself on another level of the ship. He has no idea whether it's the first or the fiftieth. He rests his hands on his knees, closing his eyes as the world tilts far more sharply than The Oasis has since he boarded it.

"Almost there."

Jiro's voice is soft. Reassuring. Like a parent encouraging their child.

"Who are you?" Fyve asks, swallowing down a wave of nausea.

"The room you're looking for is just ahead," Jiro responds, ignoring the question. *"Hurry."*

Wanting to ask what the rush is but knowing he's unlikely to get an answer to that either, Fyve lurches forward. Jiro doesn't speak until he reaches the end of the corridor and comes to a stop at a blank wall.

Fyve frowns. "You've sent me to the wrong level."

"Lift the chip and swipe it over the small square on your right."

Turning his head, Fyve discovers Jiro's right. There's a small square inlaid into the wall at about shoulder height. The surface is blank, although on closer inspection, it's slightly smoother than the wall around it. Cautious, yet curious, Fyve takes the chip from his pocket, rubbing his thumb over the metallic surface.

He's trusting Jiro, possibly with his life. Will whatever happens next really help with tomorrow's Trial?

Or has Terra set some sort of elaborate prank as she watches, amused at the lengths her gullible subjects will go to?

"Quick, Fyve."

In too much pain to have any chance of untangling those questions, Fyve swipes the chip over the square. There's a faint *click*. An almost silent *whoosh*.

And the wall slides away.

He's too stunned to blink, breathe, or move for long moments. The room that stretches on the other side is like nothing he's never seen before.

It's big. Massive.

And overwhelmingly lavish.

Every gold-colored column, the intricacies in the deep burgundy pattern woven underneath his feet, the black shiny wood that graces the large tables and plush chairs and the curling staircase on the other side of the room, is silent. Regal. Basking under the large light hanging high in the center of the room.

Thick silver ropes wind down from the domed ceiling, twisting together to create an upside-down trunk. Then, they gracefully arch out in symmetrical curves, like the branches of the tree Halo made. But hundreds of little suns glint at the tip of each branch, casting sparkling light over the beauty that has Fyve rooted to the spot.

"Sevin," he whispers. "How I wish you could see this."

"Walk toward the side wall."

Fyve doesn't move. He cranes his neck as he studies the multi-branched light. Crystals glitter among the lights, refracting fragile white into every corner of the room.

"We don't have time for you to marvel at the chandelier, Fyve," Jiro snaps. *"Go to the wall, it doesn't matter which side."*

Jolting into action, Fyve weaves through the tables.

Matching chairs circle the smooth, black surfaces, and he notes that some of them aren't tucked in and straight like the others. As if they've been sat at and not returned to their ordered place.

"See the curtains hanging down? Go to one of them."

Fyve assumes curtains are the long lengths of pale material hanging every few feet from the ceiling to the floor, so he approaches the closest one. He reaches out without thinking, awed at the copious swathes of fabric. He frowns as he touches it, glancing at his sleeve now in close proximity.

Material that's the same color as his tunic.

"See the rope tied around the curtain? Take it."

Braided strands of deep gold are indeed wrapped around the curtain. Undoing the loose knot, Fyve thinks of Halo's lucky cord and he imagines giving her this. The smooth length slips over his palm, glistening under the branched light. The chandelier. She'd smile. Be just as awed by the way the deep color seems to hold the light, the way each individual thread looks like spun gold.

Except then he'd have to explain where he got it from.

"Quick. Put it in your pocket. There's more to collect."

The curtain flutters then expands, covering a little more of the wall patterned with leaves behind it, making Fyve wonder why it's even there. It might look pretty, but what's the use of covering a blank surface?

"Beneath the stairs is a door. Go inside."

"What is this for, Jiro?"

"There's no time for questions! Get to the stairs!"

Frowning, but uneasy as Jiro's urgency only seems to be increasing, Fyve makes his way once more through the tables. The stairs are wider than any of the others he's seen, and covered in more of the intricate, burgundy flooring and edged in more black timber. Twin sets curve out and around before meeting one floor up and opening out onto a second level. He reaches out, wanting to touch the smooth, black railing. The detailed carvings seem to match the leaves that were on the walls.

"*Fyve!*"

Although it's only one word, a single syllable, Jiro's shout has pain exploding at each of Fyve's temples and shooting straight into the middle of his brain. The two streaks of pain meet somewhere deep in his skull and explode all over again. Gasping, he doubles over, clutching his head.

"*Fyve,*" Jiro pleads quietly, and even that still hurts. "*I'll keep my voice down if you hurry. Deal?*"

Straightening grimly, he nods. "Deal." The pain is only growing, meaning he just wants whatever this strange mission is over and done with.

"*Thank you,*" Jiro says, sounding genuine. "*Now, behind the doors are metal shelves to your left. Go to them.*"

Slipping through the sleek double doors, Fyve finds himself in another metal room much like the one he discovered the crates in. In fact, several crates are stacked along the back wall. Panting from the pain, Fyve doesn't let himself go to them. He's not sure how much longer he can hold himself upright. And just like Jiro said, there are shelves to the left.

Fyve staggers over, blinking as he registers several small, serrated knives lined up on it.

"*Take one. And be quick. We're almost finished.*"

His hand clamps around a wooden handle, and he's almost surprised at the cool hardness. This whole experience is starting to feel surreal.

"*Now, back in the dining room, there's a long bench just outside these doors.*"

Fyve thuds into the door, wincing as the jolt ricochets through his head. He grunts, pushing through. The doors swung easily when he entered, but they now feel like an ocean of water is on the other side, pushing back.

Just as Jiro says, there's a long bench on the other side Fyve hadn't noticed. Its top gleams softly, sleek black like every other piece of furniture.

"On the other side are bottles and shelves. Don't worry about the wine. It's what's on the shelves that you want."

Fyve isn't sure he wants any of this, but he leans against the ornate bench and discovers racks and racks of dark green bottles. Wine bottles, Jiro said. Like the wine they drank at the Trial this morning?

"See the bottle just under the bench? And the small, clear bottle beside it? You need to get it."

Fyve blinks as he tries to focus. The bottle is there, as is its companion. But Fyve doesn't pick up the fragile-looking bottle containing clear liquid. He recognizes the bottle beside it.

It's the one Terra was holding at the Trial. The one she poured the wine from.

"What's going on, Jiro?" Fyve growls, trying to shake off the pain so he can think clearly.

"Take the small bottle," he says urgently. *"Be careful. Don't let the contents touch your skin."*

Fyve instantly knows why.

It's the poison that killed five teens earlier today.

It was never in the food. Jiro knew Fyve's plate was safe because they all were. Terra poisoned their drinks.

Which means the deaths weren't random. They were targeted.

Fyve picks up the bottle, noting it fits in the palm of his hand. So small. Yet deadly. And for some reason, the voice in his head wants him to have it, along with rope and a knife.

"Jiro, what's all this for?" he demands, his voice rising.

"To protect yourself. Now, hurry! Before they're back."

Protect himself? But there's another, more urgent question. "Who's back?"

"Sh! You need to get out of here, Fyve. Now!"

The urgency in Jiro's voice borders on frantic and it makes

Fyve's pulse spike. Gingerly holding the bottle of poison, he darts around the bench, squinting as the world tilts dangerously. Pain clenches his skull like a fist.

"*Back to the door. And hurry! Please!*"

Lurching unsteadily, Fyve blindly follows the order. He doesn't know who Jiro's talking about, but it's clear he's scared of them.

Which means Fyve is, too.

He barely registers the opulent dining room with its chandelier and curtains and other marvels as he runs to the door. He hits the side as he jerks past, groaning at the corresponding bomb of agony in his head.

"*Swipe the chip!*" Jiro hisses. "*Close the door!*"

Fyve blindly obeys, barely aware of it closing silently behind him. Jiro's instructions are all he clings to as he makes his way back through The Oasis. It feels like forever before his strange new friend has him standing before another door, one he recognizes as the one to his own cabin.

"*Go inside,*" Jiro says, sounding relieved. "*You're safe, Fyve.*"

Fyve's pretty sure that's profoundly untrue, but he can barely hold himself up, let alone talk back. The running, the tension, the endless mysteries have all compounded the agony gripping his mind. It's so consuming he can barely breathe.

Staggering through, he collapses on the bed and loses his hold on consciousness.

HALO

*H*alo slides open the door to her cabin and takes the plate of food from the shelf. Retreating back inside, she pokes at the contents. After that last Trial, she's not sure she ever wants to eat again. But she also knows if she's going to survive the next Trial, she must.

She stuffs a mushy orange vegetable into her mouth, missing the familiar taste of freshly roasted rat. Forcing herself to swallow, she takes another bite. The rocking of the ship in the ocean doesn't help with her efforts to keep the food down, but she manages it. It doesn't taste any different to the salty food that's been served up so far. It has that same not-hot-not-cold temperature, and that same not-solid-not-liquid texture. Would she taste poison if it were present? The people at the Trial hadn't seemed to. Although, they'd all been pumping with such adrenaline that it was hard to tell. Ajax had thought he was poisoned when he wasn't.

She shakes away thoughts of her brother, not able to deal with the idea of him right now. It's Cloud who needs her attention.

Stuffing the rest of the food into her mouth, Halo washes it down with a glass of water and leaves her cabin. She knocks gently on Cloud's door. One of the babies is crying and she can hear Cloud making soothing noises.

"It's me," she calls. "Halo. Can I come in?"

The door opens and Cloud smiles at her. Her eyes are blood-shot and her hair's a mess. She has a very unhappy Marvel clutched to her chest.

"Have you slept?" Halo asks, reaching to take her nephew.

Cloud gladly hands her son over and checks on Miracle, who's sleeping soundly on the bed. Ajax, of course, is nowhere to be seen, having moved into Viney's cabin.

"I slept a bit," says Cloud, yawning. "I'm okay."

Halo jiggles her nephew in her arms, trying to settle him. He stops crying and she thinks she must have the magic touch, until she realizes he was just drawing breath to let out another scream.

Her head pulses at the sharp sound. The thumping she's had in her temples hasn't gone away, even if it hasn't gotten any worse. She wonders if it's something in the food that's causing it. Who knows how many years ago the vegetables she's been eating were plucked from the earth, or how long ago the animals on her plate grazed in a field.

"Have you got a headache?" she asks Cloud.

Cloud lets out a feeble laugh. "I have an everything ache this morning. But yes, my head's been hurting for a few days now."

Halo sighs, not wanting to alarm her by telling her that everyone has a sore head.

"Go and have a shower," she tells Cloud. "You might feel better."

"Are you sure?" Cloud dashes away into the bathroom before Halo can change her mind.

The sound of running water fills the small cabin and Halo paces, rubbing Marvel on his back in a circular motion. He either likes what she's doing, or he grows sick of complaining, and he lapses into sleep.

"Good boy," she whispers, dropping a kiss on the top of his fuzzy head, hoping these awful headaches haven't extended to the twins. Not daring to sit down in case he wakes, she keeps up the pacing, rubbing his back in increasingly slow circles.

Cloud exits the bathroom not long afterward, smiling to see that Marvel has settled at last.

"You're doing such a good job," says Halo, meaning it. "You're a great mom,"

Tears fill Cloud's eyes. "No, I'm really not."

"What do you mean?" Halo rocks Marvel gently. "You really are."

Cloud shakes her head, sending water droplets flying from her damp hair. "If I was a great mom, I'd never have gotten on this ship. My children would be safely back on Treasure Island."

"You were trying to give them a better life," Halo reassures, trying to keep her voice down in case she wakes Marvel. "You weren't to know how things were going to turn out."

"I trusted in Terra." Cloud's voice has a bitter tone. "And I wanted my children to grow up with a father. And look at how both those things turned out."

"Tomorrow Land is real," says Halo, desperate to give her something to cling onto. "We can make it there. Your children will have an amazing life."

"Do you believe that?" Cloud looks her directly in the eye. "Please, be honest. Because I'm sick of being lied to."

"I do…" Halo lets out a long sigh. "Or maybe I don't. Really, I don't know what to believe anymore."

She's just glad Cloud hasn't asked her about her father. That's not something she wants to burden her with given that she's already at breaking point.

"Please report to the deck immediately," says a voice inside her

head, sending Halo's pulse thumping. *"The next Trial is about to commence."*

"Not already," Cloud whimpers, clearly having heard Terra's announcement, too. "I thought we'd have more time."

"Maybe you could leave them here?" says Halo, glancing desperately from Marvel to Miracle. "They seem pretty deeply asleep. It might be safer if they're not there."

Cloud shakes her head immediately, and Halo realizes she's right. Taking her eyes off her babies even for a minute would be a very dangerous move.

"You're right," she says, carefully settling Marvel into his basket. "Ignore that suggestion."

Cloud places Miracle beside her twin and leans closer to Halo as they watch these precious children in awe.

"My brother's an idiot," says Halo, wrapping an arm around Cloud. "He's missing out big time."

"I thought he loved me." Cloud picks up the basket, fighting tears. "Then again, I thought a lot of things that weren't true."

"I know it's not the same thing," Halo says. "But you have me. You're not doing this alone, okay?"

Cloud nods, giving her a wan smile.

"And we all believed in Terra," Halo adds.

"Nobody more than me," says Cloud. "I was a fool."

"No, you weren't." She wrings her hands, desperate to find the right words. "You have a trusting heart. That's not anything to be ashamed of."

"Thank you," says Cloud in an entirely unconvincing manner. It's going to take more than a few kind words to restore her confidence again.

"Let me take that." Halo reaches for the handle of the basket, pleased that Cloud doesn't resist. She's too weak and tired to be carrying such a weight. "We have to go."

They step out into the hallway to find it filled with teens making their way to a Trial not one of them wants to compete in. Many of them are rubbing at their temples and grimacing. These headaches seem to be contagious.

It's hot on the deck, with strong beams of harsh sunlight beating down. The cool breeze as the ship moves through the water isn't enough to take out the sting of the heat. Halo sets down the basket, positioning it to shade the twins, not wanting their delicate skin to bear the anger of this scorched planet.

The rest of the teens gather, and Terra and Zake step out onto the balcony. Zake is smiling widely, while Terra remains as impassive as always.

Halo studies her, wondering again who this girl really is. She tries to imagine what she'd look like with regular clothes and a mane of hair to frame her face. She'd probably look just like any other girl. A younger version of Sevin perhaps. Her heart pangs at the memory of her old friend. She still hasn't had an opportunity to tell Fyve.

Just as she thinks of him, he appears by her side. He has dark circles under his eyes, looking almost as tired as Cloud. Iva is trailing behind him. A quick glance at her wrist reveals she's wearing Dargo's bracelet.

"There you are," he says. "I went to your cabin, but you'd already gone."

"I was helping with the babies," she explains. "Are you okay? You don't look so good."

He nods. "It's this headache. It's knocking me about a bit. But I'm sure it will settle today. Probably just the stress of the Trial."

She slips her hand into his, and he squeezes then lets go.

"Did you find your dad?" he asks.

She blinks, realizing she hadn't updated him. After sitting with her father in the brig for a while, she'd gone to find some food for him, then had fallen into her own bed, where she'd been immediately overcome by sleep.

Iva leans in, also keen to hear her answer.

"He's alive," she whispers to them. "But he's not in great shape. I'm going to check on him again after the Trial."

Fyve looks like his headache just got a whole lot worse and he grimaces. "Please don't—"

"Hey down there!" Zake claps his hands. "It's time for the next Trial if you can all shut up and listen."

"So eloquent," Fyve mutters.

"Terra has an interesting plan for ya today." Zake grins and Halo glances over at Justice whose face is screwed up in horror at just how awful her brother really is.

Cloud is holding her back stiff as she waits for whatever news is about to be delivered, and how it might impact her children.

"The rules are simple," Zake shouts. "At this same time tomorrow, you will come here to the deck where three of ya will be claimed."

There's a gasp of horror, without a single hint of surprise. How sad that they've all come to expect something as sadistic as this.

Zake holds up a hand. "There's a catch."

Halo holds her breath as she waits for what can't possibly be good news.

"If three of ya die before tomorrow, then nobody gets claimed." Zake lets out a laugh as he looks directly at Justice, whose hands are plastered over her mouth. "Doesn't matter how you die, if ya catch my drift."

"He wants us to kill each other," Fyve says between gritted teeth.

Iva shakes her head, anger boiling in her blue eyes.

Zake scans the crowd. "It's time to kill or be killed. Some targets will be easier to get than others." He looks directly at Cloud's babies as he says this last bit, and Fyve has to hold Halo back as she tries to surge forward.

"This is insane," she hisses.

"I know," he says, still holding her tight. "I'll protect the babies."

"How?" she yelps.

"I'll guard their cabin door," he says. "With my life."

She nods, accepting his help even though she doesn't want anyone to have to protect anything with their life—especially Fyve.

Halo sneers at the teens around them. "If anyone touches the babies, I'll kill you. Do you hear me? They're off limits."

The teens nod as if this is something none of them would ever consider, even though several of them hadn't been prepared to offer up their place on the ship for the babies. Halo can only hope it's different to stand back and watch someone else toss the babies into the ocean, rather than having to do the dirty work yourself.

"See ya tomorrow," Zake calls across the crowd. "The Trial is now started."

"Has started," Fyve corrects..

"We'll stick together," Halo tells Cloud. "Let's get the babies back to the cabin."

"No." Cloud shakes her head. "Let's take them to the seventh floor. The further away from everyone, the better."

"Good idea." Halo picks up the basket, and Fyve positions himself on the other side, with Cloud pressing up at the rear. Iva slots herself in the front.

A group of teens hovers on the deck, weighing up their chances of making it through the night in an open space compared to the closed walls of their cabins. Ajax and Viney are amongst them, and Halo shoots her brother a glare that he pretends not to notice. She considers telling him about their father but decides against it for now. Clearly, the guy is incapable of feelings. He's likely to do something that would get their father killed.

They head for the stairwell to find it crowded with teens.

"They've locked all the doors," someone shouts.

"Get away from me," someone else calls.

"I didn't touch you!"

"Hey! Keep your distance."

"I didn't do anything!"

Halo looks across at Fyve. It seems this is exactly what Terra wanted—to divide them. But would anyone here go as far as killing one of their peers? Halo knows for certain that she won't. She'd rather take her chances with a claiming. Although, if it's the twins' lives she's talking about...

Reminding herself that everyone here is someone's child, she tucks the basket a little closer. All they have to do is get the babies through the night.

"The door to your residential level is now open," Terra says inside their minds. *"All other levels are off limits."*

Halo hears a door click open and the teens spill out of the stairwell into the corridor.

"We'll stick together," Fyve tells them. "Head straight for Cloud's cabin. We'll board up the door."

"Can I come with you?" Justice asks from behind Fyve.

"Sure," he says, and Halo hates how she flinches at this response. Can they trust Justice? She's Zake's sister, after all. Then again, Halo is Ajax's sister and there's no way she'd want to be judged for that.

There's a commotion in the corridor and it isn't until they get there that they realize what it is.

All the doors to their cabins have been removed.

Which means, it's going to be a very long night.

FYVE

"The doors!" Halo gasps. "They're gone!"

Frowning, Fyve looks closer. "No. They're not. Just open." He digs his fingertips in, trying to pry the door from the hollow it recedes into. But it doesn't budge. "And they're stuck that way."

Cloud whimpers, clutching her twins to her chest. "My babies. How will I protect them?"

"We'll protect them," Fyve promises her, ignoring the ache in his head that's progressively growing the longer he's upright. "Nothing will happen to Marvel, Miracle, or any of us."

Halo nods, her face resolute. "We stick together. There's strength in numbers."

Cloud's lip trembles as she nods. "Okay." Someone darts past and into a nearby cabin, making her flinch. "Too bad we don't have any real way to protect ourselves."

"Back on Treasure Island we had weapons galore," Justice mutters. "I never thought I'd miss that place."

Weapons.

Although yesterday is a pain-riddled blur, it happened.

Which means Fyve now has rope, a knife, and poison in his cabin.

And the chip! It might be able to close his door!

"Quick," he urges. "My cabin is safer."

Halo frowns in confusion. "What? Why is it any different to any of ours?"

Unable to answer that question, Fyve slips his arm around Cloud and ushers her forward. "We need to hurry."

Another three teens run past them, panic tightening their faces as they dart into one cabin. Seems they've also decided to stick together.

Sica stands at the door to her cabin with her arms crossed, glowering at anyone who looks in her direction, almost daring them to take a shot at her.

Justice hurries forward, Iva with her. Halo stays with Fyve and they flank Cloud, tugging her toward his cabin. They pass two teens running the other way, and they flatten themselves against the walls, not wanting to even risk brushing the other.

Everyone has now become the enemy.

Someone to hunt. Or be hunted by.

The knowledge leaves a sour taste in Fyve's mouth. Every teen on this ship fought to be here. For a chance to live beyond the threat of death.

Although disease or starvation may not be imminent, death is still an ever-present danger on The Oasis. And now, it could be at the hands of their peers, just so they can live themselves.

Where's the sense in that?

They reach his cabin and he stands watch as everyone darts in. The corridor is now empty and silent, even though every door in both directions is open. After making sure it's staying that way, he leans in, his gaze finding Justice. "Can you stand watch for a bit?"

Looking relieved to have something to do, she nods. Fyve slips in and she stands in the doorway, arms crossed even as she leans on her crutches. He doesn't let the thumping in his head slow him down as his gaze roams over his room. Cloud is sitting on the bed, nursing the twins. Iva is on one side, Halo on the other, like two personal guards.

The scan reveals the items he collected are nowhere to be seen.

He hadn't even thought of them when he'd stumbled out of bed this morning, his only thought of Halo. But they need that chip. Fyve starts yanking cupboard doors open, then quickly shutting them when he sees they're empty. He slows down after the first, the harsh sound of wood on wood feeling like a knife blade through his temple.

Halo shoots to her feet and heads to the bathroom. "Great idea. We need to find anything we can to protect ourselves."

He nods, keeping his focus on the row of cupboards lining the wall beside the door. That's exactly what he's doing. Except he knows there are items in here no one else would have.

"*Yes, Fyve. Find them.*"

Although Jiro's voice is welcome, it makes Fyve wince. Even the softly spoken words hurt.

It takes only a handful of minutes to discover the items aren't in the cupboards. Neither is the chip. "Where is it?" he mutters. They need the chip!

"*I can't talk much during the Trial. Do what you need to survive.*"

Fyve grits his teeth, wanting to demand what Jiro's talking about. This is when he needs him the most.

"Is everything okay?" Cloud asks.

He resumes his search, realizing he paused. "It's fine. Just thinking."

"You look a little pale," she observes, clearly worried.

Because the headache is multiplying by the second.

And because Jiro just abandoned him.

Fyve throws a forced smile over his shoulder. "I'm fine," he says again, wanting to reassure her. "I haven't eaten much, that's all."

She nods, although her frown doesn't untangle from her brows.

Iva pats her shoulder. "I haven't eaten much either. Not after yesterday's Trial."

Fyve passes her a look of gratitude. Cloud has enough to worry about right now.

Halo appears from the bathroom, holding a towel. "Maybe we could put something heavy in this and swing it around?"

"Clever," Justice says from the doorway. She glances at Iva. "Pass the cover from the pillow."

Iva leaps to her feet. "Maybe we could even use the sheets!"

Halo's eyes widen. "Or block the door with the mattress!"

"Yes!" Fyve hisses, glad he has to keep his voice down because of the open door. Every word seems to get trapped in his skull. "The mattress!"

Cloud stands, holding her babies as she nods vigorously. "Yes, the mattress."

Fyve yanks it away the moment it's free, not thinking of the door. A mattress may give some protection, but it would be limited. It's what's under it that could be the key to staying alive.

That's where the chip was.

There, tucked beneath the slatted wood at the end of the bed, are the knife, rope, and bottle of poison. But no chip.

With a sinking feeling, Fyve realizes it's gone. There will be no door to protect them.

He bends over and removes the items, slipping the poison into his pocket before anyone can see it. Jiro's words are taking on a new meaning.

Do what you need to survive.

Did Jiro have him find these items so Fyve could protect himself?

Or to kill...

Halo steps up beside him, staring at the knife and rope. "Where did you get those, Fyve?"

Fyve stills, frantically trying to think up a response. One that isn't the truth. Jiro has helped him in ways he hadn't realized. He's given Fyve a way to protect Halo, Cloud and her babies, even Justice and Iva.

Although the thought of lying to Halo makes his gut tighten, he can't tell her the truth.

"I found them," he says. "Here, you take the rope."

She does, slipping the smooth, golden length over her palm. "Where?"

He tries for a smile. "Your new lucky cord."

Halo doesn't smile back. "Where did you find these, Fyve?"

"On the ship, obviously," he hedges, his head hurting too much to think of anything else. In all likelihood, he doubts he could come up with a reason that Halo would find plausible. Her smart mind will zero in on any holes or inconsistencies.

She steps closer. "You're hiding something," she says softly. "You know you can trust me."

"No, you can't. Not if you want her to live."

Fyve stiffens. Images of Halo collapsing as she'd clutched her head, the pain of being claimed multiplying, blood running from her nose, makes him physically ill.

"And are you forgetting that she has her own secrets?" Jiro sneers. *"She asks for trust but hasn't earned it."*

Frowning, Fyve studies Halo closely as he says the next words. "Are you saying that you have no secrets, Halo?"

She winces. "That's not the point—"

"Double standards aren't the point?" Fyve asks, the words harsher than he intended. The pain, the need for her to stop asking questions, and Jiro's insinuations clearly being true are becoming harder and harder to ignore.

Halo steps back. "That's not fair."

"None of this is," he snaps back, then spears his fingers

through his hair. "How about you don't ask any questions, and neither will I?"

"Is that what you want?" she asks, studying him for long seconds.

No.

"Yes. It is."

Something shutters closed in her eyes. "Okay."

Iva clears her throat. "Let's get through tonight, shall we?"

Fyve turns away, knowing that's exactly what he aims to do.

He just has to hope his relationship with Halo survives, too.

"Let's move the mattress to the door like Halo suggested," he says, not looking at her. "Then we take turns being lookout. We don't let anyone in until this Trial is over."

A round of solemn nods is his answer. Fyve lifts the mattress and is about to jam it into the doorway when footsteps echo down the corridor.

Everyone freezes.

It's been silent since everyone holed up in their cabins, either alone or in small groups. It was too much to hope it would remain like that during the night, but movement so soon doesn't bode well.

"Is this how ya gonna to spend all day and night?" Zake's voice booms. "Cowering in ya cabins, hoping no one attacks ya?"

"Ignore him," Fyve whispers. "He's trying to goad us." And anyone else on The Oasis.

Fyve, Halo, Justice and Iva creep forward, peering through the doorway as Cloud remains sitting on the slatted bed.

Zake leaps into the cabin on his right. "Boo!"

The frightened cry that follows makes him chuckle. Fyve's stomach clenches in disgust even as the shouted word punches pain through his head. How could Zake enjoy being like this?

He stops several cabins away, hitting one wall then the other. "Hoping and praying ya won't be claimed tomorrow?" He snorts in disgust. "Or ya could show Terra you actually have some guts and that ya want to see Tomorrow Land."

To Fyve's surprise, a girl with long dark hair slips out of an open doorway not far from Zake, clutching something wrapped in cloth. Tension coils through Fyve's muscles. Has this girl who looks only a year or two older than Sevin created a weapon just like Halo suggested?

"Zake," she says timidly. "I have some food I've been keeping. I want you to have it."

His eyes flare as she holds up her offering, the cloth falling away to reveal several chunks of meat. Meat she would've stockpiled.

"You want Terra to go easy on ya, huh?" He grins, wiping his mouth as he leers at the meat. Or is it the girl...

She nods eagerly. "Terra likes you because you're strong and smart. She'll listen to you."

Zake swipes the chunks of meat, shoving two in his mouth as the others disappear into his pockets. "You're right," he growls around a full mouth. "Terra chose me, and for good reason."

The girl sidles closer, dropping her gaze as she cautiously smiles. "You're everything she's looking for." She trembles. "Even handsome."

Zake's chest expands and Fyve's sickened that he's going to take advantage of this girl's desperation. The need to grab her and yank her into this cabin is strong, but Fyve remains still. Seems everyone has to make their own decision about how far they'll go to survive these treacherous trials.

Zake leans forward as his hand reaches out to caress the girl's face. She tenses but doesn't move. His grin grows, pleasure already sparking in his hard gaze.

A split-second before Zake's hand reaches the girl's cheek, it twists. Lowers a little. And snaps around her neck.

In a blink, she's pushed against the wall, pinned there by the clamp around her throat. She gasps and gurgles, but it's too tight for her to form any words.

"Stupid girl," he snarls in her reddening face. "You just became the most hated person on this ship."

She shakes her head frantically, her panicked eyes pleading with him.

Zake chuckles, leaning back so he can shout to everyone in the corridor. "She wanted ta buy her way out," he says loudly as a few teens poke their heads out. "The little whore didn't care about playing fair. Is that someone who should live?"

He looks one way down the corridor, then the other. More and more teens are standing in their open doorways, watching this unfold.

And none of them are answering the question.

Zake presses his hand in, cutting off the girl's garbled objections. "Should she be the first one ta go?" he calls out. "Does Terra really want people like her in Tomorrow Land?"

Silence.

A few teens even slip back into their cabin, their actions speaking far louder than their lack of response.

Zake's eyes flash with victory. And a sickening dose of excitement.

A low, pained moan escapes Halo. "We can't let this happen."

She goes to push past Fyve, but he's already moving. Her words echoed the very same thought he just had.

They can't let this happen.

Fyve and Halo break into a run simultaneously. It'll only take a handful of seconds to reach Zake and push him off the girl. Then she can come into their cabin.

There's a flash of movement and Halo cries out as she stumbles forward, her momentum sending her careening as she hits the ground.

"Halo!" Fyve shouts, going to help her up after she tripped.

Something big and heavy plows into his side, slamming him

into the wall. A groan is yanked up his throat at the impact, but he fights back despite the pain. Hands push into his shoulders, then his chest.

Two boys have pinned him to the wall.

"Just let him do it," one hisses. "You could be saving your own life."

Fyve blinks past the pain and shock. They're stopping him and Halo from saving the girl, so they can save themselves?

"Get off me," he snarls. "This isn't right."

"None of it is right," snaps the other guy, echoing Fyve's words to Halo. "Stayin' alive is all that matters now."

Fyve struggles against the hands pushing him into the wall, panting through the pain in his head. "Not like this, it doesn't. Let me go!"

Zake's laughter punctures Fyve's haze of pain and fury. "Number Boy just doesn't get it. He don't care if ya all die, he just wants to be some hero so he can impress the girl he's so hot for."

Halo pushes to her feet, looking between Fyve and Zake. She's clearly weighing up her options—free Fyve or attack Zake on her own. Even if neither situation is likely to end well for her.

Fyve pins his captors with his gaze. "Do you really want to live, knowing someone else has to die?"

They glance at each other, clearly hesitating. Then their lips turn into grim lines. "I've come too far to die now," one mutters.

"And she was tryin' to buy her way out," says the other.

A faint thud has Fyve and Halo looking back at Zake. The girl's head has lolled to the side, her eyes rolling back to reveal blood-shot white. She's dying.

To everyone's surprise, Zake releases her and steps back. She crumples to the ground, one hand reaching out as if she's going to crawl away before she falls unconscious.

Zake's rabid gaze roams over the corridor as teens appear,

looking to see if it's over. "I ain't doin' your dirty work for ya," he sneers. "You want to save your sorry asses, do it yourselves."

He takes another step back, glancing at the unconscious girl with disgust, before razing every teen with a daring look.

If they want one less person claimed tomorrow, they'll have to ensure it happens.

The hands trapping Fyve slacken as the two guys blanche. Watching Zake kill the girl was far more palatable than doing it themselves.

Fyve shoves them back, turns, and stalks toward Zake. "No one is going to touch her," he shouts.

Zake's hands form into fists. "You don't get ta decide that, Number Boy."

"I just did," Fyve snarls back, moving forward unflinchingly.

"If ya come near me, I ain't gonna stop like I did with the girl." Zake lifts his fists. "I'll be enjoyin' meself too much."

"I'm not scared, Zake." Fyve realizes he's telling the truth. He's too angry. And knowing Jiro is watching over him helps.

Zake must see something in Fyve's stony face because he curls his lip. "I ain't wasting my time. You obviously don't wanna see Tomorrow Land." He takes a step back, his eyes darting around their audience.

Fyve continues his determined walk, his temples pounding with each step.

Zake glares at him, turns, and walks stiffly away.

Fyve reaches the girl, not surprised to find Halo right behind him. She kneels down as the girl's lashes flutter. "She's alive."

He leans down to help the girl up when Zake shouts from the stairs at the end of the corridor. "Have fun wondering who's gonna be claimed tomorrow, cowards."

Those parting words have Fyve straightening. Blood rushes to his head, bringing with it a flood of pain.

And fury.

Zake's parting words are designed to fuel the claim-or-be-claimed thinking the Trials are breeding. He's goading the other teens to finish what he started—kill the girl, and anyone else they see as a weakness.

Like Cloud or her babies.

Or any other vulnerable soul on this ship.

"I've had enough," Fyve growls.

And then he's running, his feet thudding down the corridor. The girl isn't the most hated person on The Oasis.

Zake is.

"Fyve!" Halo calls desperately.

"Stay there and look after the girl," he shouts back, not looking over his shoulder. "And protect Cloud!"

Zake's halfway up the stairs when he realizes Fyve is coming after him. Like the coward he claims everyone else is, he breaks into a panicked run, sprinting up to the next floor, then the next one.

The exertion only fuels Fyve's blinding headache, but he uses the pain to power his determination. Zake doesn't deserve Tomorrow Land. He doesn't deserve for someone to die just so he can live.

Fyve reaches him just as he clears the stairs and he launches himself forward with a grunt. He crashes into Zake, who stumbles forward and slams into the wall, his hands bracing his fall. He pushes off, spins away, then turns to face Fyve as he shakes his head, trying to blink away the pain.

Zake's face twists with something ugly. "Fine, then, Number Boy. Let's do this."

Fyve slips the knife out of his pocket, adjusting the weight of it in his palm. Despite the pain sapping his strength, he has the advantage. "Great idea."

To his surprise, Zake sneers. "You think I ain't seen a knife before?" He yanks up his shirt, revealing a scar across his side. "Got this one from me dad."

And then he's running at Fyve, his gaze darting to the stairs behind him, clearly unafraid. Clearly intending on pushing Fyve down them.

Fyve has no choice but to run, too, holding the knife with everything he has as he creates as much distance between himself and the one story fall. His head thunders with the jolt of motion, and for a split-second, the corridor tilts and blurs. When it comes into focus, he realizes two things as Zake's fist powers toward his head.

He underestimated Zake's familiarity with violence.

And his ability to recognize weaknesses.

Zake's thick hand is a weapon in itself, and the moment it connects with Fyve's temple, a new pain is unleashed. An overwhelming one. A voracious one.

His knees give out.

Everything goes black.

And one last bolt of understanding pierces the agony devouring him.

He's about to die. Which means he's left Halo unprotected.

HALO

"*Y*ou're safe," Halo says as the girl's bloodshot eyes spring open. "You're okay."

The girl glances around, her fear palpable inside the tiny cabin they've dragged her into. If Cloud weren't perched on the bedframe with the twins in their basket, and Justice not pressed against the mattress that's leaning on the doorway, there wouldn't be enough room for Halo and Iva to squat beside the girl.

"Your name's Coda, isn't it?" Iva asks, gently holding her hand.

The girl nods weakly, angry red marks streaking down her neck like an invisible force is clawing at her skin. She's going to have an impressive set of bruises.

"I'm going to take your pulse," says Iva, moving her hand to press her fingertips against Coda's narrow wrist. "Lie there and rest. There's no need for you to move."

Halo stands, seeing that Iva's a natural at this whole nursing routine. She's got this.

"I need to go out for a minute." Halo pulls at the edge of the mattress, but Justice plants herself on her good leg and keeps the barrier firmly in place.

"We need to keep the cabin sealed off." Justice shoulders her out of the way, while she leans on the wooden crutches she's been using to get around.

Halo rakes a hand through her hair. "Fyve should be back by now. I don't know what's taking so long."

Justice looks at Halo, her eyes filled with the kind of knowing that nobody her age should have. "Halo, he's not coming back."

"What do you mean?" she snaps. "Of course, he is. He's just dealing with your no-good brother."

"Halo—"

"He's fine." She crosses her arms and glares, not willing to accept what Justice is insinuating.

Justice swallows. "You don't know my brother."

"And you don't know Fyve," she retorts. "He's strong. And when he's protecting people he loves, nobody can stop him."

"I hope you're right," Justice mutters. "But I doubt it."

Anger burns in the pit of Halo's gut. "We have enough happening here right now without that kind of negativity."

"Halo," Iva warns. "We're all on the same side here."

"Did you hear what she said?" Halo spins around. "She pretty much said Fyve's dead."

"Halo." This time it's Cloud who says her name, as her eyes spill over with tears. "It's you who needs to listen. Justice is right. Physically, Fyve has the advantage over Zake, but fighting isn't always about physical strength."

Halo's head spins as her anger mingles with fear and confusion. "You think Fyve hasn't had to fight for survival his whole life? You're all grossly underestimating him."

"You're the one underestimating Zake," Coda croaks from the floor. "Like I did."

Iva nods, beseeching Halo with her eyes to listen.

"Let me out." Halo goes to the mattress and pulls at the edge.

"No." Justice holds on tight, not prepared to let it budge. "It's not safe out there."

"Which is exactly why I need to go." Halo pries back the heavy mattress, sending Justice stumbling on her crutches, creating just the gap she needs to get out.

"Halo!" Cloud screams. "No!"

She's beyond listening. There's no way she can stay in that cabin knowing Fyve is out there somewhere, fighting for his life.

"I'll be back in a minute," she says, sliding out.

Justice curses at her as she presses the mattress back against the door. It's flimsy protection, but at least it's something. And judging by all the other mattresses she can see leaning against other cabin entrances, it's all anyone can think up.

Cloud and the babies will be fine for a short while. The best way Halo can protect them is to get Fyve back. And from what she witnessed earlier, she's not concerned about anyone stalking the corridors just yet. They're all waiting for someone else to make the kill so that they don't have to. Those two guys who'd tripped Halo and hauled Fyve back had made that clear. They were perfectly okay with Zake killing Coda, just as long as they didn't have to do it themselves. The danger hours will be when night falls and true desperation kicks in. The closer they draw to gathering again on the deck, the more chance there is of death. Which is why she needs Fyve back.

She creeps down the silent corridor, reaching in her pocket for her new lucky cord. It's more like a rope than a cord, but it's better than nothing in terms of a weapon. Her fingers instinctively wind through it as its golden length drapes to the floor. How she'd love to wrap this around Zake's neck and scare him in the way he did to Coda. Although, she's not sure she'd be able to let go…

Her eyes flare at the primal urge for violence seeping into

her veins. This isn't like her. She grew up surrounded by words of peace and gratitude that wove the fabric of her soul. Fyve's upbringing was a little more complicated, but still, he knows the meaning of the word love. Whereas Zake is made from hate and greed and brutality. Is that what Cloud meant when she said physical strength isn't what wins a fight?

She heads up the staircase, trying a few different doors and finding them locked. As she suspected, the only one open is the one leading to the pool deck.

Blinking in the afternoon sun, she scans the deck, looking for any sign of Fyve. It's even quieter than the corridor. It doesn't seem that anyone has chosen to wait out the Trial here. It's far too exposed.

She takes a few steps toward the pool when she's hit by a force that sends her crashing to the deck. She flips to her back and looks up to find she's tangled in a net.

"What are you doing?" she cries, thrashing about. "Get this thing off me!"

The more she struggles, the more entangled she becomes, so she stills her movements, deciding to buy herself some time to figure her way out of this.

The figures of several teens emerge from the shadows. It's hard to see who they are through the thick mesh.

"We got one!" a girl shouts.

"I can't believe it worked," says someone else.

"One down, two more to go," says another.

The teens reach Halo and start dragging the net toward the pool, and she realizes they intend to drown her.

"No!" she screams, resuming her efforts to free herself. She needs to find Fyve. She needs to get back to Cloud to keep the babies safe. It can't end like this!

"Let's do this fast," says a much more familiar voice. "Then we can reset the trap."

"Ajax!" Halo shouts. "It's me!"

"I know who it is," he replies as the net continues to bring her closer to the edge of the pool. "My idiot sister who decided to take an afternoon stroll on the deck. You never were very smart."

"We're family," she sobs, as she feels the edge of the pool underneath her hip. "Please don't do this. I need to get back to protect your children."

"That's exactly what I'm doing," he says. "If we kill three now, the babies will be allowed to live. I'm being a good father. How about you be a good aunt and let me get this over with?"

He's doing it again. He's twisting the truth to suit his purpose. He's not protecting his children. He's protecting himself. But she knows better than to call him out on this. Not now. Her brain scrambles to think of something else.

"Mom used to talk about us leaving our mark on the world," she says as he prepares to give her the final shove with his foot. "Do you think killing your sister is what she meant? Would she want you to do this?"

Her words have him pausing. He loved their mother, she knows that. She was probably the one person he ever loved. Apart from himself.

"Make Mom proud," she says. "Leave your mark. This isn't what she'd want."

"Just get on with it," a female shouts. "You're overthinking it."

His foot pushes at her and she accepts that not even their mother was enough to convince him.

"Ajax!" she hisses in one last desperate attempt. "If you kill me, Terra will only have one thing she can use against Dad to punish him. You. She'll use you to get at him. Torture you or kill you, even. She already tried to claim you once. Maybe next time she'll follow through."

There are a few rough and hurried movements and Halo braces herself for the water. She can't move her arms or legs, which means she'll have no hope of making her way back up to the surface. She thinks of Coal and how brave he was in his final moments, even though he hadn't known that death had been about to sneak up on him. If only she could be more like him.

But instead of hitting the water, the net falls away and she's hauled roughly to her feet.

She blinks up at Ajax's tortured expression.

"Get out of here," he sneers, pushing her away from the pool.

She stumbles forward.

"What are you doing?" several of the teens complain at once.

"Leave her!" Ajax demands. "She's so pathetic she barely counts as a kill. Let's find ourselves a real victim. Consider that a test run."

The other teens grumble, but nobody reaches for Halo, and she dashes for the stairwell before they can change their mind. Coming up here was foolish. Just as leaving the twins had been. She'd underestimated the teens on this ship, thinking they couldn't kill when they made it more than clear just now that's not the case.

She bursts into the stairwell and decides she has no choice but to make her way back to the cabin and hope that Fyve appears from wherever he's hiding. She's never going to find him like this. Panting heavily, and her head throbbing, she wipes sweat from her brow as she makes her way down the stairs. When she reaches the landing to the residential floor, she comes to an abrupt halt.

Zake is waiting for her, leaning against the door with a lecherous smile. He has dried blood on his face and another trickle coming from each ear, like Terra had warned him with the beginnings of one of her claimings. Or maybe Fyve had boxed him in the head a few times. Either option sounds good to Halo.

She yelps as she turns, realizing she has nowhere to go. The deck will lead to certain death. Ajax's friends won't let her go again. And all the other doors are locked.

It's time to face this knucklehead on her own.

Reminding herself that she's not the same person she was when he attacked her on the beach, she pulls back her shoulders and faces him. She's grown stronger, both physically and mentally since that day. And she has a fire burning in her belly that hadn't sparked before. One built with kindling made from fear and desperation. Whatever it is that's fueling the hatred in Zake's soul, she's certain she can match it.

"Where's Fyve?" she asks.

He seems to find this question amusing and tips back his head and laughs.

"You worried he's gonna find us?" Zake asks. "Don't worry. Nobody gonna bother us here, not even your pretty boyfriend—'specially not him."

Halo narrows her eyes, doing her best to look intimidating. "I'll ask you again. Where is he?"

"Well," he says, clearly enjoying this moment. "I know I said I wasn't gonna do ya dirty work for ya, but Number Boy forced me to make a sepshun."

Halo frowns, taking two beats to figure out he means *exception*. Then her frown grows to a scowl as she takes in what he's saying.

"You couldn't kill Fyve with your little finger," she says. "I bet he's back in his cabin."

"What ya gonna bet?" He pushes off from the door and steps closer, sending her reeling with the stench of his foul body odor.

Feeling in her pocket for her lucky cord, she removes it as subtly as she can, determined not to be taken by surprise like she was on the deck.

"Ya know something?" he asks, licking at his cracked lips. "You're special. That's why I knocked back that udder girl. The one who wanted me bad. I did that special for ya."

"Coda didn't want you," Halo says, holding her position.

"She called me handsome." He rubs at the sparse bristles on his chin. "Sounds to me like she wanted me real bad."

"She just wanted to live real bad," Halo snaps back. "We all do."

"I coulda broken her neck," he says, holding up his hand toward Halo's own throat. "I could feel her life right in me hand. Maybe I'll finish the job afta this Trial's over. I'll kill her like I killed ya boyfriend."

That's all it takes for Halo to make her move. She lunges forward, wrapping the lucky cord around Zake's neck in one swift action.

His eyes bulge as his hands fly to his throat. The need to protect Coda, along with everyone else on this ship, overpowers Halo and she twists the cord and strains on it with every ounce of her strength. She may have been raised with love but right now the only emotion pulsing through her veins is hatred. She has to kill this guy to protect every other soul on this ship.

Zake makes a gurgling noise that reminds her of the sound Coda had made when he'd first gripped her by the throat.

"It's not so fun being on the other side, is it?" she snarls.

His body convulses and she can only hope this doesn't take much longer. Her hands are already burning from the cord as she keeps the pressure up. As the next horrifying seconds pass, she realizes he's not convulsing from lack of oxygen.

He's laughing.

With a swift kick, he sends Halo flying across the landing and he tears the cord from his neck.

She turns to run up the stairs, but one of his meaty hands grabs her by the ankle and sends her slamming forward, her knees connecting painfully with one of the steps. She spins to her back and Zake wastes no time climbing on top of her, pinning her down, and wrapping the cord around her neck.

Oxygen is choked from her lungs as he licks her face, his revolting tongue like a sea slug sliding up her cheek. "Might wait til ya not breathing to have me way, I reckon. Less fuss dat way."

Halo freezes in terror, in much the same way she had when he'd attacked her on the beach. She'd thought she was a different person, but somehow, here she is, reacting in exactly the same way. He has her in an impossible position and without help, she's never going to be able to get herself out of this situation.

He tightens the cord and over his shoulder she sees a movement at the door to the stairwell.

Oh, please, let that be Fyve!

Focusing on Zake's blotchy face, she dares not look back at the door to see who it is. If they're here to help her, there's no way she wants to destroy the element of surprise. She just hopes whoever it is realizes she needs their help. As in, now!

She draws in the biggest breath she can with her restricted airway and holds it, hoping this isn't the last oxygen her tired body ever gets.

"That's da way," says Zake. "Ya gonna look even prettier when you're dead. Time ta say bye bye."

There's an almighty roar and Halo looks up to see Justice standing behind Zake with her weight on her good leg and one of her wooden crutches in the air. She tears off a cloth wrapped around the end to reveal she's sharpened the tip into a spike.

Halo's eyes widen. She's seen this before…

Justice slams the crutch down, seeming to channel the fourteen years of abuse she received at the hands of her father and brother. The crutch impales Zake from his back right through to his front, until Halo can feel the point of the spike against her belly. Warm blood gushes over her and the cord around her neck goes slack.

"You bi—!" Zake cries, his words turning to a gurgle as he slumps over Halo.

She concentrates on her breathing, trying to build the strength to push him off as she rips the cord from her throat.

"Are you okay?" Justice asks, rushing over to help. They send Zake rolling down the stairs to the landing, the crutch further skewering him through the middle.

"I am now," says Halo, sitting up. "Thank you."

Justice sits on the step beside her and stares at the evidence of what she just did.

"I got the idea from Sevin," she says. "From the oars we used on the rafts. I thought it might be useful to have a weapon."

"I figured that." Halo shakes her head in amazement. Sevin may not have made it onto this ship, but here she is, saving Halo from Zake once more.

"Do you think he'll count as a kill?" Justice asks. "You know, for the Trial."

"Is that why you did it?" Halo is surprised. She'd thought there was more to it than that.

Justice shakes her head, her expression devoid of emotion. "I've wanted to do that for a very long time. It was Cloud who gave me the courage when she said that winning a fight isn't about strength. She meant that Zake had grown up differently to Fyve so he could win a fight with him because of all the terrible things he's seen. I realized that I've seen those same things. I can be strong, too."

"You're different to Zake," says Halo, thinking of her own brother. "You're so much better than him."

Justice nods. "Let's get back to your family."

She tucks the cord in her pocket and wraps an arm around this complicated girl who just saved her life. "We're your family too, now."

Justice breaks into a wide grin, the first real emotion she's shown since she killed her brother. "Massive upgrade."

They get to their feet, knowing they can't stay where they

are. The danger of this Trial is far from over. And she still hasn't found Fyve. If he's even still alive.

"I'm sorry for what I said earlier about Fyve," says Justice, grimacing as she pulls the crutch out of Zake's back then leans heavily on it.

Halo nods. "And I'm sorry I got mad at you for saying it. Zake said he killed him. I'm just not going to believe it until I see for myself."

There's no way she can let go of her hope that he's still alive. He'd never give up on her.

"*Please remove all barriers from your doorway,*" a voice echoes inside Halo's head. "*Anyone with a blocked doorway is obstructing the Trial and will be claimed immediately.*"

Halo and Justice look at each other in panic.

She'll have to look for Fyve later. They have to get back to Cloud and the babies.

As in, now!

FYVE

"Wake up, Fyve."

Jiro's voice floats through Fyve's mind, tugging at his consciousness. He frowns, sensing something is wrong. He shouldn't be asleep. He needs to—

Adrenaline spikes through his system, making his pulse surge.

Zake!

The Trial!

Halo!

Fyve sits up as his eyes fly open, groaning when the room spins fast enough to make his stomach twist. He grips the mattress, willing it to stop. He needs to get to Halo.

"Take it easy, Fyve. You're safe."

Fyve goes from heart thundering and mind spinning to pulse nonexistent and body frozen.

The words weren't spoken in his mind. They were outside of him. He *heard* them in the same way he can hear his harsh breathing.

And the slow, steady footsteps approaching him.

He turns his head slowly even as his eyelids flutter faster

180

than they ever have. The room comes into focus, and it's nowhere he's ever seen before. It's mostly white with cupboards and drawers everywhere. He has no idea what they contain.

The slow sweep of Fyve's head stops just as the footsteps do. A man stands a few feet away, his dark skin almost as dark as his tunic. His black hair is cropped close to his head, and his beard is neat and trimmed in a way Fyve didn't know was possible. Beards have always been messy, wiry growths that can reach a man's chest. He's also…wider than any person Fyve's ever seen. His middle is rounded, his jowls soft and jelly-looking. The man's dark eyes are as still as the rest of him.

He smiles. "Hello, Fyve."

The voice is unmistakably familiar. "Jiro?"

He nods. "Yes, it's me."

The blinking slows, then stops. Fyve stares, wide eyed. "You're real."

Even as he says the words, he knows he's stating the obvious. He knew Jiro was as real as Terra is. They've seen the girl who speaks in their mind.

But the man standing in front of him is still a shock. Someone he knows, who's protected and helped him, yet is a complete stranger.

Jiro nods as if he understands. "I won't hurt you."

Fyve instinctively knows that's true. Jiro has shown that over and over, but there's also a gentle quality about him. An inexplicable desire to befriend him.

"Where am I?" he asks, glancing around.

"It's called the infirmary," Jiro says. "It's where injured and sick people would be taken so they can get better."

Fyve climbs off the narrow bed he's on, discovering something else.

His head no longer hurts.

He brings his fingertips to his temples, surprised to find a small cut on the right side. It's painful to touch, although the deep throb that had become a part of his skull is gone.

"Zake struck you there," Jiro explains. "So I cleaned up the wound."

Fyve frowns. His memory is still a pain-filled haze, but it doesn't align with what Jiro's saying. "Didn't he hit me on the other side?"

"There was probably more than one punch." Jiro takes a step closer. "What's important is that you're alive and well."

The assurance has Fyve jolting into action. "Exactly. Thanks, but I need to go help Halo and the others."

He takes a step forward, only to have Jiro move in closer and block him. "They're fine."

Fyve goes still, conscious he needs to slow down and understand what's happening here. Jiro's revealed himself. And although he's helped Fyve, it's also been at a cost. He hasn't extended his protection to Halo or anyone else.

"What's going on, Jiro?" he asks, staring as he pays close attention. He may finally be getting some answers.

"You almost lost a fight to Zake." Jiro shrugs a little. "He was about to finish you off when he blacked out and I got you out of there."

"You saved my life." Possibly more than once.

"I wouldn't have had to if you followed instructions," Jiro says, a hint of exasperation bringing his brows together.

Fyve takes a step back as something else hits him. "You made Zake black out. You can control the pain. You can claim people!"

Jiro doesn't answer. He barely moves. Yet the acknowledgement is there in the way his shoulders contract an inch. In the way his head ducks as if he's trying to dodge the truth.

Although it's a realization he knew on some level, the knowledge still shocks Fyve. Jiro may look peaceful and unthreatening, but so does the little girl posing as Terra. Looks are deceiving.

"Of course you can," Fyve says, his voice taking a bitter edge. "Are you the real Terra?"

"I am." Jiro's mouth tightens. "But I'm also not."

"What does that even mean?"

Jiro shakes his head. "I cannot answer that."

"What's going on, Jiro? What's happening on this ship?"

Jiro's lips press into a thin line.

"I deserve to know," Fyve growls, taking a step closer. "Teens are dying out there."

Halo could be next. Or Cloud. Or her babies.

He can't lose them like he did Coal and Sevin and everyone else he's cared about.

Jiro's dark eyes flash. "This is how you thank me? I saved your life, and you make demands?"

Fyve refuses to be intimidated. He's faced death over and over in the past weeks. He's lost close to everything.

And he came here for answers.

Fyve glances past him, noting the door on the other side of the room. "Well, if you're not interested in talking, then I'm going back to my cabin. I have another Trial I'm taking part in, whether I choose to or not."

A Trial Jiro knows about. And is part of.

Fyve needs to remember that.

He takes a step to the side, only to find that Jiro mirrors him. "You can't go yet, Fyve."

"Watch me," he growls.

He steps to the other side, but Jiro is there with him, looking both pained yet determined. He doesn't intend on letting Fyve leave.

Fyve's hands curl into tight fists. "If I have to choose between you or Halo, then the decision's already been made. I'm going back to her."

Jiro's face twists. "You can't go to Halo. Not yet."

"Like hell I'm not—"

"First, you need to know the truth about her."

Jiro steps around before Fyve can ask what he means. He walks to a door he hadn't noticed at the back of the infirmary and opens it, pausing to glance over his shoulder. "There are some answers I can give you," he says, then steps through.

Leaving Fyve with a choice.

He can go back to Halo, carrying more secrets.

Knowing she has some of her own.

Or discover what's in the next room.

The possibility of knowing some semblance of the truth, of having some answers, along with Jiro's assurance that Halo is fine, makes the decision for Fyve. He follows Jiro with purposeful steps.

If he gets nothing more than hedging and tight lips, he leaves.

The moment Fyve enters the adjacent room, he knows he won't be doing that. First, shock has him rooted to the spot.

Second, it's going to take some time to process what he's seeing.

Every wall of the small room they're standing in is covered in squares holding small, moving images. Fyve cautiously steps closer, eyes growing wider and wider. There are people in the images. People he knows.

Teens in their cabins, some holding each other, some holding anything that could resemble a weapon. The leg of a bed. A cupboard door. What looks like a metal plate that's been twisted and shaped into a point.

Fyve moves slowly from one image to the other. "What…"

"They're screens," Jiro says. "They project what's happening on the ship as it occurs."

They're being watched. Constantly.

The thought makes Fyve sick.

He's about to say as much when he reaches the next screen, and all thoughts are stalled. Halo is pacing his cabin, chewing on the side of her thumb, even though it's only a few steps from one to the other. Justice is guarding the door with her wooden crutch. Cloud and Iva are holding a twin each as they sit on the hard slats of the bed. The girl Zake almost choked to death is lying on the floor.

"See? I told you they're fine," Jiro says.

Fyve reaches out and brushes his fingertips over the cool glass. "Nothing about this is fine," he mutters.

Jiro moves three screens over and points at a still outline. "And Zake's dead."

Fyve joins him, registering he's right. Zake is lying at the bottom of a set of stairs, a dark pool of blood stretched across his torso.

Good riddance.

"He'll no longer be a threat."

Fyve turns to Jiro, trying to understand what this all means. Why is everyone being watched so closely?

And by whom?

"What's going on, Jiro?" He watches the man who's somehow part ally, part enemy. "Tell me."

"I didn't bring you here for that." He indicates to a dozen screens in the bottom right corner. "It was to show you this."

At first, Fyve doesn't look. By doing so, he's allowing Jiro to change the subject, and that's not why he followed him into this disgusting spying room.

Except, even from the corner of his eye he can tell there's something familiar about the images on those screens. They're not full of the smooth, geometric lines of The Oasis. Everything is jagged and uneven, messy and chaotic.

Fyve's drawn to the images. They just became his new center of focus. The only thing he sees.

Treasure Island.

A wave of homesickness is the first to rock through him. It

stings his eyes. Clenches his heart. He can almost smell the faint rotting, hear the crying and laughter that coexisted.

But it's quickly replaced by another tidal wave of emotion.

And this one is far more devastating. Raw anger. Unadulterated outrage. Gut-twisting revulsion.

"How..."

Watching the teens didn't start on The Oasis. It goes back so much further than that.

Treasure Island was some sort of play or exhibition or... entertainment.

Is that all these Trials have been?

A roar builds inside Fyve, clawing at his chest, searing his throat, clamoring behind his gritted teeth. Jiro is no ally. Whatever he's part of is sadistic and disgusting. Fyve's about to let his rage explode when someone enters one of the screens.

Just when he thought the shocks, the soul-shaking revelations were over, there's one more.

Fyve leans closer. "It can't be..."

But it is. His sister, Sevin, is standing beneath Halo's fake tree, staring out at the ocean.

Fyve's legs give out and he drops to his knees. "Sevin," he moans.

She's alive!

"How?" he chokes out.

Jiro moves behind him and there's a soft *tap* as he touches something. The screen changes, revealing Fyve and Halo and all the teens standing on the deck of The Oasis. Everyone is smiling and cheering.

It has to be the day they left. No one has done much of that since.

He quickly realizes he's right when he sees himself and Halo near the railing as they watch Treasure Island recede. He's holding her from behind, a broad smile on his face. It had been hard to leave Cee and her children behind, but he made the right decision, which is apparent in the soft joy molding his features. Despite everything they've faced, he's never regretted that choice.

Halo is his family now.

Fyve feels it in his heart. Their love is proof that life doesn't have to be defined by what you've lost. Not when he has Halo. Her existence brings hope and purpose and a future. Their argument suddenly seems petty and foolish. The desire to apologize and tell her he loves her returns the strength to his muscles.

He's about to stand when the image shifts, and Treasure Island grows to fill the screen, despite the increasing distance. Fyve makes out the serrated, barbed horizon, the frail, feeble huts, then the hill that Halo built her fake tree on.

A strangled moan grates through the air, and Fyve realizes it's his own. If he hadn't already lost the ability to stand, he would've collapsed.

Sevin has climbed to the top of the tree. And she's waving. At Halo.

The girl that naive, trusting Fyve is holding turns in his arms and kisses him, drawing his attention away from what he was leaving behind.

"She saw her," he whispers hoarsely. "She knows."

Jiro was telling the truth. Halo has a secret.

Sevin, the sister he swore to protect, is alive.

And because of Halo, he left her behind.

HALO

*J*ustice stands in the doorway like a sentinel. The wooden crutch is gripped tightly in her hand, the tip of it stained a deep crimson. The front of Halo's tunic is the same color and she tries not to look down as she paces the tiny cabin. Cloud and Iva are perched on the bed frame, each with a baby in their arms, while Coda sleeps off her injuries at their feet.

"He's still not back," says Halo, unable to accept Fyve is dead no matter how many hours he's been missing. She's certain she'd feel his absence if he'd left this earth. Their souls have become entwined since the Trials began. She'd barely know herself without him. Nor would she want to.

Justice remains silent, clearly deciding to keep her skepticism about Fyve's survival to herself. And for that, Halo's grateful.

"And I'd like to check on my dad." Halo rubs at her temples as she wishes this headache would hurry up and go away.

Justice shoots her a glare and waves her crutch. "Don't make me use this thing again."

Halo holds up her hands. "It's okay. I'm not going anywhere.

It's not even possible to check on him while the Trial's still running. But what if they're not bringing him food?"

"Your dad's a survivor," says Cloud firmly. "He'll be okay."

Iva turns to Cloud. "You don't blame Elijah for sneaking you on the ship?"

Cloud shakes her head. "He didn't make me come. I wanted to. I was a complete and total fool."

"No, you weren't," says Iva. "We all fought hard to get on this ship. If you're a fool, then so are we."

A piercing scream rattles down the corridor and Justice pokes out her head.

"I can't see anything," she reports back. "It's okay."

Halo's eyes brim with tears. None of this is remotely okay. The only way the seven of them in this cabin can be guaranteed safety is for someone else to die. Three of them, in fact. In what kind of messed up world is that okay?

There are footsteps and Justice takes another peek outside. Her back stiffens and she widens her stance to fill the doorway with the sharp tip of the crutch pointed out.

"Get back," she hisses to Halo, making her wonder when this young girl got so brave. She's come a long way since she'd joined them at their precariously placed pile of metal poles in the first Trial. That memory feels like a thousand years ago now.

Halo steps behind Justice where she's unseen but ready to strike if needed. There's no way she's going to let Justice put herself in danger again to save her. They're in this together. It's the only way.

The same two guys who'd interfered when Halo and Fyve had tried to save Coda appear at the door. One is tall and the other short, but other than that they have the same mousy features that distinguish them as brothers.

Justice brandishes the crutch. "Go away!"

"Give us the babies and we'll be gone," the tall brother says.

Halo balls her hands into fists. She'll make what happened to Zake look like a party.

"Nobody has to get hurt," the short brother shouts.

"Except the babies," sneers Justice. "Or you two, if you don't get out of my sight right now."

Justice leaps forward with the crutch. Halo steps out into their line of sight and clutches her stomach in the center of the giant bloodstain on her tunic. Hopefully these guys aren't smart enough to notice the blood is dried.

"She's not joking," moans Halo, screwing up her face in a painful grimace. "She's crazy. She killed Fyve and Coda, and now she's after me."

The brothers look to Coda lying on the ground, then back at Halo's tunic, their faces filling with panic.

"Help me!" Halo cries, dropping to her knees, still clutching her stomach. "Please!"

Justice brandishes the crutch. "Get out of here and let me finish my kill."

The taller guy grabs his brother by the arm and they run off, no doubt to hide in a cabin and pray for Halo's demise. If they believe Fyve, Halo and Coda are all dead, there'll be no need for them to return.

Justice leans back on her crutch and turns to Halo with a wide grin as she shakes her head.

She smiles back. If the situation weren't so dire, they might even laugh.

"You're both my heroes," says Cloud, holding Marvel tightly to her chest. "I can't thank you enough."

"You can thank us if we make it to the morning," says Justice, resuming her stance at the entrance.

This wipes the smile from Halo's face. But Justice is right. Now isn't the time to get complacent.

The night crawls past. Each minute of each hour is excruci-

190

ating and it's almost a relief when eventually Terra speaks to them.

"The Trial has now finished," she says. *"Gather on the deck for the results."*

There's cheering further down the corridor, and Halo wonders if it's the two brothers.

"They're not going to be happy to see you," mutters Justice, clearly thinking the same thing. "Or her."

Justice nudges Coda with her foot. She's so deeply asleep, she hadn't even seemed to have heard Terra's message. Halo bends down and jostles her gently awake.

Coda blinks up at her, seeming confused. Then the memories must come flooding back and she groans.

"It's time to go to the deck," Halo says. "Do you need help?"

"You're hurt!" Coda sees the state of Halo's tunic and sits up. "What happened?"

"I'm okay," she says. "It's not my blood."

"Whose is it?" Coda gets to her feet. She's a little wobbly and her neck is bruised purple, but she seems otherwise fine.

"Zake won't bother you again," says Justice, in answer to her question.

Coda's dark eyes widen and she nods her understanding. "I'm glad."

"Come on." Justice steps out into the corridor while Cloud and Iva get the babies settled into their basket.

"I'll meet you up there," says Halo, pointing at her tunic. "I need to get changed quickly."

She can't stand having that knucklehead's blood on her for another moment.

"Justice, can you help me with something?" Cloud calls from the bathroom.

Justice returns to the cabin and Halo slips out, looking left and right, a feeling of unease still winding through her. She's not sure she'll ever feel safe again, even though the Trial is over, which means they should be out of danger for now.

As she walks down the corridor, there's the sound of breaking glass. She looks back to the cabin but sees Coda in the doorway, not looking like anything is wrong, so she continues on. She's being jumpy, that's all.

Her shoulders slump to find her cabin empty. She'd half expected to find Fyve waiting for her. Taking a spare tunic from her cupboard, she goes to the bathroom and uses a cloth to sponge herself down. It turns a deep brown color as she wipes away Zake's blood. She'd wipe her skin away if she could. She slips the fresh tunic over her head and smooths down her hair with damp hands.

"Where are you, Fyve?" she asks her reflection in the mirror. "Where are you?"

Leaving her room, she heads directly for the deck. Terra isn't known for her patience. And besides, this is her chance to find out if Fyve is alive. He still doesn't *feel* dead to her, though. Is this how he felt when he found Sevin? Had some part of him been screaming at him that she was still right there with him?

As soon as she sees him again, she has to tell him the truth. She's waited far too long already. And if Justice is right, she's missed her chance completely.

"She's not right," Halo growls to herself as she slides open the door to the deck.

Even though it's crowded outside, she can't help notice the difference since the very first day. With each Trial they've endured, losses have been incurred. If Terra only wanted fifty of them, why couldn't she have left the other fifty behind on Treasure Island instead of using them as unwilling participants in her sick game?

The sky is gray and angry, almost as if it's protesting the injustice of the crimes being committed on this ship. A drop of rain lands on Halo's cheek and she puts her hand to it, feeling the sadness of the planet deep in her heart. Is there anything good left in the world?

She sees the twins in their basket with Cloud and Iva fussing over them from either side and decides there are still plenty of good things left. They're just getting harder to find, the further they head out to sea.

She takes a step toward the basket only for the two brothers from last night to step out in front of her.

"What are you doing here?" the tall brother asks, looking at her like she's a ghost.

"Same thing as you." She tries to step past them, but they block her way.

"She doesn't look injured," the short brother says. "Which makes her a liar."

"Better than being a baby killer." She pushes past only for the tall brother to grip her by the arm.

"I hope you get claimed," he hisses in her ear.

She swallows but remains quiet, deciding some people aren't worthy of a reply.

Eventually, he lets go of her arm and she holds her head high as she walks to join her people.

Her people. She turns those words over in her mind. That's exactly what this small group has become. Justice. Iva. Cloud. Miracle. Marvel. And now Coda. The only one who's missing is Fyve. And her father. If Tomorrow Land is real, she knows they could make themselves a wonderful life. But she also knows it would never be worth the price they had to pay for it.

Terra steps out onto the balcony. She's alone, as Halo knew she would be. She looks tired as she pulls the hood of her cape tighter around her bald head. The ship rears up over a wave and Terra grips the railing to steady herself.

"The rules of the Trial were simple," Terra's voice says inside their heads.

Halo winces, concentrating on keeping her feet stable. Each

word of Terra's had punched at the pain in her temples, reminding her that her headache hasn't gone anywhere.

"You were asked to take the lives of three of your own," Terra continues. *"And I can report that while we experienced death during the night, it didn't count toward your quota."*

"What does that mean?" Halo whispers to Justice, her heart soaring. Fyve's death would surely count. Which can only mean he's still alive. "Where's Fyve then?"

Justice slips her hand into Halo's. "Not counting doesn't necessarily mean he's still alive. Zake wasn't a competitor, so his kills wouldn't count."

Halo's heart immediately crashes back to the ocean, feeling like it's being swallowed up by the angry waves. Iva moves to stand a little closer to Halo, giving her a heartbreakingly sad smile. She knows exactly how Halo feels right now. The leather bracelet she's wearing around her wrist is proof of that. And just like Halo, Iva hasn't given up on Dargo.

"I gave you every opportunity to save yourself," says Terra. *"Once again, you proved that you were unable to make a decision. Which means it falls in my hands to claim three of you at my will."*

"Your will," Halo mutters. All her life she's heard stories about Terra's will. But not one of them was like this.

There's a scream and Halo spins around to see the tall brother has a young teenage boy slung over his shoulder. The boy is beating at his back with his fists.

"Let me go!" he screams as he's carried to the railing.

"I'm not going to die," the tall brother shouts. "I worked too hard for this."

Halo is just about to race over to help the boy when she sees the short brother eyeing Cloud's basket. She can't leave the twins now. Not even to help that innocent boy.

"Do something, Terra!" Halo shouts to the girl on the balcony. "I don't know who you are. Who you *really* are. But whoever you are and whatever power you have, do something now!"

Terra flinches—or at least Halo thinks she does—yet remains staring straight ahead as if people's lives aren't at stake here.

The tall brother steps up on a crate near the railing and tries to pry the terrified boy from his shoulder. But the boy isn't having any of it and he grips on tight.

"Just let go," the tall brother growls. "Do it for everyone here. Die a hero, not a coward."

To Halo's shock, the boy stills his fight and goes limp.

"That's the way," the tall brother coos, his face filling with victory. "You're a hero."

He lifts the boy from his shoulder and raises him in the air like a sacrifice, preparing to throw him into the ocean. Momentum gathers as the boy is flung through the air, but at the last moment, he reaches out and grips the tall brother by the shoulders of his tunic, sending him toppling.

"Two heroes now!" the boy shouts as they both fly over the railing and hurtle out of sight.

Halo's hand goes to her mouth as she shakes her head at the horror, deciding she'll never get used to witnessing this kind of death.

"Good for him," says Justice. "Although really there was only one hero."

Halo nods. That poor boy knew he didn't stand a chance. And there was no way he was going to go without taking his killer with him.

The short brother chooses this moment of distraction to make a lunge for the basket. He picks up Miracle and dashes across the deck.

"No!" screams Cloud, as she chases after him. Halo is following right behind her.

But the short brother is fast and gets to the railing first.

"No!" screams Cloud again. "Stop!"

"If you do this, I'll kill you," shouts Halo, meaning every word. "Whether it's part of the Trial or not."

The short brother hesitates, holding Miracle far too close to the railing for Halo's liking. Miracle lets out a cry, even though she can't possibly realize the danger she's in.

"You throw that baby and it's your guaranteed death," says Halo, stepping forward. "You give her to me, and you have a one in ninety chance of being claimed. I know what odds I'd take."

"You won't kill me," the short brother snarls, lifting Miracle higher. "You don't have the guts."

Cloud is creeping toward him, and Halo knows she has to keep his attention so she can get just a little closer.

"What do you think that blood was on my tunic last night?" asks Halo. "Terra said there were deaths. And I caused them. Now give me the baby or you'll be next."

"No!" the short brother shouts as he makes a move to propel Miracle over the edge.

Cloud lets out a roar and Halo jumps forward, getting her hands on Miracle just as Cloud slams something into the back of his neck. He falls slack and Halo tightens her grip on Miracle as he lets go, bringing the screaming child to her chest.

The short brother gurgles from the deck with blood blooming from his mouth, as Cloud stands over him with a jagged shard of a broken mirror in her hand. Her own blood is running down her hand and across her forearm.

That had been the breaking glass Halo had heard. Cloud had decided to make her own weapon to protect her babies. It reminds Halo to never ever underestimate what a mother will do to protect her child.

"Is she okay?" Cloud asks, looking at her daughter pressed to Halo's chest.

Halo nods. "She is now."

The short brother lets out one final gurgle then lapses into unconsciousness as he bleeds out at their feet. In another life-time, back on Treasure Island, Halo would have felt bad about his death. But not now. She doesn't want to share oxygen on this ship with the likes of anyone who would hurt a child.

Cloud lets her weapon drop and Halo hands her Miracle, stooping to pick up the piece of mirror and throwing it over the railing. She watches as it drops to the ocean to join the fins of the two leatherskins who just had an unexpected feed and are waiting to see if dessert is on offer. She blinks as one of the sharks leaps out of the water, certain it only has one eye.

Could that be…

"Well done," says Terra, interrupting her thoughts. *"That's three deaths. However, they did not take place during the Trial and do not count."*

Instantaneously, three teens cry out as they fall to the deck. All males. All older than Halo, perhaps eighteen or nineteen.

"No," Halo gasps, as she watches blood seep from their nose and eyes.

Two die almost immediately, but the third seems to hang on to life, his convulsions worsening then lessening as his final words are gurgled through his blood-stained lips.

"Don't let her," he moans. "No…"

Halo wraps her arms around Cloud, pressing her sweet niece between them and holds them both tight. She has to find a better way to protect her people.

And until she finds Fyve, she has to do it all by herself.

FYVE

There are cameras all over Treasure Island. A few angled toward the beach where Gratitude happens every evening. One aimed at Elijah's cabin, which has remained empty since The Oasis departed. Several capturing the movements around the village.

But it's the one inside Fyve's family hut that has him entranced.

It had been nothing but a grainy, gritty image throughout the night, yet Fyve had barely taken his gaze off it once he discovered its existence. And the small form curled up on the sleeping mat.

His heart aches. Yet it's thudding with joy.

Sevin's alive.

And he's not with her.

Fyve shifts the chair he's sitting on closer to the screens. His knees bump the wall, but he ignores the discomfort. He'd climb straight through if he could. Especially now that Sevin's waking up.

He was surprised to find she's remained in their hut rather than moving in with Cee and her children. The knowledge she's alone wraps around his chest and strangles the heart that's already hurting. She must be so lonely.

She sits up, scratching her messy hair in a way that's achingly familiar. She rubs her nose, stretches, and scratches again. All mannerisms he knew would happen before they did.

Suddenly, the flap of material that poses as their door is yanked back. Pale slivers of light illuminate Bloo racing into the hut. A delighted smile spears across Fyve's face as his cousin hugs Sevin. They talk for long minutes, smiling and even giggling a couple of times. How Fyve wishes he could hear what they're saying. He'd forgotten those mornings before most people were up where they'd laugh about something that happened the day before or joke about how many dozen rats may have fallen into their trap overnight.

Sevin crawls over to the other side of the hut, Bloo dancing alongside her. Together they move Halo's motor from the lid of the barrel that's buried in the ground. For the first time Fyve's brow contracts.

Halo.

She knows Sevin is alive. She saw her on the fake tree as they were pulling away from Treasure Island.

And she chose not to tell him. Just so he'd stay by her side.

She didn't care that he was leaving his vulnerable younger sister behind. The last of his family.

Leaving Sevin to starve. To probably die of disease. To most definitely live a short, lonely life.

Bitter anger burns in his gut. He can never forgive Halo for that. She robbed him of choosing his future.

Sevin leans into the barrel and Bloo watches, her hands clasped to her chin. Sevin straightens, then settles into a cross-legged position as she uncurls her palm. Bloo bounces on her knees and Fyve can practically hear her squeal of excitement. It has him leaning even closer, wanting to know what Sevin's holding.

She opens her hand, shoulders curled almost protectively as she reveals what's sitting in her palm. Baby rats!

It's too soon to have bred them, meaning Sevin must've caught a pregnant female. But she didn't kill it and eat it. She kept it alive and is seeing the rewards far quicker than she would've expected.

"That's my smart girl," Fyve murmurs proudly.

She holds out the tiny, squirming creatures to show Bloo, whose face rounds with wonder. Sevin strokes a gentle finger down a fragile back, her face soft.

"Don't get too attached, Sevin," he says fondly. "They're food."

As if she heard him, she slips the baby rat back into the barrel and with Bloo's help, they replace the lid and the motor, hiding it from view. Sevin's realized that if others discover these tasty morsels are here, they'll be stolen before the rats are old enough to continue the cycle.

She rises to her feet and says something to Bloo, who nods enthusiastically. They exit the hut hand in hand. Fyve immediately scans the other screens capturing Treasure Island, desperately wanting to keep them in view.

But they're either empty or slowly coming alive with movement as the village wakes to another day.

"Where have you gone, Sevin?" Fyve asks aloud, sitting back with a huff. If she's heading out to the trap, he won't be able to see her. Heck, if she's in another hut he won't be able to see her. Theirs is the only one that seems to have a camera.

A sharp movement on one of the other screens draws his attention and the tension between his eyebrows contracts some more.

The teens have congregated on the deck, no doubt for the announcement now that the Trial is finished. But a young man has forcibly lifted another and is carrying him to the side of the ship. Fyve watches, horrified, as the taller male tries to throw the other overboard, only for the two of them to fall.

Suddenly, the short guy Fyve recognizes as the one of the two who stopped him from getting to the girl Zake was strangling grabs one of Cloud's babies. Clutching the child that would no doubt be screaming, he runs for the railing, too.

"No!" Fyve shouts, shooting to his feet, knowing he could never reach them in time to be of any help.

Then Halo and Cloud are there, and Halo looks like she's trying to talk to him. He draws in a harsh breath as she slowly edges closer, clearly intent on saving little Miracle or Marvel.

Just seeing her is a knife in the chest. So is the knowledge that despite it all, he doesn't want to see her hurt.

The short brother lurches as he tries to throw the baby into the water below. Halo moves first, grabbing the baby. Then Cloud leaps, slamming something into the back of the boy's neck. He crumples, blood flowing from the wound that was just inflicted.

Now that the baby is safe, Fyve turns away, his gut churning once more. He may be relieved Halo is fine, but he's also relieved Cloud is. In fact, all this proves is exactly how savage life is now. In ways Treasure Island never was.

And this is what Halo chose for him. A world of brutality. Of kill or be killed. And unlike Treasure Island, it's one where he's no longer sure what he's fighting for.

He thought it was what he had with Halo.

But that was founded on lies. It never would've survived.

There's a flicker of movement in one of the screens and Fyve gladly returns to his newfound connection to Sevin. Especially considering it's been largely still as it's angled at the outskirts of the village, on the way to the beach. It catches Fyve's attention, then completely ensnares it. It's Sevin! With Bloo skipping alongside her as they hold hands.

Fyve's once more leaning close, watching with rapt attention. Although it feels like a lifetime since The Oasis left, it can't have been more than a week. Still, Sevin looks older. Well on her way to being a young woman. She's been forced to grow up in that short space of time.

Releasing Bloo's hand, she squats down and lifts something up. She straightens, holding a long pole like they used in the first Trial. She's frowning with strain as she maneuvers it, Bloo holding it further down although she'd be of little help. Sevin's cheeks puff out as she jostles a little to the left, then a little more. The pole slips forward and then she's pushing it into a standing position. Within minutes, it's upright.

There's a rope dangling down and Fyve instantly knows what it is. Another tree. But this one is closer to the village. He quickly realizes there's another pole a few feet away, and another on the other side. As if Sevin's intending on building a forest.

"She's quite determined, that sister of yours."

Fyve spins around to find Jiro standing behind him, smiling. "She's also been digging something further west and using the soil to build a wall of some sort."

"The waterfall," Fyve breathes. "She always wanted a waterfall."

"I suspect that's exactly what she'll have, then."

"Well, she has to fill her time, somehow, doesn't she?" Fyve says, bitterness staining his tongue. "She's practically alone."

Jiro glances at the screen. "She doesn't look alone to me."

"That's because she's now responsible for looking after our cousins!"

Jiro clasps his hands on his rounded middle. "She's breeding rats. She's building the world she wants to live in. She doesn't look unhappy to me."

Fyve's arms explode out to the sides. "She shouldn't be doing it alone, Jiro!"

Jiro doesn't flinch from Fyve's angry gaze. "Don't you see she's at peace with the decision she made?"

"Of course you'd say that," Fyve snarls, rounding on him. "You're one of the people who left her behind."

Jiro stiffens so sharply that his jowls wobble. "That was not my choice."

"Then whose was it?"

Jiro pulls himself up, drawing in a slow breath. "This isn't what I came here to discuss. You can't stay in this room, Fyve. It's time to return to your cabin."

Fyve takes a step back, then another. He's almost tempted to use his body like a shield to protect the screens from Jiro's words. "No. I'm not leaving her."

"You already have." Jiro's lashes flutter at Fyve's gasp, but he doesn't break eye contact. "And it was the right decision."

Fyve's lip curls. Jiro's part of whatever's happening on The Oasis. He's just as self-serving as Halo. They'll never understand that he was supposed to stay. "I'm not leaving," he grinds out, digging his feet into the floor.

"There's one more Trial," Jiro continues. "But you don't need to worry. You'll be safe."

"I'm also safe here. If that's really your priority, you'd let me stay."

Jiro shakes his head. "You're far from safe here, Fyve." He steps forward as he pulls something out of his pocket. "Here's your knife. You dropped it when Zake attacked."

Fyve takes it, thinking that moment feels like a lifetime ago. So much has changed. His world has shifted, the assumptions it was founded on forever altered.

Sevin's alive.

Halo lied to him.

Another thought strikes Fyve. Another assumption that's been annihilated. "What are the Trials for, Jiro?" he demands. The promise that he'll be safe is evidence they're not random.

That it's not just about being strong and smart. Teens are being chosen for something.

"Tomorrow," Jiro says simply. "The Trials are about our future in Tomorrow Land."

Fyve's about to demand he actually give an answer that makes sense when Jiro moves toward the door. "There will be time to explain. For now, you must return to your cabin as if none of this ever happened. No one else can know."

"You can't ask that of me," Fyve says, shaking his head. "Nothing is the same."

"You need to act as if it is." Jiro frowns. "For both our sakes."

Fyve crosses his arms. Not only does he not want to leave the only connection he has to Sevin, but he also doesn't want to see Halo. The anger and betrayal are just too raw.

Jiro stills, his eyes widening. He glances at the door behind him, his breath suddenly rasping in and out. Fyve can practically hear his heart thundering in his chest. For some reason, Jiro's terrified.

And then Fyve definitely hears something.

Voices! There's a deep voice, a man's voice, then a woman's. They don't belong to the teens who have been forced to endure the continuation of the Trials.

And they're approaching the door.

Fyve whispers the same question he's asked more than once. "What's going on, Jiro?"

"You need to go!" Jiro says frantically, his beard a stark contrast to his pale skin.

Except there's only one door to this room. It's both the entrance those voices are on the other side of, and the exit Fyve would need to escape through. He's about to meet whoever's on the other side, whether Jiro likes it or not.

Jiro rushes to the wall of screens behind Fyve, runs his hand down the side of one and presses it. To Fyve's surprise, it swings open like a door. Behind is a smooth, square panel and Jiro yanks off the bracelet that's around his wrist and swipes it over it.

This time, the whole wall opens like a door.

"Quick!" Jiro hisses. He shoves the bracelet in Fyve's hand. "Take this and open the door on the other side. It'll take you to the kitchen where you saw the crates. From there, go back to your cabin."

Fyve hesitates. If he stays, he'll find out who's approaching. He'll finally know who's behind all of this.

"Please, Fyve," Jiro moans. "Go."

But if he stays, it's obvious the consequences will be bad for Jiro. Fyve can't repay everything this man has done for him by waiting to see what those consequences would be.

With a last glance at the one link he has to Sevin, he slips past the wall of screens and Jiro instantly closes it behind him, shutting off any light in the process. As darkness envelops Fyve, he also discovers it also cuts off any sound. He has no idea what's happening on the other side.

Feeling his way, he finds he's in a narrow corridor. Keeping his hand on the smooth wall, he slowly creeps forward, his breath sounding loud in the black space. His outstretched arm soon hits another surface in front of him. Running his hands over it, he discovers it's a wall like many of the ones they've seen on The Oasis.

Walls that have sometimes been doors.

Fyve waves the bracelet around, realizing it must contain a chip, like the one Jiro hid for him and then was used to reveal the dining room. Which means he needs to find a panel like the one Jiro swiped over. Squinting even though he can't see anything, Fyve feels the wall to his left, then his right. It's there that his fingers bump over the raised, square shape he's looking for.

One swipe of the bracelet and it silently slides open.

The kitchen—as Jiro called it—is exactly what Fyve finds on

the other side. He steps through, noticing another panel tucked beneath some shelves to his right. Another swipe and the door closes, once more looking like a wall. He stands still as his heart thuds. Just like the last time he was here, the crates are gone, but now he has some idea how they disappeared. Just not where.

He's finally getting answers, and yet, never before has a victory been so hollow.

The answers came at an unimaginable price.

Tucking the bracelet into his pocket, Fyve quickly makes his way back to his cabin. There's no one in the corridors, for which he's grateful. They must be in their cabins, trying to process the last Trial.

Just like he's trying to process what to do next.

He slips into his cabin, quickly shutting the door behind him and leaning against it. The moment he draws in a breath, the moment his mind realizes he now has to do what he was told— pretend nothing's changed—Fyve's knees give out. He slides down, curling up once he hits the floor, a low choking sound scraping past his throat. He pulls his knees in close, resting his head on his arms.

He blinks. Swallows. Tries to hold back the waves of devastation.

There's one more Trial to go, but what's the point?

He abandoned Sevin, the one person he swore to protect.

Whatever he had with Halo is a lie. The ship he's on is little more than a set of cruel games where the outcome has already been decided.

There's nothing worth fighting for.

HALO

*I*t's afternoon when Halo goes looking for Fyve. She'd returned to her cabin after the Trial and had collapsed into a deep sleep. The rest had restored some of her energy, but it had done nothing for her headache. It feels worse than ever, like Terra herself has taken up residence inside her skull and is tapping out messages in morse code, making every nerve in her brain throb.

She slides open her door, glad it's started working again after the conclusion of that hellish Trial. It's quiet outside in the corridor. Even the babies seem to be asleep, which is a blessing for Cloud. Halo tiptoes toward Fyve's cabin, deciding it's the best place to start, even though she doesn't rate her chances of finding him there. But maybe he's left her a clue, like Dargo with his bracelet.

As expected, his cabin is empty, barely any sign of the night they all spent in here fearing for their lives. She goes to his bed, straightens the mattress and picks up his pillow, holding it to her chest.

"Where are you?" she whispers, knowing only too well how

Iva must feel. Maybe she should have slept in here. She already feels closer to him just by standing in this room. There's no way she can accept Fyve's dead, even if that's what everyone else thinks. She'll never believe it. Not unless she's shown some hard evidence. Something a lot more convincing than him simply being gone.

Putting down the pillow, Halo decides to head up to the deck. Having spent a lifetime living in the outdoors, she needs to feel the sun on her face. If she can't have the comfort of being with the guy she loves, then at least she can close her eyes and pretend she's at home for a few precious minutes. And who knows, maybe the sun will help relieve this relentless ache in her head.

She goes to the stairwell and climbs, keeping one hand on the railing and the other on her head. The fresh air hits her as she opens the door. The storm that had been brewing when the results of the Trial had been announced has passed. The gray clouds have been chased away by bright rays of light and the wind has died down. But the memory of what took place on this deck remains. It's like fear and death have seeped into the boards beneath her feet. She can barely remember that feeling of excitement when she'd first come aboard The Oasis. She wants to scream at her younger self to turn the other way and run.

Walking to the edge of the pool, she sits down and tucks up her knees, watching the pods swim underneath the plankton. Their tiny translucent wings are outstretched as they perform the steps to their intricate dance, passing each other in a series of sweeping circles and dives. The teens haven't been fed any of these creatures yet. Maybe Terra is saving them for when times are really tough. Or maybe she's letting their numbers thrive before they start thinning them out.

A sharp pain pierces Halo's head and she lets out a whimper

as she drops her face into her hands. She can't take much more of this. Maybe once they get off this ship with its incessant rocking, the pain will subside? That's assuming she ever gets off this ship. Her father seemed certain Tomorrow Land exists, but it's not like he's seen it. They'd all thought Terra existed, too, and that's looking more and more like a lie with every day that passes.

"Are you okay?"

Halo's hands fall from her face as she looks up and gasps, hardly daring to believe who had spoken to her.

"Fyve!" She jumps to her feet and throws her arms around him, only to find he doesn't hug her back. "I knew you were alive! I knew it!"

He doesn't reply. Nor does he move. But he doesn't push her away, so she continues to hold him close, drawing in the scent of him.

"Are you in pain?" she asks, forcing herself to step back. "What's wrong?"

"I thought you were the one in pain." He points to her head, and she notices he's not meeting her eye. He has a few bruises and a cut on the side of his head, but otherwise he seems in good shape.

"I was in pain," she says. "I mean, I am. My headache is worse. But that doesn't matter now. You're here! You're alive! And I have something important I have to tell you."

She'd made a promise to herself that if she ever saw him again, she'd tell him immediately about Sevin. No more excuses. No more waiting. He needs to know.

He lets out a frustrated sigh and takes a few steps away, and she realizes he's heading for the door.

"Fyve!" She chases after him. "What's going on? I said I have to tell you something."

He stops and turns, meeting her gaze at last, and she almost wishes he hadn't. Because he's looking at her with what feels very much like disappointment.

"Sevin's alive," she says, the words feeling like a magic spell on her lips. One that will bring back the guy she loves instead of this robot who seems to have returned to her.

He doesn't react. He doesn't so much as flinch. Whatever she'd been expecting from him, it wasn't this.

"Did you hear what I said?" she asks. "Sevin's alive. I wanted to tell you earlier but—"

"Enough!" He holds up a hand.

"What happened to you, Fyve?" Her voice quavers as she realizes something big has taken place while he was missing. "Where have you been? What were you told?"

He shakes his head. "Nobody *told* me anything."

She sighs. Something has changed between them. Which means he heard or saw something. Yet clearly, he doesn't want to talk about it.

"Okay, so what did you see then?" she pushes. "You knew about Sevin, didn't you?"

He winces and goes to walk away again. This time she grabs his arm and holds him to the spot.

"What did *you* see, Halo?" he asks, his voice even more bitter than the beautiful creatures circling the pool beside them. "When we left Treasure Island. What did you see?"

Her hand falls from his arm. He definitely already knew. She has no idea how, but he knew about Sevin.

"I saw Sevin," she whispers, dropping her gaze to his feet. "She's alive. That's what I just told you."

"Yet you kept it from me all this time," he says. "You tricked me into staying on the boat."

This has Halo's head snapping up. "That's not fair."

"You knew I'd go back if I saw Sevin," he says. "And you were too selfish to tell me."

Anger builds in her gut at the injustice of that accusation. "It wasn't like that. Sevin didn't want you to know. If she had, she'd never have faked her death in the first place. I did it for her, not for me. It hurt so much not to tell you."

She raises her face to look at him and sees his jaw fall open as he tries to take in what she's saying.

"I've always been honest with you," he says. "I thought we could trust each other. I could never keep something like that from you."

"I was put in an impossible position." She throws out her hands. "It was either betray you or betray Sevin. Your sister saved my life. I couldn't do it to her. She'd never have forgiven me if you gave up your place on the ship for her. It was what she wanted."

"And look how much better off my life is since I got on this ship," he snarls.

"I wasn't to know that." She crosses her arms. "We all thought this ship was our ticket to a better life. And that we'd be able to return home to bring our families with us."

"Do you still believe that?" he asks. "That we'll return for everyone else?"

She shakes her head, having realized long ago that this journey is a one-way ticket.

"I'll never see Sevin again," he says. "And it's all because of you."

She nods, too exhausted and her head in too much pain for her to summon the energy to argue. Especially when he's right.

"I should have told you," she says. "And I'm sorry. Really, I am. I wanted to tell you. There were so many times that I almost did."

"Then why didn't you?" His entire soul visibly breaks with the pain of his loss.

"Because of this." She points at his shaking hands. "Because I didn't want you to feel like this."

"She needs me," he almost whimpers. "I'm supposed to look after her."

Halo swallows. "She doesn't need you, Fyve. Not anymore. She's capable of so much more than you think she is. I wouldn't have tried to honor her by keeping her secret, if I didn't believe that."

He recoils at these words, but she knows they had to be said. The Sevin that Halo had known was clever and resourceful. She didn't need her older brother following her every move. She proved time and time again that she could take care of herself. If she'd wanted Fyve to stay, she wouldn't have gone to such lengths to make sure he didn't.

"She's just a little kid," Fyve says. "You don't know her like I do."

Tears sting Halo's eyes as she questions if she'd done the right thing. It's true that Fyve knows his sister so much better than she does. But is it also possible there's another side to her that he can't see? The fierce, independent young woman that Halo had witnessed during the Trials. It seems like whatever choice Halo made when she saw Sevin waving at her, was going to be wrong.

"I'm sorry," she says again, daring to reach out and put a hand on his arm. "I was always going to tell you. I think that's what Sevin wanted, too. That's why she made sure I saw her. Honestly, I was just doing what I thought was right. I never meant to hurt you."

"You did hurt me," he says, plainly.

"Can you forgive me?" she asks. "I really am very sorry."

He blinks once. Twice. Three times. "I don't know."

She nods. That's not the answer she wanted, but it's a start.

"You missed one heck of a Trial," she says, desperate to return the conversation to something that resembles normality.

He nods, not taking her bait by offering her a reply.

"You should have seen Justice." She smiles gently, aware she's rambling. "A tip for future...don't mess with that girl. She's tougher than she looks. Cloud, too."

Fyve doesn't give so much as a shell of a smile at her attempt at humor.

"Oh, and we killed Zake," she adds.

"What?" Fyve's eyes widen. Now she has his attention...

"Well, technically Justice killed him," she continues. "But he was trying to kill me at the time, so he totally deserved it."

Fyve shakes his head and she sees his protective instincts kick in. "I should never have left. I just thought—"

"No!" Halo presses a fingertip to his lips. "Don't do that. Let's not go back on what we should have done in the past. We all have so many regrets since getting on this ship. Let's concentrate on what we do from now on. I want to move forward."

He brings his hand to hers, and her heart sinks when he lifts it from his face and lets it fall.

"I love you, Fyve," she says.

He winces, seems to hesitate, then a shutter falls over his face. "We should return to our cabins." He steps away. "The next Trial is tomorrow. You have to rest."

"I've been resting all day," she complains, more interested in sorting things out with him than she is in closing her eyes. "I need to check on my dad. You go back if you want to."

His head shakes, almost as if it happens against his will. "I'll come with you."

"I thought you were mad with me." She furrows her brows.

"I *am* mad with you," he practically growls. "But that doesn't mean I'm going to let you get yourself killed."

She grins, yet just like with her declaration of love, he refuses to return her smile. If actions really do speak louder than words, she already has all she needs. He won't let her check on her dad alone. Which means that even if he's still furious with her, there's still something left in his heart that shows he cares.

Unless he's just being the protective Fyve she's fallen for…

A sharp stabbing pain slices through her brain, sending her hands flying to her temples. She hears a whimper climb out of her throat almost like someone else made the sound.

"Fyve," she gasps, unable to pretend the pain isn't a problem anymore. "It hurts."

"We need to get you back to your cabin." He goes to put a steadying arm around her, his first move to touch her since he found her here on the deck, but still, something stops him.

"No." She blinks at him through glassy eyes. "My dad. He needs me. I can do this."

"I'll check on him," he says firmly, letting his arm fall back to his side.

She takes her hands from her head, trying to steel herself against the pain. "I need to see him for myself. Surely, you of all people can understand that."

He lets out a sigh, and she knows he's thinking of Sevin. "Then we do it fast. Come on."

He surges forward, leading the way, not taking her hand as he normally would. She swears a silent vow to never keep anything from him ever again. No matter whose trust she has to betray. He's the most important person in her life.

She feels in her pocket for the piece of bread and slices of dried fruit she'd saved from the plate that had been left outside her cabin after the Trial. She'd eaten only what she needed, saving the rest for her father who needs it so much more. His body is damaged from the beating he took, even more than his broken mind. Food will help him heal. It's the one thing she can do for him right now.

Fyve winds his way through The Oasis and Halo follows. Her head hurts far too much to bring forward the map of the ship she's been building in her mind. They walk in silence, keeping their footsteps light and a few times Halo has to bite down on her lip as another wave of pain grips her by the temples. Fyve's words of resting in her cabin come back to her as she wishes to do exactly that. But first, she needs to see her father. Only then can she properly rest.

They reach the brig and Fyve opens the door.

"Elijah," he calls softly. "It's Fyve and Halo."

Halo pushes past him and blinks in the dim light, unable to find the familiar shape of the man who raised her. Hurrying to the bed, she runs her hands across the thin blanket as if she expects him to appear from its crumpled shape.

"Where have they taken him?" she gasps, like she expects Fyve to have an answer.

"Same place they took Dargo, maybe?" Fyve shrugs.

She shakes her head, the movement sending more waves of pain through her skull. "We need to go to the door. The wall. Or whatever it is now."

She knows she's not making a lot of sense but also that Fyve will understand exactly where she means. The place where Iva found Dargo's bracelet is the best place to start.

"Halo, you need to rest first." He urges her toward the door. "And you need to eat whatever food you saved for your dad."

They step out of the brig and blink in the brighter light that feels like fire behind her throbbing temples.

"I can't eat it, Fyve," she tells him. "He needs it."

"Will you eat it if we check out that door-wall-thing and can't get through?" he asks.

"Yes," she says feeling better immediately that she gets to look for her dad and that Fyve is so worried about her. It seems that his protective instincts are so much more powerful than his anger. *That* she can work with. It's the only bit of hope she has right now.

He walks down the corridor, once again not taking her hand, but she's not going to complain. He's here with her when only a short while ago, she'd thought there was a chance he might be dead. He still hasn't told her where he was or who he spoke to, but now's not the time to push him on that. All she can hope is that, with time, he'll tell her everything.

Just like she did. Surely, their relationship is stronger than this.

The Oasis feels like even more of a maze and by the time they reach the right spot, she's almost wondering if it is indeed the place she remembers. She looks around, squinting through her pain to inspect the wall. Even the dim light here feels like hot needles poking her eyeballs.

"We need to break a hole in it," she says, knocking on the panel. "It sounds like it could be hollow."

"Let's try this first." Fyve holds up a bracelet. Not a primitive one like Dargo's leather strap, but more like something made on another planet. "It has some kind of chip in it that can open doors. Maybe there's one of those square things hidden somewhere that will trigger it. They're normally beside the doors, but I can't see one here."

Halo steps back, biting down on her tongue to stop herself from asking him where he got such a thing. He's keeping a lot of secrets from her right now. Although, in fairness, the secret she'd kept from him had been worth a thousand of his. There must be a reason he's not telling her whatever it is that's going on with him. If only she knew what it was.

Fyve waves the bracelet methodically over the door, starting on the left and working his way to the right. With every one of his calculated movements, Halo's head thumps a little harder.

She leans against the wall behind her, sliding down until she's seated with her knees tucked up. Resting her head in her hands, she blocks out all light with the balls of her palms. It provides no relief from the pain, so she tries massaging her temples, but that only seems to make it worse.

"I've got it!" Fyve says.

Halo's head snaps up as the wall begins to slide. The sudden movement makes her dizzy, like her brain can't reconcile what's happening.

"Fyve," she groans as black spots cloud her vision.

Unwanted darkness takes hold, shattering her agony into a thousand pieces, each one of them tearing at her skull and she feels herself tipping sideways.

FYVE

$\mathcal{F}$yve only gets a brief glance at the expanse on the other side of the door before he has to catch Halo. He grabs hold of her a second before her head hits the hard floor, then quickly lowers her the rest of the way, cradling her protectively.

"Halo," he gasps. "Halo!"

All the anger and betrayal he'd been nursing evaporates as it's clear she's desperately unwell.

"Wake up, please!"

Her pale lashes don't move as her head lolls against his arm. He checks her pulse, finding the rapid flutter beneath the skin of her throat, then notes her short, gasping breaths. She may be unconscious, but her body's still in pain.

He looks around frantically, as if help is going to materialize. The corridor they came down is empty. The large space that's opened on the other side is just as empty. But in a far more ominous way.

The oval space is somehow cleaner, brighter. And surrounded by closed doors.

"We need to get out of here," he murmurs to Halo as if she can hear him.

With little choice, he slips one arm under her shoulders and another beneath her knees. They can't stay here. One of those screens in the room could be capturing their presence right now. The people Jiro's so terrified of could storm in any second.

As if it heard Fyve, a door to the immediate right begins to move. It slides silently open, seeming to constrict his chest tighter and tighter. His gaze is unblinking as he waits and watches. And decides.

Run. Or fight.

Whatever's necessary to keep Halo safe.

The figure that steps through has him stiffening in shock. At first, he almost doesn't recognize her. "Terra," he whispers.

The little girl isn't encased in her voluminous robes. Instead, she's wearing the same tunic and pants that Fyve and Halo have, the outfit making her look smaller. More fragile. Yet her bald head is wrapped in a colorful scarf, which humanizes her in a way Fyve hasn't seen.

She freezes the moment she sees them on the ground near the entrance to this secret section of the ship. She blinks. Sniffs. Then wipes her nose. The gestures are so childlike, so…human, that it takes Fyve a moment to realize she's been crying. Tears glisten on her cheeks, looking just as vulnerable as she does.

He has no idea whether or not she's a threat.

Fyve indicates to Halo. "She needs help. She's in a lot of pain."

Terra simply stares at him. Yet her eyes don't seem vacant. They seem undecided.

"Please. I don't know how to help her."

And the last words he spoke to Halo were angry, unforgiving ones. He has to make it right.

Terra frowns as her eyes dart to Halo. But she doesn't move.

"Please," Fyve begs, having no idea if this is going to help. He goes to stand, and the moment he moves, Terra flinches. She curls into herself, retreating a foot back into the room she exited.

It's Fyve's turn to still. She's scared. Judging from the way her hands tremble before they clasp the other, she's really scared.

Realizing she can't, or won't, help him, Fyve turns his attention back to Halo. She's still deathly pale. Still breathing as if agony has a hold of her lungs. He scoops her up, unsure of what to do next, but knowing he needs to get away from here.

He turns back to Terra, Halo in his arms. "Please don't tell them we were here."

Even as he makes this request, he wonders what he's doing. This girl can't speak. Except she nods, the movement subtle but undeniable.

Fyve blinks. She understood his request. And she agreed to it.

A soft moan from Halo has him jolting into action. He turns and walks as quickly as he can without jostling her too much. He's halfway down the corridor when he realizes he's left the door open. He spins around, surprised to find Terra framed by the rectangular space that's not supposed to exist, watching him. She swipes the bracelet on her wrist over a sensor and the door slides shut, cutting her off from view.

With no time to process what just happened, Fyve hurries back to his cabin. Inside, he carefully places Halo on his bed, then shuts the door, closing them off from the rest of The Oasis. Within moments, he's pacing. What does he do now? He has no idea how to help Halo. It's like she's slowly, excruciatingly, being claimed.

Kneeling beside her, he lifts the blankets a little higher, softly murmuring her name.

The moment he speaks, her eyes fly open. They widen as she

registers the pain she's in. "Fyve," she gasps, blindly reaching out. "It hurts."

He clasps her hand, his gut clenching. "Just your head?"

"Yes," she whimpers. "Even talking…it hurts so bad."

A baby's cry carries down the hall signaling Marvel or Miracle are awake and Halo arches her back as her face contorts. "Fyve." His name is a breathless gasp. "I lov—"

She collapses back onto the bed as she falls unconscious once more, the pain too much to bear.

"I love you, too," he chokes, wishing she could hear him but glad she can't. He remembers what the pain of these headaches was like at its peak. It consumed his mind with such totality that loss of consciousness was the only peace to be found.

Except Halo will wake up again, tortured by agony.

It's only the finality of death that will bring her peace.

Fyve jams his hand through his hair, silently cursing. He stills, wincing, as his fingers rake over the cut at his temple. But as the sharp pain quickly fades, he doesn't move.

The cut.

The headache was gone after he woke up in the infirmary. With this wound on the side of his head. The one Jiro claimed was because Zake struck him there, even though Fyve was sure it was the other side.

That is, if he's going to believe Jiro…

Fyve leans forward, his fingers gently running over Halo's temples. He almost draws back when he feels a faint ridge on the right-hand side. The same side his cut is on. He touches his own again, feeling nothing beneath the cut less than an inch long. Yet there's been no headaches since. No voices in his head.

Trying to be as gentle as possible, he returns to probing Halo's temple, quickly discovering the bump is a small rectangle. A shape that shouldn't exist inside her. A man-made shape.

Fyve retracts his hand as he tries to understand what this

means. And how he can fix it. If there was something inside his head, and taking it out cured him, he has to do the same for Halo...

He shoots to his feet, his stomach rebelling at the thought. He wouldn't even know how to!

Before the thought is finished, he feels the knife sitting in his pocket. His stomach downright revolts. The thought of what he has to do makes him physically ill.

But what choice does he have? If his hunch is right, whatever's inside Halo's head is killing her, just like it was him.

Gritting his teeth, Fyve withdraws the knife and stares at the sharp edge. The pointed tip. All it will take is a small cut and he'll know. If he's right, Halo's pain will disappear.

If he's wrong, he'll slice her open and risk infection for nothing.

One glance at her still form, the fluttering pulse at her throat evident even from here, and his decision is made. He has to do this before she regains consciousness again.

Moving quickly, he kneels beside her and once more feels for the small rectangle just beneath the skin of her temple. His throat tightens as a ball of bile climbs up, and he swallows. Steady mind. Steady hands. That's what he needs right now.

He pushes aside Halo's blonde strands, tucking some behind her ear, and spreading the rest over the pillow. He desperately hopes she doesn't wake up during this. With a fortifying breath he does what needs to be done.

The knife tip pierces her skin and a bead of blood instantly appears, tugging at his gut. One sharp movement and the cut grows, crimson blood ballooning up and running into Halo's hair.

Bringing with it a smooth, rectangular piece of metal.

Fyve carefully picks it up, staring at it in shock. "A chip," he murmurs.

Snapping himself out of his dismay, he quickly rushes to the bathroom and grabs the towels in there. Returning, he folds one over and presses the wad against Halo's temple as he lets out a breath. It's done. And she didn't wake up.

Thank Terra for small mercies.

He frowns as the thought filters through his mind. He's spent all his life thanking Terra for the small blessings in his life. He'd assumed, like everyone else on Treasure Island, that she was looking over them, waiting for them to do right by her so she could reward it just as much as punish the transgressions.

The image of the little girl in the pale tunic and bright scarf quickly follows. The chip that just came out of Halo's head rests heavily in his palm.

Terra isn't real.

And she never has been.

Fyve carefully pulls back the towel, relieved to see that the bleeding has already stopped. Refolding it, he presses it back, wadding it up so it stays in place. He leans down to brush a soft kiss on her forehead. The worst is over for Halo.

Her face is calm. Peaceful. Free of the overwhelming pain she couldn't escape.

Gripping the alien piece of metal that Jiro must've also removed from his own head, Fyve slips out of his cabin and strides down the corridor. He memorized the way back to the infirmary because he wanted to be able to visit Sevin again. But now, following the twists of turns and series of stairs is about something completely different.

It's time for him to get some answers.

The blank wall that he reaches looks exactly like the one he and Halo visited not long ago. Innocuous. Like a dead end. Yet nothing on The Oasis has been what it seemed. It's always hidden secrets. Sinister ones. Fyve swipes the chip Jiro gave him without hesitation. Seeing Halo almost die has burned away any fear or uncertainty. He won't accept deflection or half-answers.

They need to know what's happening on The Oasis. And why.

Fyve discovers he's not alone in the infirmary the moment he enters, and it's not Jiro who's there. It's Elijah.

Halo's father is lying in the same bed Fyve woke up in. Although the bruises have faded and the streaks of blood have gone, he looks very much like a broken man. The great leader of Treasure Island is frail, the bed more of a presence than he is. He wakes up as the door behind Fyve closes even though it was almost silent. He's just as hyper-vigilant as the teens on this ship.

"What are you doing here, Fyve?" he asks, frowning. "How did you know it's even here?"

"I'm here to talk to Jiro," he growls, deciding to answer the first question.

To his surprise, Elijah relaxes back into the bed as if that makes sense. "He's gone and he won't be back. He's preparing for the final Trial."

Cursing, Fyve spins on his heel. He'll go looking for Jiro if he has to. He'll go back to that secret space with all the doors. At least he knows Elijah's being taken care of. Bringing Halo back some good news will be nice alongside whatever else he finds. Although he'll have to tell her that her father is part of this. Elijah knows who Jiro is.

"Is Halo okay?" Elijah asks behind him.

Fyve turns back, disgusted that Elijah is asking about his daughter as if he cares, and yet allowed her to come on The Oasis in the first place. "She almost died," he says, knowing he's being harsh, but the last few hours have been harsh. He holds up the tiny chip. "I had to cut this out of her head."

He's once again surprised as Elijah looks at the chip as if he recognizes it. In fact, he winces, opens his mouth to speak, then looks away.

Fyve stalks forward. "You know what this is, don't you?"

Elijah clamps his lips shut.

"Tell me, Elijah. Halo deserves to know what someone did to her body."

The mention of his daughter has Elijah turning back, his eyes a strange mix of defiance and regret. "I didn't do it alone. Your mother was also a part of this."

Fyve has to stop himself from reeling back. "My mother?"

"Yes," Elijah spits. "Dee knew everything."

"What...what are you talking about?"

Elijah glares at the chip. "Every child on Treasure Island has one of those in their head." His gaze slips away. "I inserted them not long after they were born."

Because he would visit every baby, ensuring he remembered their names. "You..." Fyve can't even voice the blow that knowledge is. "And my mother knew?" he chokes.

"She did more than that," Elijah says. "She initiated some of the claimings."

This time Fyve steps back, unable to suppress the horror that slams through him. His mother knew the truth about Terra. Not only that, she killed in Terra's name. "But...she was claimed herself."

"Something you shouldn't forget, Fyve. It's what I've been trying to tell you. She did everything Terra asked of her, and yet Terra showed no mercy the moment she disobeyed." Elijah grips the sheets, his face tightening. "No one is safe."

Fyve curls his lip. "That's why you keep obeying her like the good servant you are? Because you're scared?" He shakes his head in disgust. "No matter what it means for your daughter? She almost died!"

Elijah flinches, then quickly scowls. "You have no idea what we're up against. I'm doing everything I can to keep her safe!"

Still shaking his head, Fyve turns away. His stomach is back to churning in the same way it did when he was about to slice Halo's skin open. "How many times have you had to tell yourself that to believe it?" he spits over his shoulder. "Because just like everything else, it's a lie."

Fyve leaves the infirmary, conscious he has some more answers, yet his world is again turned upside down. His mother was a part of this. Is that why she disappeared so often? Because it was too hard for her to be on Treasure Island, even though her children were there?

Staggering, he finds himself back at his cabin rather than the secret wall, but he doesn't fight it. He feels unbalanced. Unsteady.

And Halo's the only one who can fix that.

He falls to his knees beside the bed, taking her hand in his. "I'm so sorry," he whispers as he rests his forehead against their interlinked fingers.

"No, I'm sorry."

He looks up, finding Halo blinking groggily at him. The color has returned to her cheeks, her breath is even and regular. It means when she smiles softly, it's one of the most beautiful things he's ever seen.

"Halo," he breathes, saying her name like a prayer. "I understand why you kept the truth from me. I shouldn't have been angry." Not when she's the only one who can turn his world the right way up.

She reaches out with her other hand to brush his cheek. "You love hard, Fyve. It's one of the things that had me falling so fast for you."

He leans into her touch, feeling the caress somewhere deep in his chest. "And I love your remarkable strength and your amazing mind and your generous heart."

Halo's smile grows, blossoming across her face like a breathtaking dawn. "See? You don't love in halves. Sevin knew you'd never be able to leave her."

For the first time since he saw his sister on the screen, Fyve can't wait to tell someone. Halo would want to know Sevin's okay just as much as he did. "In the same way I'll never leave you," he murmurs huskily.

Their kiss is soft. Tender. A reconnection, an affirmation of what they'd almost lost. Of what was too strong for even Terra to destroy.

Halo pulls back, brushing her fingers over the cut at her temple. "The pain's gone."

"And it won't be coming back," Fyve promises.

She nods, relief relaxing her face. "Lie with me," she murmurs sleepily.

He climbs into bed and pulls her into his arms. He'll tell her what he's learned in the morning. He'll tell her everything. About Jiro. The cameras. Terra in the secret rooms.

But right now, they both need their rest.

Tomorrow they'll be facing the final Trial united. No secrets between them.

And they'll find out if that's enough.

HALO

*H*alo stirs, taking a few moments to realize she's in Fyve's cabin. Muddled memories of the night before rush back to her in small snatches. They'd been looking for her father and her head had felt like it was going to split in two. Then she was being carried, although at the time she'd thought she was floating through space. Then Fyve had been there, his face breaking through the darkness in intervals, telling her he loved her.

He's curled around her now with his chest pressed to her back, evidence that she hadn't dreamed it. He forgave the unforgivable. He said he understood why she hadn't told him about Sevin. That it didn't matter, when of course, it matters. A lot.

She snuggles into his warmth and he wakes, his hold on her tightening as he keeps her pressed to his chest.

"How are you?" he asks, his breath tickling her ear.

"I'm fine," she says, realizing it's true. "My headache has completely gone."

She puts a hand to her temple where there's a slight sting. But this pain is mild and on the surface, rather than buried deep inside her skull.

"Don't touch it." Fyve props himself up on his elbow to inspect the side of her head. "Let it heal."

"Let what heal?" she asks. "What happened?"

He lets out a sigh. "So much happened."

Halo turns over so she can look at him. "Can you start with what happened to my head?"

He winces. "I cut it open."

This has Halo sitting up. She braces herself for the agony the sudden movement will have in her head, but...nothing.

"What are you?" she asks, her hand going back to her wound. "A brain surgeon?"

"I didn't go near your brain!" He sits up beside her and gently removes her hand from her temple. "You had a chip inside your head. I had to get it out before it killed you."

"A chip?" She furrows her brow, not understanding. "Like the thing you use to open doors?"

He nods as he reaches over to the small table beside the bed and picks up a tiny rectangular shaped object and passes it to her. "We all have one. Well, not you or me anymore, but everyone else."

"How did it get there?" she asks, turning it over in her hand. This isn't making any sense. She's sure she'd remember if someone put this thing in her head.

"I'm still figuring it all out," he says. "But it looks like your dad might have put it there. My mom played a part in it, too, although I'm not sure what. We've had them since we were babies."

"Why?" She goes to touch her temple again, only for Fyve to catch her hand and bring it to his lips.

"I don't know," he says. "It has something to do with the claimings. There must be a way for the chip to detonate."

Images of people dropping to their knees with blood pouring from their eyes and nose come racing into Halo's mind. Could a tiny chip really do that? And could her father really have been responsible for putting it there? It puts her at a loss for words.

"I think it's how Terra's been talking to us," he says. "I haven't heard any messages since mine was removed."

"Who took yours out?" she asks. "Was it my father?"

Fyve shakes his head, but before he can tell her anything else, Iva bursts into Fyve's cabin.

"There you are," she exclaims. She steps out of the room and calls down the corridor. "I found her!"

Halo tucks the chip in her pocket and swings her legs out of Fyve's bed.

Coda and Justice appear moments later, along with Cloud who's carrying the twins in their basket.

"Fyve!" says Justice. "You're...alive."

"Of course," he says, getting to his feet.

"We could have used your help in the Trial." Justice rolls her eyes.

"It wasn't his fault," says Halo, even though she still has no idea where he'd disappeared to. But she does know if he could have found his way back to her during the Trial, he would have.

"We have to go," says Iva, avoiding looking at either Halo or Fyve. It must be hard for her to witness the reunion that she herself is still hoping to have. "Didn't you hear Terra's message? The final Trial is about to begin."

"No," says Halo, fear building deep inside her at the thought of another Trial so soon. "We missed that one."

"We thought you'd disappeared," says Cloud, smiling at Halo, even though she must be just as scared as she is. "I'm so glad you're okay. Both of you."

"Come on," says Justice, hobbling away on her crutches, the one with the sharp tip wrapped back up with a cloth. "We're late."

"You two should eat something," says Coda, pointing at the

plate on the shelf outside Fyve's room, as she begins to follow Justice. "You'll need your strength."

Fyve takes his plate and gives it to Halo. "Eat this. Quickly. I'll go and get yours."

"We'll catch up," Halo tells Cloud and Iva, who nod before hurrying away.

Halo sets down the plate and takes the opportunity to go to the bathroom to use that strange thing she's learned is called a toilet, and to smooth down her hair. She peers at a section of the mirror that survived being broken in the last Trial. The cut on her temple is weeping a little, but it's clean and should hopefully heal without trouble. Could a chip really have been in there without her knowing? She combs down her hair to cover it, not wanting to attract any unwanted attention.

"Halo!" Fyve calls.

She steps out and sees him chewing on a piece of bread.

"You didn't eat," he says, picking up the plate and thrusting it at her. "Come on. You barely ate yesterday either."

Realizing she's actually starving, Halo scoops up a portion of food with her fingers. Coda is right. They need their strength. This Trial could have them doing just about anything. She'll be of no use to anyone if she faints before it even starts.

"Use the bread as your plate," says Fyve. "We'll have to eat while we walk."

Following his lead, Halo piles the bread with food and they scurry off down the corridor. Without any way of hearing what Terra has to say, they're not sure just how late they really are.

"How will we know what the Trial is about?" asks Halo, swallowing the last of her food. "If we can't hear Terra, I mean."

Fyve slips his hand into hers and she tries to focus on his comfort rather than the way her food seems to have turned into a lead weight. Without instructions, this Trial is going to be even more dangerous than any other they've faced.

"We'll be okay," he tells her. "I'm not going to let anything bad happen to you."

"It's not me I'm worried about." She squeezes his hand. "It's all of us. Cloud and the babies. Justice. Iva. Coda. You..."

Before he opens the door to the deck, he pulls her into a hug and brushes his lips across hers.

"We'll be okay," he says again. "We have each other."

She melts into his touch, relieved to have both his love and his forgiveness.

The door to the deck swings open and a tide of teens rushes toward them, pushing them back down the stairs. They're too late. Whatever it was that Terra had to tell them, they've missed it. The disadvantage they had just got even bigger. The Trial has begun and they have absolutely no idea what they're supposed to do.

"What's happening?" Halo asks the girl closest to her.

The girl looks at her like she's her enemy, refusing to answer as she brushes past.

Halo and Fyve are caught up in the swell, spilling into the corridor where they'd just come from.

"Justice!" Fyve calls over the crowd, scanning the faces. "Iva!"

"They're over there." Halo tugs on his arm, pointing to the very back of the crowd.

Pressing themselves against the wall, they wait as the rest of the teens head for their cabins. Once the corridor is mostly clear, they rush to Justice, Iva, Cloud and Coda.

"What's going on?" Fyve asks. "What did she say?"

"We have to hurry back to our cabins," says Cloud, seeming to be struggling with the weight of the basket.

"Anyone not in their cabins before the next announcement will be eliminated," says Iva, not pausing her steps. "Come on. Hurry!"

Halo glances at Fyve in panic. This is the worst-case

scenario. How are they going to know what the next announcement says if they're in their individual cabins?

"Don't wait for me!" Justice says, hobbling along behind Coda. "Go to your cabins. Quickly."

Fyve loops an arm around Justice and helps her to her cabin, while Halo helps Cloud carry the basket.

"Good luck," Cloud says, her eyes spilling over with tears as she stands at her doorway.

Ajax appears beside Halo, pushing his way past her into what used to be his cabin. Cloud steps inside to give him room.

"What are you doing?" Halo asks.

"Terra said we have to be in our own cabins." He begins sliding the door as he speaks. "This was the one I was assigned."

Halo sticks her arm through the gap in the door, wincing as Ajax attempts to close it.

"Get to your cabin!" he says, tilting his head toward the next door. "You heard Terra. I'm not helping you pass another Trial."

"I didn't hear Terra," Halo says, panic climbing up her throat. "I can't hear her anymore."

He scrunches up his face. "How can you not hear her? She spoke to everyone."

"You have to help me," Halo pleads. "What did she say?"

"To wait in our cabins." He sighs. "Now get to yours before you get eliminated. Hurry!"

Halo is frozen. This whole thing feels so hopeless. She can't possibly pass a Trial when she can't hear the instructions.

Fyve grabs Halo by the waist and hauls her away from the door, dragging her to her cabin.

"You can't get eliminated now," he says, as he pushes her gently inside her door and steps outside. "I need you."

"Go," says Halo, knowing she doesn't have the time to say all the words that need to be said. "Go."

Fyve turns and runs down the corridor, leaving Halo alone in her cabin with nothing but silence for company. She doesn't even know if they made it back in time. This Trial could already be over.

The muffled sound of arguing from the cabin next door breaks through the wall.

"Good for you, Cloud," Halo mutters. It's about time she stood up to Ajax. It's just a shame it took him completely abandoning her for that to happen.

Halo goes to the bathroom to check on the cut on her forehead to see how it's healing. A drop of blood has seeped from it, and she dabs at it with the corner of a cloth. Then the sound of sobbing fills the room.

"Cloud?" she says, loudly, realizing she must be in her own bathroom next door. "Is that you?"

"Halo?" says Cloud, her voice floating through the vent in the ceiling. "Are you okay?"

"I'm fine," she lies. "Are you okay?"

"I'm fine," Cloud lies in return.

"Has Terra spoken to us again?" Halo projects her voice in the direction of the vent.

"Yes," says Cloud, sniffing. "We have to do the next Trial alone. She's going to call us one-by-one to go to the deck."

Halo leans against the wall and groans. How will she know when Terra calls her?

There's a long pause.

"Halo," Cloud whimpers. "She just called me. I have to go."

"You'll be okay," Halo says, fighting back tears. "I'll see you when this is over."

"I love you, Halo," Cloud says before there's the sound of a door sliding open as she leaves the bathroom.

"I love you, too," Halo whispers back, knowing Cloud can't hear. So many things have changed since she stepped foot on this ship, and most of them for the worse. But her relationship with Cloud has been one of the positives. They'd never seen eye-to-eye back on Treasure Island. Cloud had been so devout.

So wrapped up in her love for both Terra and Ajax. She'd irritated Halo, who'd kept herself at a distance. And yet now Cloud's one of the people she respects most.

Going to her bed, Halo flops down. If Cloud has just been called, then it's not Halo's turn yet. At the very least, she doesn't have to worry about being claimed now that Fyve has removed the chip from inside her head. If Terra wants to kill her, she'll have to find another way. Which might give her the opportunity to fight back.

Thoughts of everything Fyve told her swirl inside her mind. Could her father really have been responsible for inserting the chips? She has to admit it's possible. He visits every baby when they're born, which would give him the opportunity. And if he didn't realize what he was doing was wrong, he could justify it. Terra would have fed him a story to make him believe it was necessary. No matter what Halo hears about her father, she just can't see him as a bad person. There's good in his heart. He was just misguided in much the same way as Cloud was.

After staring at the ceiling for several minutes, Halo reaches into her pocket. She finds the tiny chip Fyve had said he removed from her head and rests it in her palm. It's hard to believe something artificial like this had sat beneath her skin for such a long time. And that it had come so close to killing her. Even though having it removed has put her at risk in this Trial, she's so glad it's no longer in her body.

A faint pulse of energy emanates from the chip. It's so faint that she wonders if she imagined it. Holding still, she concentrates on the chip and feels it again. It's not quite a buzzing. Not quite a vibration. Just a very small movement that she would miss if she weren't concentrating on it.

Terra must be talking to her. Either that or the chip is somehow reacting to being outside her skull.

Cloud has only been gone for maybe ten minutes or so. Is

that long enough for her to complete whatever this Trial is and for Halo to be called?

Maybe, she decides, getting to her feet and tucking the chip back in her pocket. It's a risk she's going to have to take. Because turning up when she wasn't called has got to be less catastrophic than staying in her cabin when Terra has asked for her.

Halo slides open her cabin door and heads for the stairwell. She takes the stairs cautiously, aware her heart is racing and her breath is coming in short gasps. The door to the deck opens and Cloud walks in, the twins' basket held so tightly in her hand that her knuckles are white.

"What happened?" Halo asks, rushing to the door.

"I'm not allowed to tell you," Cloud says. "But you'll be okay. If I got through, then so will you."

Halo breaks into a smile as she realizes Miracle and Marvel are now safe. "You passed."

Cloud nods, although whatever it was that she had to do has clearly shaken her up. She's not in the mood to celebrate her success just yet.

"Go," says Cloud. "Don't keep her waiting."

Halo gives her a quick kiss on the cheek and hurries out onto the deck. Terra is standing off to one side and it's only when Halo gets closer that she sees part of the railing has been removed and a long wooden plank has been positioned, leading directly off the edge of the ship.

Terra motions for Halo to approach. While she's relieved she'd correctly guessed that she'd been called to participate in the Trial, she doesn't like what she's seeing one little bit. But if Cloud made it through, then surely, she can, too. She has to. If not for herself, then for Fyve.

It's windy on the deck and the ship tilts rhythmically as it slices through the water. Halo concentrates on breathing deeply, doing her best to feed her cells with oxygen and reduce the shaking of her hands and legs.

Terra tilts her head, raising her brow slightly in a question.

"I can't hear you," Halo says, deciding she has nothing to lose. "I bumped my head and now I can't hear what you're saying."

Terra stares at the cut on the side of Halo's head, and while her expression is neutral, there's something brewing in her eyes. Curiosity? Pity? Concern?

Holding out a steady hand, Terra points to Halo and then the plank.

"You want me to walk out on that thing?" Halo asks on a gasp. "What if I fall off?"

She leans over the railing. If the sheer height of the fall isn't enough to kill her, the leatherskins that are following in the ship's wake are sure to. And it's not like there are any tropical islands or other vessels that could rescue her before the acid water eats away her flesh. No matter what happens, she can't fall.

Terra remains pointing at the plank.

"What happens if I refuse?" Halo asks.

Terra's eyes flare in what can only be described as shock or fear, and Halo decides that the consequences of not walking the plank must be far worse than giving it a shot. Reminding herself that Cloud must have managed to do exactly that, while carrying her twins in the basket, she decides she can do it.

"Okay, okay." Halo holds up her shaking hands and steps up to the plank. It's wide enough for her to comfortably place her foot, but not enough for her to position two feet side-by-side. Thankfully it feels sturdy enough and as long as a big wave doesn't hit, she should be able to get out to the end.

Deciding the best approach is to get this over with quickly, Halo looks straight ahead and takes a few steps, feeling with each foot before putting her weight on it just in case she's misjudged how quickly she'll reach the end.

How in sweet Terra did Cloud manage this while carrying a basket? Then again, there's nothing Cloud wouldn't do to ensure the safety of her children.

She takes a few more steps, then hears a splash in the water below. Making the mistake of looking down, she sees a giant leatherskin leaping from the water with its jaws snapping. She's high enough up to be safe. But only just.

Her stomach contracts and the food she'd only just eaten threatens to make another appearance. This causes her to wobble and her hands fly out as she tries to steady herself.

Looking back up, she imagines Fyve is standing at the end of the plank, beckoning her. She focuses on this image and walks forward, reaching the end and slowly spinning to face Terra again.

Terra locks eyes with her, no doubt issuing her with instructions she can't hear.

"What happens now?" she calls out. "Please don't tell me you want me to jump!"

Terra moves her head the tiniest amount from left to right. It's a bit like the pulse in the chip—if Halo hadn't been watching for it, she wouldn't have noticed. Is she telling Halo she's allowed to just walk straight back?

Not liking any other possible option, Halo keeps her eyes on Terra and walks forward. She moves quickly, and as the ship begins to rear up on a wave, her steps turn into a leap and she flings herself back onto the safety of the deck. Collapsing to her back, she pants for breath, hardly daring to believe she survived, and hoping desperately she passed.

Terra stands over her, blinking. Halo tries to see the young girl underneath the robes, and once again she's reminded of Sevin. Her heart aches with how much she misses that girl.

"Please tell me I passed," Halo pants, as she hauls herself to her feet. "I know you're a regular girl just like me. I know you're a human with thoughts and feelings and wishes for your future. I don't know who's making you do all this, but I want to help you. First, though, I need you to help me. Please, Terra, tell me… did I pass?"

Terra glances to her left then shifts so that she has her back to the ship's structure. Pulling her hood over her face a little more, she gives Halo a small nod.

But it's not the nod that has Halo gasping in shock—it's what accompanies it.

Terra gives Halo the widest, sweetest, world's most beautiful smile.

"You passed," she whispers. "Go back to your cabin and wait."

FYVE

*F*yve paces in his cabin, grinding his teeth in frustration that it's only three steps before he has to turn and stalk over the tiny distance he just covered. How's Halo? What's the Trial going to ask of them this time?

And if she can't hear Terra either, then how will she know she's being called?

He's heard people walk past on their way to the deck. A couple came back, sobbing. He swears some haven't returned at all. He has no idea what that's supposed to mean.

The need to yank open his door and find out is strong. The need to go to Halo is overwhelming. He's had enough of playing by these arbitrary rules. He's had enough of waiting to learn if he's going to live or die.

He pauses, listening hard. He's not sure which is more gut-wrenching. The crying and the stumbling as someone returns.

Or the silence when they don't.

At least thirty teens have gone up to the deck, and there are more on the floors below. It's possible most have already endured the Trial. Which means he's almost last.

Or has he been called, and he didn't know because his chip has been removed?

Which means he's already defied Terra.

Fyve brushes his temple, the next thought blazing through him. Terra can't claim him. Whatever or whoever she is can no longer kill him with a glance. She's no longer in his head, in more ways than one.

He reaches out for the door with a fierce frown. No more waiting. No more letting someone else decide where he goes or when. He needs to see if Halo's okay.

They're stronger together. Now that he's realized that, it's time to honor it.

"Fyve." Jiro's hushed voice comes through the mesh in the ceiling above him. "It's your turn."

The frown deepens. "For what?"

"The final Trial," Jiro says, sounding confused that it's not obvious. "I know you can't hear Terra's commands anymore."

Which confirms that Jiro knew what he was doing when he removed Fyve's chip.

"So, I'm letting you know," Jiro continues. "You need to go up on deck. There, Terra will point to a plank."

"A plank?" Fyve asks. "What do you mean, a plank?"

"It's not as bad as it sounds. You're expected to walk to the end of the plank, turn around and come back. That's it. Your final Trial will be over."

Fyve shakes his head. "That's what you're asking us to do? As some twisted show of faith in Terra?"

"You'll be safe, I promise," Jiro assures. "You know I'll look after you."

"What about Halo?" Fyve's hand closes around the handle of his door, clenching it tightly.

"She's fine," Jiro huffs impatiently. "You really need to get over that girl."

That has Fyve stiffening. Jiro has made it very clear that he'll look out for Fyve and no one else. Why is that?

As the question forms, he realizes it doesn't matter. He's not playing this game anymore.

He takes a step back from the door, gazes up at the mesh, and speaks one word. "No."

There's a pause. "What?"

"You heard me," Fyve growls. "Take your plank and shove it up your—"

"Now isn't the time to rebel, Fyve," Jiro hisses as if he's working to keep his voice under control. "You have to get up there. Now!"

Except Fyve doesn't move, and he knows Jiro can see him. He even crosses his arms for good measure.

"Please, Fyve." This time, Jiro's voice is quiet. Pleading. "This is the last Trial. All you have to do is what you're told and this will be all over."

"Will it, Jiro? Will I finally learn what's happening on this ship?"

There's another pause. "Yes. I'll tell you everything." The resignation in Jiro's voice is unmistakable. "After the Trial, you'll know the truth."

Fyve has the door open in a blink. He strides down the corridor, his head held high, his shoulders back. In a complete turn around, he's actually looking forward to this Trial.

The truth is waiting for him at the end of it.

There's a briny, sulfurous breeze up on the deck and he draws it deeply into his lungs as he scans the space. Terra is standing off to one side, a part of the railing missing beyond her. Jiro was telling the truth. Fyve's expected to walk off the edge of The Oasis.

The ship bobs gently, the rhythm now so familiar he barely notices it as he continues forward. The plank comes into view, narrower and longer than he expected. He glances over his shoulder at the young girl who calls herself Terra.

"Is this what you really want?" he asks her. "For me to risk my life to prove that you have total control over me?"

But she's unmoving. Emotionless. The whisper of humanity he saw in the secret space with all the doors is gone. She simply points to the plank, her gaze now fastened on the horizon, as if she's not even here anymore.

The breeze whips Fyve's hair back as he focuses back on the plank. The end hovers over the red ocean, piercing nothing but air. A part of him considers refusing. Whoever Jiro's so scared of will have to hunt him down to kill him.

But the promise of the truth is too strong a draw.

He has to know.

Once more straightening his shoulders, Fyve places a foot on the plank. Jiro promised he'd be safe, and he's proven that over and over. The Trial with the plates of food. Ensuring he had weapons to protect himself. Saving him from Zake. Then removing the chip. Jiro has gone to lengths to ensure Fyve stays alive.

It will be the same in this Trial.

The narrow wood isn't wide enough to put two feet side by side, so Fyve takes a cautious step forward. Behind him, he wonders if Terra's even watching. Isn't this all about her? About proving their faith?

Although that's not why he's here. There's a prize dangling at the end of this ridiculous, treacherous task.

Once he makes it to the end of the plank and back.

Fyve takes another cautious step, feeling with his toes to make sure he's stepping onto solid wood as he keeps his gaze on the horizon. For the next step, he decides to look down. He's never been worried by heights, and he can't afford to slip now. Not when he's so close.

Not when he has Halo.

One glance down and Fyve freezes. Denial has him shaking his head, his eyes wide. "I can't be..." he whispers.

But the refusal is quickly razed away by the reality of what he's seeing. Blood. An arm. Leatherskins thrashing about, turning the ocean into a cauldron of death.

Horror clenches Fyve's gut like a vice. Others have fallen.

All the ones who never returned to their cabin.

A mottled gray-black fin slices through the water that's sickly shades of red. One surges forward and the arm that was floating on the bloody surface disappears into its gaping mouth. It dives, taking the morsel to be consumed down in the depths. The others circle, creating a gentle whirlpool of human blood.

Throughout it all, the leatherskins are silent. Ominous.

Waiting.

Fyve looks back at Terra. "What have you done?" he gasps.

She flinches. Tucks her hands deeper into her sleeves. And says nothing.

Horrified at the painful, awful death his peers have been subjected to, Fyve turns back to look at the end of the plank. All he needs to do is make it there and back. Slow, steady steps.

Then he finds a way to end this.

One step, then another, and he's more than half way. Fyve's heart thuds hard against his ribs, almost making him light-headed. He blinks rapidly, tearing his gaze from the grizzly sight below.

Slow. Steady. Steps.

He's so hyper-focused on what he has to do that he swears he feels the plank wobble. A bead of sweat zigzags down his temple, instantly cooling in the soft breeze. That must be what he felt. The breeze tugging at his clothes.

Fyve reaches the end of the plank and he seamlessly turns and begins the journey back to safety. The plank shudders and he gasps as he looks down. There's nothing but air in the space between him and the leatherskins below. He must've imagined it.

The next shudder ripples right up his body, pulsing fear through his veins. He glances at Terra and the sunlight glints off the single tear resting on her cheek. She knows what's coming next.

And she's already grieving his death.

The other teens didn't slip or fall. They were shaken off the plank. They were murdered.

The next shake has Fyve wobbling. He throws his arms out to steady himself, his toes curling in as if they can grip the smooth wood. There's another shudder, even bigger than the last. It freezes Fyve's blood. It sends his pulse hurtling into overdrive.

He has to get off.

Before the next thought, he's running, trying to cover the plank with as few strides as possible.

The plank shifts again, wobbling from side to side, shifting the path that will take him to safety. As Fyve's foot comes down to take the next stride, it glances off the edge of the timber. Slips into nothingness.

And then he's falling.

He cries out as he crashes into the plank, bounces slightly, then honors gravity once more. He throws his arms out desperately, clamping them closed the moment they feel something hard. His breath rasping through his tight throat, he grips the plank and holds on.

It shudders, like a beast trying to shake him, but he tightens his legs along with his arms. The next shake jars him yet doesn't loosen his hold. He's wrapped around the plank like his life depends on it.

Because it does.

Drawing in sharp breaths, he takes in the remaining distance he needs to cover. Several feet extend between him and the edge of The Oasis. The moment the next round of shakes are over, Fyve shuffles forward. Almost crab-like, he slips along the length of the plank, still keeping a tight hold with his arms and legs. The rough wood scrapes his biceps and thighs, but he almost welcomes the pain. It means he's not staying still, waiting to be thrown off. He pulls himself along a few inches before he's forced to stop because the plank is moving once more.

Fyve presses the side of his face into the wood as it wobbles from side to side and convulses up and down. And it goes for endless seconds. His arms are aching by the time it finishes and he realizes he doesn't have much longer.

The shakes are getting harder. More protracted.

Someone wants him off this plank.

Scooting forward, he pants as he tries to move as quickly as he can considering he can't loosen his hold. There's a splash somewhere beneath him and he's glad he can't see below. He already knows what's waiting for him if he lets go. He doesn't need to see the small, predatory eyes or the large, knife-like teeth.

He covers almost half the distance before the next shake shudders through the plank, and therefore him. This time he closes his eyes, thinking of Halo. Sevin. Coal. Even his mother.

Each one of them a reason for him to live.

It stops after what feels like a lifetime and Fyve resumes the gripping shuffle forward. He can see the edge of the ship, the railing to his right and left, the solid floor that he always took for granted.

When the plank shudders again almost instantly, he cries out in frustration. Then he realizes the shudder came from behind him. It didn't originate from the base of the plank joined to The Oasis.

He risks letting go enough to look around the plank, a scream of terror lodging in his constricted throat.

A leatherskin is powering toward him, its body out of the water at an impossible height, its mouth open to reveal rows upon rows of deadly teeth. Fyve instinctively kicks at it and his foot connects with its blunt snout. The beast barely changes trajectory, but it's enough for its mouth to clamp shut. The monstrous shark lands back in the water with a splash.

Knowing he won't be so lucky the next time around, Fyve remembers the knife in his pocket. It's the only way he can protect himself. But if he lets go of the plank, he'll fall with the next round of rattles.

As if on cue, the shaking begins again. Fyve clamps his arms back around the wood, no longer able to see when the leatherskin leaps again, ravenous to continue its human feast. Instead, he lifts his head enough to look at the base of the plank. At the point he needs to reach to escape this hell.

It means he sees when a line appears along the width of the plank, just past the edge of the ship. A straight slice that widens as the plank jolts down an inch.

"No!" Fyve screams.

A release mechanism has been triggered. The plank's dropping.

And so is Fyve.

Air rushes past him as the plank swings in a long arc, taking him with it. He has seconds before it slams into the side of The Oasis, knocking him off and throwing him to the waiting leatherskins below.

Crying out, he simultaneously releases his hold and yanks the knife out of his pocket. Whipping his arm up, he slams the blade into the wood at the same moment the plank crashes into the white wall of The Oasis. Fyve's body collides with the plank, thrusting the air out of his lungs and cutting off his shout. The knife impales the plank then gouges a deep line in the wood as his weight drags him down. He slides several inches, gasping and praying, before it stops.

He hangs, suspended from the one hand gripping the knife, his legs wheeling through thin air. But he's alive. He's not in the water, becoming another tortured victim of these brutal Trials.

Breathing hard, Fyve looks up. The edge of the ship is half a body length away. If the knife had scraped down any further, he probably wouldn't be able to reach. "Thank Terra," he whispers, not even caring that he's praying to a deity he's lost all faith in.

Conscious he doesn't have long before his hand, the single point of contact keeping him out of the water, tires from the strain of holding his weight, Fyve takes in a steadying breath. Then another. One leap and he'll be safe.

He coils his muscles, contracting everything like a spring, just as something slams into his legs.

Fyve gasps, instantly realizing what hit him. A solid body. A powerful one. A leatherskin.

He looks down, instinctively pulling up his legs as another leaps from the water, its massive jaws snapping shut an inch from his feet. Droplets of water hit him as it lands back in the water with a splash.

Another leaps before he can blink, a little smaller than the last but just as vicious looking. Fyve cries out as it spears straight toward him, mouth opening in anticipation. He swings right and it sails straight past, also landing in the water. Fyve dangles from his hand, conscious his grip is weakening as his palm grows sweaty, unable to drag his gaze from the sight below.

The leatherskins are circling, snapping at each other in annoyance.

They're fighting for the first bite. To be the first to kill.

Another leaps, and Fyve kicks out, knocking it off course. The impact has the shark returning to the water empty-mouthed, but it jerks Fyve's arm. The motion has the knife gouging down another few inches, lengthening the jagged groove in the wood above it.

He doesn't need to look up to know it's too far for him to reach now. Dread pools in his stomach. It's only a matter of time before the blade loses its grip in the wood. Or his hold slips. Or a leatherskin is successful.

"Terra!" Fyve screams. "Help!"

Even though he knows it's useless—she won't help, and even if she could, she's not strong enough to help pull him up—he tries again. "Please! Help!"

No one appears above.

A motion below catches his attention, and Fyve watches in horror as the largest leatherskin so far launches up from the water. It freezes him with its empty, feral stare, serrated cuts circling a whitish eye. Its monstrous jaws open, glistening white teeth as long as his forearm making his heart stutter.

No kick will stop this beast. Its bite will be the fatal blow.

"Fyve! Take my hand!"

He looks up, wondering if he's hallucinating as Halo leans over the edge of the ship, extending her hand.

"Quick!" she screams, her wide eyes looking past him then back. "Now!"

With a mighty roar, Fyve swings. His free arm arcs through the air and clamps onto Halo's outstretched hand. Their fingers lock around the other's wrist. Then Halo's pulling, her face twisting with the strain.

And Fyve's scrabbling, his toes slipping on the smooth wood but gaining enough traction to push himself up. One heave from Halo, and a leap of faith as Fyve releases the knife, and he grips the edge of The Oasis. There's a snap as the leatherskin's jaws slam closed beneath him, then a splash as it returns to the sea, unsuccessful.

The feeling of the hard edge is one of the most beautiful things Fyve's ever experienced.

He pulls himself up with Halo's help, then collapses on the deck, drawing great gulps of air into his lungs.

Halo flops beside him, also panting.

"How did you..." he asks, his mind whirling too hard to finish the sentence.

She smiles weakly. "I realized I was sitting in my cabin, just waiting to see what my—your— fate was after I went through the walk on the plank. It was just...wrong. I was waiting to see what my future would be."

The same conclusion Fyve came to.

She rolls over, her gaze steady on his. "So, I came to warn you or stop you or something. Anything to show that I'm no longer letting someone else dictate my tomorrows."

Fyve reaches a hand to stroke her cheek, noting that his hand is trembling thanks to the adrenaline still coursing through his veins. "I love you," he says, then grins. "And thank you."

Her face softens. "You're my heart, Fyve. I'm not doing this without you."

They get to their feet, looking at the open space where the plank once was. Fyve shakes his head. "Jiro said I'd be safe," he murmurs.

He either lied, or someone overruled him.

Halo frowns. "Who's Jiro?"

Fyve takes her hand and tugs her toward the door that will take them below. "We're about to find out," he says, determination settling like rocks in his gut.

It's time.

Except the door opens and the other teens make their way out. Cloud sees them as soon as she's exited and rushes over, clutching the basket with her twins.

"You passed," she says, relieved.

Iva is there. So is Justice.

Fyve looks beyond them at the crowd. The one that stops growing far sooner than it should. "Where's everyone else?"

Cloud's face shutters. "There isn't anyone else. This is all that's left."

Elijah's words back when this all started echo in Fyve's mind.

At the end of the Trials, Terra will choose fifty teens who will go on to forge the future of humankind.

He quickly counts the pale faces surrounding him, realizing Halo's doing the same. They finish at the same time. They glance at each other, the need to deny the number they both reached is there in their trapped breaths. Their parted mouths.

And their tightly held hands.

There are only fifty teens left.

HALO

*H*alo scans the group, checking off the faces as she tries to process who made it through to the final fifty. The number has never felt smaller.

She sees Ajax with his arm around Viney. As complicated as her relationship is with her brother, and the way he's treated her during these Trials, she can't wish him dead. It's a bitter relief to see him.

Justice is leaning on her crutches, and Halo lets out a sigh. She has no idea how she navigated that plank with her injured leg, but it seems her determination alone was enough to keep her balanced. Just like Cloud.

Iva has made it, too. And Sica. Although, the newest member of their group is missing.

"Where's Coda?" Halo whispers to Iva, who shrugs sadly in response.

Halo winces. Coda hasn't made it. They saved her from Zake's clutches only for her to be fed to the leatherskins. That hardly seems fair. She looks out at the ocean, giving Coda a nod of respect as she pushes down the familiar feeling of grief that builds in her stomach. She deserves to be standing right here with them.

Halo notices something as she looks across the group of teens—most of them are female. She can only count Ajax, Fyve and four other males in the final selection. And Fyve wasn't even supposed to make it through.

Something isn't right here.

Pulling back her shoulders, she acknowledges that nothing ever was.

"Halo," Fyve says, slipping his hand into hers and looking up at the balcony. "Look."

She lifts her face and sees her father standing beside Terra.

Gripping Fyve's hand tightly, she stares at the man who raised her, barely able to recognize him. Covered in bruises, his long gray hair hangs limply over his shoulders. His beard is patchy like he's had chunks of it torn from his chin. He's thinner and hunched over, using the railing to support himself, refusing to meet anyone's gaze.

"They broke him," Halo says, finding it almost impossible now to keep her grief in check. "He's broken."

"Elijah," the crowd murmurs as they stare at the man who used to lead them.

Terra looks to Halo's father on the balcony, as if waiting for him to speak. But he says nothing. So, Terra raises one of her arms, the long sleeve of her robe draping down, and she touches him on the elbow.

"She can talk," Halo whispers to Fyve, remembering her promise never to keep another secret from him again. "She spoke to me in the Trial."

Fyve's brows shoot up. "In your mind?"

"No." Halo shakes her head. "With her voice, out loud."

Fyve seems surprised by this, but not as shocked as she expected. Perhaps they've discovered so many secrets already that nothing can rattle them anymore.

"My people," Halo's father calls out, his voice weak and shaky. He doesn't even have the strength to lift his hands in his usual pose. "You are the fifty who've…"

The teens strain their necks, trying to hear his words as his voice fades out.

"What have they done to him?" a girl near Halo asks.

"He looks terrible," another girl mutters.

"You're the fifty who made it through the Trials," Halo's father continues with great effort. He lifts his eyes and searches the crowd, steadying his gaze when he finds Halo, locking eyes on her.

"You are the people of Tomorrow Land." His cloudy eyes glisten and she knows that right now he's talking only to her. "You will have a bright future. You will have happiness."

"So will you," she calls back.

A few teens in front of her turn look at her like she's gone mad. In fairness, he doesn't look like a man with a bright future, but Halo's desperate to give him something to cling onto.

"You will make everything I did worthwhile," her father continues, both hands gripping the railing of the balcony. "All the things Terra forced me to do."

Halo frowns. He's going off script. There's no way Terra would have him say any of that. She holds up a hand, warning him to be silent.

"Terra convinced me what I was doing was right," he says. "But I was wrong. So wrong. My own people have died at my hands. I thought it was for the greater good when it was nothing but pure ev—"

His hands fly to his temples and Halo whimpers as she realizes what's about to happen.

"No, Dad," she cries. "No!"

"Halo." He leans forward, his eyes still locked on hers as blood pours from his nose. "Don't trust Terra."

Fyve lets out a gasp beside Halo to hear the same final words that his own mom had uttered when she'd been claimed.

Halo sobs as her father topples over the railing and sails down to the deck below. The teens jump apart to create a space. Halo lurches forward, wanting to break his fall, even though she knows it's already too late.

"You'll get hurt," Fyve says, trying to hold her back. But his words are a vortex in her ears and she's unable to process their meaning.

She wrenches herself free just as her father's body hits the deck with a sickening thud. And now it's hard to tell the difference between the injuries from his claiming and those from his fall. Let alone the ones he sustained beforehand.

Halo crouches beside her father's bloodied body, wanting to run her hands over him, yet not wanting to cause him further pain. She takes his left hand, remembering how he used to hold her hand as a child. Then she notices his fourth finger has been cut off and a strange howling sound erupts from her chest. Her father had done some terrible things but as he'd only just said, he truly believed he was doing the right thing. He didn't deserve to be mutilated like that.

She's aware of sobbing coming from around her as the teens process the shock that the man they've known as their leader all their lives is dead.

"Dad." Halo clutches at his hand, hoping some part of him can still hear even though his eyelids don't flicker. "You're a good person. You're such a good person."

"He really wasn't that great." Ajax is standing beside her with his arms crossed and a scowl beneath his blond curls. "You always thought he was better than he was."

"Oh, piss off, Ajax," says Halo, her patience for him finally snapping.

Ajax's nostrils flare and he retreats back to his precious Viney. Fyve takes his place beside Halo.

"You know, I really don't like that guy," she says, not caring if Ajax can hear.

"Come on," says Fyve, trying to urge her to stand. "There's nothing more we can do for your father now."

"There is," she says, not wanting whoever's controlling this ship from hell to get their hands on his body. They've already cut off one finger. What else might they do to him after his death? "Can you help me get him into the ocean?"

"Are you sure?" Fyve seems concerned by this. "The leatherskins—"

"Are a better option than the alternative," Halo finishes firmly. "I'm sure."

Fyve stoops and lifts her father's frail frame in his arms. Blood seeps into Fyve's pale tunic as he clutches him to his chest. The crowd gathers around him. Some are openly crying. Others are shaking their heads in disbelief.

"Elijah," they mutter, not seeming to be able to get more than just his name to leave their lips.

"I need some space," says Fyve as he stands.

The teens part as he walks to the railing. Some reach out to touch Elijah as if they can't believe what they've just witnessed.

"Any last words?" Fyve asks as Halo reaches him at the railing.

She shakes her head, having said everything she needed to say, whether her father had been able to hear or not.

Fyve gently raises her father's body over the railing and with a nod of respect, he lets go. Halo swallows as she forces herself to watch him fall. This had been her call. She needs to see it through.

He hits the surface of the ocean, but before he can disappear into its depths, a scream has Halo spinning around.

A group of teens has run up the stairs to the balcony and Sica has Terra in a headlock.

"What are you going to do now?" Sica growls. "I have you, Terra! Elijah told us not to trust you. And I don't."

Terra wriggles in panic, trying to free herself.

"Don't!" Halo cries out. "That's not who my father meant. She's just a little girl. You're scaring her."

Sica falters for just a moment but doesn't let go. "Then who did he mean?"

"I don't know," Halo pleads. "But not her. She's just a scared little girl."

More teens run up to the balcony, all with a murderous look in their eyes. They've put up with so much since these Trials began. And they've put up with even more since they got onto this ship. It seems that claiming Halo's father was the final straw. They're no longer wishing to listen to Terra. And even though Halo knows exactly how they feel, they're taking out their frustration on the wrong person.

Fyve leans into Halo. "You said Terra spoke to you?"

"She really is just a girl," Halo whimpers. "No different to Sevin. We have to do something."

Fyve nods at Halo and together they run to the stairs, pushing their way through the group on the balcony to get to Terra.

Sica glares at them, and Terra moans as she tightens the grip around her neck. If she keeps this up much longer she'll choke her. "I'm not letting her go. I thought you'd be happy after what she just did to your own father."

"You have to let her go," says Halo firmly. "Because you're tough and you're brave, but you're also kind. You don't want to kill a little girl. She's not Terra."

Sica loosens her hold just a little. "Then who is she?"

"I don't know," Halo says. "But I do know you've got the wrong person. She's just a girl who's been caught up in all this. She's exactly the same as us."

"Kill her!" a guy in the crowd sneers. "Snap her skinny neck!"

There are jeers of agreement and Halo looks desperately at Fyve.

"Halo's telling the truth," says Fyve. "Don't hurt her. There has to be another way."

"Fine." Sica lets go of Terra and cracks her knuckles. "But you'd better be right about this or it's you I'll come after next."

Halo pulls Terra to her side and to her surprise the girl wraps her arms around her waist, trembling against Halo's body.

"We're going to look after you," Halo promises, believing with all her heart this hadn't been who her father had been talking about. "You're going to be okay."

"So, what's your plan?" Sica asks Fyve. "Because I'm sick of being treated like this. No more! Do you hear me? NO MORE!"

"No more!" the crowd of teens echo, raising their fists in the air. "No more!"

"We're taking over this ship," says Sica. "As much food as we like! And we're turning around and going back to Treasure Island."

The crowd is overflowing with joy. It's the happiest Halo's seen them since the day they boarded The Oasis. Is this really possible? Can they turn this ship around and return for all the loved ones they left behind? Might Fyve get to see Sevin again? And might they be able to bring their people more tins of food than they could ever have imagined in their lifetime?

"Let's go!" shouts Sica, pointing to the deck.

The teens stream down the staircase and spill out onto the larger deck below. Some go directly to the pool of pods and scoop them out, shoveling them into their mouths. Others are too busy whooping and cheering at the turn of events.

Halo follows Fyve down the stairs, her arm still wrapped firmly around Terra.

"I want to stand up and fight," she says to Fyve. "But I'm not sure about all of this."

"I am," he replies. "I'm sure this is a terrible idea. They don't understand. This is bigger than just that little girl. There's so much they don't know ab—"

They freeze as half a dozen men burst through the door from the stairwell with large weapons held out in front of them. They're unlike any men Halo's seen before.

Pale, pockmarked skin.

Rolls of excess fat around their bellies.

Manicured beards.

Clothes that look so new the black fabric seems to stand up all on its own.

It's clear that war on The Oasis just broke out. And the invisible army they've been fighting all along have just shown themselves.

"Bring it on," Halo mutters, looking at her pasty opponents. Her father being claimed lit a fire in her belly. Then Ajax threw fuel on that flame and made the rage inside her burn. She's ready for whatever it's going to take to bring an end to this madness.

The men start herding the teens into a corner, pointing their weapons and cursing.

"Everyone over there!" one of the men shouts.

"We need to do as they say for now," Halo says quietly, not liking the look of those weapons.

Fyve leads Halo and Terra to the other teens. "You need to stay alive. Don't do anything stupid."

Halo bites her tongue. She can't promise him that. Her whole life she's done as she was told. All her actions have been the opposite of stupid. And look where that's gotten her! Nope. You can't repeat the same actions and expect a different result. She's not going to allow herself to continue to be a pawn in this sick game.

Sica sneers at one of the men, refusing to budge. "I'm not doing what you say. It's about time you started doing what we say!"

She looks to the crowd of teens, clearly expecting to see them cheer their support. They all remain quiet. They might have been ready to rebel, but the game just took a new and far more dangerous turn.

"Get back!" the man warns.

"Or what?" Sica cries out. "How can you punish any of us any further? I refuse to do anything you say ever again."

The man pulls on the trigger of his weapon and a flame pours from the end. Sica dives out of the way just in time before she's roasted like one of their rats back on Treasure Island. But one of the other nearby teens isn't so lucky and her tunic catches fire. The girl beside her pushes her to the ground and rolls her over to smother the flames.

The man lifts his weapon in the air as more flames pour out.

"Who's next?" he asks, as Sica reluctantly joins the other teens.

"What is that thing?" Fyve asks, his eyes wide as he stares at the weapon.

Halo shakes her head, trying to breathe through her panic. She's heard of guns but never has she heard of one that spews fire. How do they fight against that? Maybe her promise to stand up to these men is going to have to wait until she has an actual plan. They might have weapons, but they don't look all that smart to Halo. Surely, she can outsmart them if she bides her time…

Once they're all corralled in a corner of the deck, their captors pace in front of them, looking them up and down.

"Well, isn't that sweet," says one of the men. "Little Terra has joined the gang. It seems we have fifty-one of you bloodsuckers to take care of now."

"Unless we claim the tough one," a man says, pointing his weapon at Sica.

"No!" one of the other men shouts, his rounded belly shaking with the force of his words. "I told you. I can tame her. She's mine."

"Like hell I am!" Sica calls back with a fist raised.

Halo looks across at Fyve. This is worse than any of them feared. These people are claiming ownership over them. Is that what all this has been about? Has one of these revolting men placed a claim on Halo for himself?

Half a dozen more men and one woman emerge from the stairwell and step out onto the deck. The man standing in the middle is the only one who isn't armed. He's also the only male without a beard. He has a rounded face with a square jawline and short brown hair flecked with gray. Like his compatriots, he looks like he's eaten a few too many tins of food. But unlike the others, he has an aura about him that leaves no doubt in Halo's mind he's in charge.

His men fan out beside him, and he looks over the quivering crowd of teens with an expression of pride. His gaze lingers on Halo and she tucks Terra closer.

"We know each of you like you're our own children," the man says. "There's Sica, Fyve, and Halo. Then we have Cloud with Miracle and Marvel, and her constant shadows of Iva and Justice. And let's not forget Ajax and Viney, along with Antic and Bloss."

He continues on, naming every teen standing on the deck, proving that Halo's father hadn't been the only one with a knack for remembering names. When he's finished, he puffs out his chest like he's expecting an applause.

Instead, he's greeted with stunned silence.

"You know us," says Fyve, the only one with enough courage to speak. "But who are you?"

This amuses the man, who tips his head back and laughs. "*We are the real Terra.*"

THE END
Ready for the next installment?
Check out The Last Oasis, now!
http://mybook.to/LastOasis

BOOK 13 - THE LAST OASIS

THE THAW CHRONICLES

A doomed ship. An explosion of lies. One last Oasis.

Fyve and Halo have never felt more vulnerable than when The Oasis becomes lost at sea. The ship was supposed to be a beacon of hope, a way to reach Tomorrow Land. But war is breaking out within its confines. Terra was never who they thought she was. And now the ship itself is dying.

With no food, water, or fuel to power the ship, the search for Tomorrow Land has become futile. And now deadly. As lie upon lie is uncovered, they begin to wonder if the mysterious land they've been searching for even exists.

When the sky turns black and a storm threatens, Fyve and Halo must face one final battle. The future they were promised may not exist, but there's something more important to fight for...the truth.

You will be blown away by this epic dystopian adventure brought to you by Tamar Sloan and Heidi Catherine, authors of the smash hit series, The Thaw Chronicles.

Grab your copy now!
http://mybook.to/LastOasis

WANT TO STAY IN TOUCH?

If you'd like to be the first for to hear all the news from Tamar and Heidi, be sure to sign up to our newsletter. Subscribers receive bonus content, early cover reveals and sneaky snippets of upcoming books. We'd love you to join us!

SIGN UP HERE:

https://sendfox.com/tamarandheidi

ABOUT THE AUTHORS

Tamar Sloan hasn't decided whether she's a psychologist who loves writing, or a writer with a lifelong fascination with psychology. She must have been someone pretty awesome in a previous life (past life regression indicated a Care Bear), because she gets to do both. When not reading, writing or working with teens, Tamar can be found with her husband and two children enjoying country life in their small slice of the Australian bush.

Heidi Catherine loves the way her books give her the opportunity to escape into worlds vastly different to her own life in the burbs. While she quite enjoys killing her characters (especially the awful ones), she promises she's far better behaved in real life. Other than writing and reading, Heidi's current obsessions include watching far too much reality TV with the excuse that it's research for her books.

MORE SERIES TO FALL IN LOVE WITH...

ALSO BY TAMAR SLOAN AND HEIDI CATHERINE

The Sovereign Code

Elemental Games

ALSO BY TAMAR SLOAN

Keepers of the Grail

Keepers of the Light

Keepers of the Chalice

Keepers of Excalibur

Zodiac Guardians

Descendants of the Gods

Prime Prophecy

ALSO BY HEIDI CATHERINE

The Kingdoms of Evernow

The Soulweaver